D0207779

continued ...

Moonlight Kiss

A CRICKET CREEK NOVEL

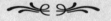

LuAnn McLane

A SIGNET ECLIPSE BOOK

SIGNET ECLIPSE
Published by the Penguin Group
Penguin Group (USA) LLC, 375 Hudson Street,
New York, New York 10014

USA | Canada | UK | Ireland | Australia | New Zealand | India | South Africa | China
penguin.com
A Penguin Random House Company

First published by Signet Eclipse, an imprint of New American Library,
a division of Penguin Group (USA) LLC

First Printing, November 2013

Copyright © LuAnn McLane, 2013
Excerpt from *Whisper's Edge* copyright © LuAnn McLane, 2013

ISBN 978-0-451-41558-5

Printed in the United States of America
10 9 8 7 6 5 4 3 2 1

This book is dedicated to my beautiful granddaughter, Emilie.
May all of your dreams and wishes come true!

Acknowledgments

I want to extend a heartfelt thanks to the editorial staff at New American Library. I truly appreciate the time, effort and care that you put into getting a book on the shelf. I have loved all of my covers but this one in particular made my breath catch. Publishing is such a team effort and the attention given to detail shows in the finished product. Coming up with a story is just the beginning!

Once again, I want to give a very special thanks to my dear editor, Jesse Feldman. You've helped me find a blend of lighthearted humor and deeply felt emotion that brings this series to life. Working with you is a joy!

As always, I want to thank my wonderful agent, Jenny Bent. Having you with me every step of the way has been such a blessing.

Of course, a great big thank-you always goes out to my readers. My wish is to give you a story that brings a smile to your face and joy in your heart.

1

Breaking Up Is Hard to Do

"WHAT? GARRET, PLEASE TELL ME YOU'RE JOKING." Addison put down her fork and stared across the table at her fiancé. "You want to do a reality show about our marriage? Really? Why?"

"Why not? My agent is working on a sweet deal. With my rock-star father and your finance-guru mother, we would have a built-in audience." Garret gave Addison his megawatt smile, and when that didn't sway her, he quickly followed up with the *pretty-please* pout that always worked.

Not this time. Addison shook her head. "I don't want our life together to have an audience."

"Addison . . ." Garret drew out her name and put his hand over hers. "Would you at least give it some thought?"

Addison tilted her head to the side. "Don't you want to be known for something other than being Rick Ruleman's son?" she asked gently.

Garret waited for the server to refill his water glass and then said, "Well, *yeah*, and this show would make us both famous in our own right."

"So we would simply be famous for being famous,"

Addison answered flatly. "That's not really in our own right."

Garret shrugged.

"You know how hard I've tried to stay out of the public eye. And, seriously, you of all people know that it's not easy being the child of a celebrity. Remember that my mother's fame came much later in my life. I didn't grow up being followed around by the paparazzi and I don't think I'll ever get used to the idea. I'm not interested in having my life played out on the television screen." Leaning forward, Addison gave Garret a pleading look that he didn't even seem to notice, and her heart sank. "Garret, please don't ask this of me."

"You'd be so good in front of the camera. Addison, you're so pretty and you have that, you know, sincere thing going on. And look how good your mom is in front of the camera."

Addison gestured to her long jet-black hair and her chocolate brown eyes, all courtesy of her mother's Native American heritage. "I look like my mom, so people expect me to have the same personality as Melinda Monroe and to enjoy the spotlight, but I don't. Not one bit. I never told you this, but I was asked to be her sidekick on *Melinda Knows Money*. The producers wanted us to be a team." Her mother's show was hard-hitting and funny, and she helped viewers straighten out their financial messes. The difference between it and some other shows was that Addison's mother wasn't mean-spirited and she actually helped families improve their lives and get back on track. Melinda Monroe boosted self-esteem rather than exploiting people's problems.

Garret's jaw dropped and his mouth gaped open. "And you turned it down?"

"Of course I did." Addison put a hand to her chest. "Because it's not *me*. Garret, if you're not true to yourself, you're simply living a lie."

"But you're smart and have a business degree. You could have rocked it, Addison."

"Thanks for saying so, but you know I'm more reserved, like my dad. That's why I work at his art gallery." Garret couldn't be surprised that she wouldn't want to be on TV, and the lack of compassion in his eyes hurt her to the core.

"Yeah, but don't you see?" Garret smiled. "We're the same way as your mom and dad! I'm outgoing and you keep me in check. That's why we would be so damned entertaining. Addison, all you would have to be is your beautiful, wonderful self and rake in the money. Pretty easy, huh?"

"I *don't* want to do a reality show." She hoped her firm tone would set him straight and he would drop this nonsense.

"You won't do this for me?" Garret gave her his very best puppy-dog look and then smiled oh so slowly. "Come on. What do you have to lose?"

"What's left of my privacy, for starters." Addison sighed. "But most of all, my dignity." Her pointed look had him shifting in his chair. Addison felt a sense of dread.

"Well, would you just look at yourself way up there on your high horse?" Garret scooted closer and leaned forward. The puppy-dog expression vanished. "For someone who supposedly values her privacy, you sure do like dating celebrities. It was splashed all over the place when Aiden Anderson cheated on you with his costar and broke off your first engagement."

"How lovely for you to bring that up." Addison felt a hot flash of anger. "Aiden was the son of a family friend and I knew him most of my life . . . way before he became a famous actor. And I met *you* at a party at my parents' house. I don't go *chasing* after celebrities, Garret."

She wanted to add that Garret wasn't actually a celebrity, only the son of one, but she didn't see the point in being mean, especially when Garret's attempt at his own music career was a crushing failure. The critics had been harsh, and Garret had taken it hard. One of the reasons

Addison fell for him was his vulnerable side, which most people never witnessed. She knew all too well that it wasn't easy being the child of someone in the spotlight, and she thought it was part of their common bond. Apparently Garret had other aspirations that he had kept pretty well hidden until now. "That was a really nasty thing to say."

He shrugged again. "It's the circles we run in, Addison."

"So if you can't beat 'em, join 'em?"

"And make a shit ton of money at the same time."

"But we talked about how it sucks to be followed around just because of who our parents are. The paparazzi are just waiting for us to do something stupid so they can take pictures. Garret, my breakup with Aiden was difficult enough without having it played out in the media. Most of what was reported was false, anyway. It really sucked."

"Come on, Addison!" Garret pleaded, shoving his long bangs out of his eyes. He had an artfully messy haircut that required lots of product. "Why are you being so stubborn?" he asked tightly. When he glanced down at Addison's engagement ring and sighed, she felt a jolt of alarm.

"Garret . . ." Addison leaned forward and continued softly so other diners wouldn't hear. "Did you ask me to marry you because you wanted to do this show?"

"Of course not!" Garret sputtered hotly, but when he glanced down and started toying with the straw poking out of his drink, Addison wondered if she had guessed correctly.

"Really? Because that's what this feels like." Addison looked at him expectantly and waited for the profession of love that never came. Her heart sank. "Oh boy." Addison closed her eyes and inhaled a sharp breath. She was torn between feeling sorry for him and tossing ice water in his handsome face. She glanced at her water glass and her fingers twitched. "Wow . . . I was right, wasn't I? You might as well come clean."

"No, baby, you've got it all wrong," Garret insisted in that soulful, charming voice that had sucked her in from the first time they met. He followed it up with a wounded look.

Addison stared across the table at him. She searched his face and looked into his blue eyes, wanting so badly to believe him. But the lack of love she saw in his expression convinced her. Her heart sank. "No, I think I've got it totally right."

Addison tossed her napkin on the table and then stood up.

"Where are you going?" Garret's eyes widened as if he couldn't believe how fast this was going south, and he actually followed her through the restaurant and out the door. Addison was so glad that she had driven to meet him for lunch, and hurried toward the parking lot while frantically fishing her keys out of her purse.

"Addison!"

She kept on walking until she spotted her red Mustang convertible. The muscle car made her feel just a little bit badass, and she picked up her pace.

"Wait . . . *please*." Garret's gentle pleading tone caused a little spark of hope to blossom in her chest. Maybe he'd tell her that the show meant nothing and that she meant everything. That this was an insane idea and that he'd squash it.

Holding her breath, she slowly turned to face him.

"Would you at least sleep on it? We can revisit this tomorrow, after you've had the chance to think it over."

Addison let out the held breath and her shoulders slumped. "There's nothing to think about. I won't do it, Garret. I'm sorry, but it's just not in me to make a fool of myself in front of a big audience."

"Who cares? We'd laugh all the way to the bank."

"There's not enough money in the world."

A muscle jumped in his jaw. "Well, then, I guess we're through," Garret announced as if this was his ace in the hole, which would surely win her over.

It didn't.

"If this show means more to you than me, then I guess so," she conceded, giving him one last chance to turn this thing around, but only got a stubborn lift of his chin.

"I guess you just answered my question." With shaking fingers Addison tugged the engagement ring off. Oh, how she wished she were a bit tougher, like her mother, because she was having trouble holding her emotions in check. "Then here." Sunlight glinted off of the diamond solitaire when she thrust it toward him.

Garret swallowed hard and his eyes widened, as if he couldn't believe that he'd called her bluff and it blew up in his face. He glanced at the ring and then back at her. "Addison, let's talk about this. We can't call off the wedding! Everything has been ordered. Invitations sent out." He looked at her in a bit of a panic. "We . . . we had that couples shower. What the hell will people think?"

"That's a really poor reason for getting married. You have to care." She tried to sound angry, but her voice shook.

"I . . . I *care*!" His raised voice negated the sentiment.

"Do you love me?" Addison asked quietly.

"Of course I do!" Garret protested loudly but the word *love* never touched his lips.

"Then say it . . . and not in your offhand, cutesy way like you always do, but like you mean it. Like I mean the world to you like I thought I did." She patted her chest. "Like *I'm* more important to you than some silly show."

"If you loved me, you'd do the show," Garret tossed back at her.

Addison looked at him and had a sudden moment of clarity. "You have a point."

"See . . ." Garret said, but his sudden smile faltered when she remained silent. "Wait. What are you saying? That . . . that you don't love me?"

Addison gave him a sad shake of her head. "You're right, Garret. If I loved you the way I should, I might consider doing this with you. On the other hand, if you loved me the way you should, you would never ask me to do something I would hate doing. It's pretty simple. We're not meant for each other after all."

"No, wait, Addison. Seriously. I've handled this all wrong!" Garret shoved his fingers through his no longer carefully styled hair once more. He'd be appalled if he knew it was standing on end. But she finally saw real sorrow in his eyes. "I'm sorry. I was being an ass because I wasn't getting my way."

"Yeah, you were." Addison nodded her agreement. "And you're not usually like that. Or maybe I haven't seen it because I always agree with whatever you want to do. But, Garret, this just shows that we want way different things out of life." She reached out and put a hand on his forearm. "We had such fun together. You made me laugh and enjoy so many things I would never have tried." She smiled softly . . . sadly.

"We can still do that," Garret said in a pleading tone. "You know, just with cameras," he added with a little wince.

Addison looked down at her ruby red toenails peeking through the top of her black sandals. She swallowed hard and then looked back at Garret. "Be honest. Did you ask me to marry you just to be in the reality show?"

"No." Garret reached out and ran a fingertip down her cheek. "I loved being with you, making you laugh, smile. You made me feel good about myself even when I didn't always deserve it." He shrugged and Addison saw raw emotion cloud his eyes.

"We're both breathing down the neck of our thirties, Garret. Maybe it's time to grow up."

"Eh . . . growing up is overrated," he answered with another cocky shrug. But Addison wasn't really fooled. "Just look at my dad, still rockin' long hair and leather. I guess the apple doesn't fall far from the tree and all that crap." His nonchalant tone didn't match the rather haunted look in his eyes. "My mother called it something . . ."

"The Peter Pan syndrome?"

"Yeah . . . *that*."

Addison hitched her purse strap higher on her shoulder. "You know, Garret, maybe your father wishes he'd been around more when you were growing up. Maybe he'd still be married to your mom. Being a rock star might not be all that it's cracked up to be either."

"Yeah, right. Said no one *ever*." Garret chuckled but it sounded a bit forced. "Trust me, my dad loves his life," he added with a touch of bitterness. But then he sighed. "Damn. So, you're really breaking up with me? Calling the wedding off? For real?"

"For real."

He remained silent for a moment. "So, what do you want out of life?" Garret finally asked in a rare serious moment. And she had to wonder if he was asking himself the same question.

"Oh, I don't know." Addison sighed. "Undying, everlasting, all-consuming, crazy love. Is that asking too much?" Her small laugh ended with a slight hitch.

"Does that really exist?"

"I'm not sure." She toyed with the heart charm on her key chain. "But I want to find out. Don't you?"

Garret shrugged but for once seemed at a loss for words. Addison supposed that he was as stunned as she was at the sudden, very sad turn of events.

"Good-bye, Garret." But when she turned to open her car door he put a hand on her shoulder.

"Hey . . ."

Addison turned around.

"I'm going to really miss you. This is my loss. You deserve better," he said, and Addison could tell that he meant it.

"We both do. I hope someday you'll figure that out too."

Garret looked down at the ground and then back at her. "Then promise me one thing."

"What?"

"That you won't settle for anything less than undying, everlasting, all-consuming, crazy love. Go for it. All or nothing at all. Don't let my sorry ass turn you into a cynic."

Addison chuckled softly. "You know, Garret, there's more to you than you let on or than you even realize. I've seen it. Like right now." She stepped forward and tapped on his chest. "Just have the courage to dig deep and find it."

With a sigh Garret leaned in and kissed her on the cheek. "Like I said, you give me much more credit than I deserve, but that's the way you are," he said. "Now promise me."

Addison blinked at him for a minute. "I promise." She had to push the words past the emotion clogging her throat.

"Good," Garret said gruffly, and stood there for a long moment, as if knowing this might be the last time they spoke.

Addison reached up and cupped his chin. "This was easier when I was super-pissed and wanted to toss water in your face."

"Right . . ." He gave her a slight grin. "You'd never do that."

"No . . . probably not." She dropped her hand. "But it crossed my mind."

"You're making this damned difficult," Garret admitted with an unexpected tremor in his voice. But he inhaled a deep breath and seemed to regain his composure. "The thought of not having you in my life anymore just, well . . . sucks." He jammed his thumb over his shoulder. "Can't we just head back in there and start over?"

"No . . ." Addison shook her head. "This is hard but I really think it's for the best, for both our sakes. Good-bye, Garret."

"Ahh, Addison . . . dammit." He opened his clenched fist and looked down at the ring before gazing back up at her.

Addison reached over and gently folded his fingers upward and then over the ring. She knew that he really did care about her, probably more than he actually realized until now. But it wasn't enough, and they both knew it. Without another word, he turned and walked away.

Addison watched him depart and felt warm tears sliding down her face. She felt an empty ache settle in her heart and wondered why love had once again eluded her. "Godspeed, Garret," she whispered, and then slid behind the wheel. "And so the journey begins. . . ."

Again.

2

The Long and Winding Road

WHILE DRIVING AROUND AIMLESSLY, ADDISON TRIED TO make sense of what had just happened. "Too bad life doesn't have a GPS, because I sure as hell don't know where I'm going after this mess," she mused. Two broken engagements in less than five years was, well, too many. And both times she'd been convinced she was in love—Addison was serious when she told Garret she wanted the real deal. "Right. Like that's going to happen," she grumbled. Clearly, she couldn't trust her own judgment. The reality of calling off another wedding settled into the pit of her stomach, disturbing the Cobb salad she'd consumed.

Addison finally pulled into the parking lot of her father's art and music gallery. Beauty and the Beat showcased affordable artwork and music from lesser-known but extremely talented artists and musicians from all around the country. Her father had one entire room dedicated to Native American art and music, in honor of her mother's heritage. Paul Monroe loved discovering new talent, and Addison had developed a deep appreciation for the arts from him. But while she truly enjoyed working there, Addison secretly longed to find her own passion. She just didn't quite know what it was, and maybe that's why she kept falling for the wrong guys. Maybe she needed to discover herself first.

But who was she?

Addison frowned and considered her own question. While she had gotten the creative gene from her father, Addison also had a nose for numbers and a degree in business to show for it. Would it be possible to find some sort of career where she could combine the two?

For a few minutes she simply sat in her car and stared out the window. This breakup with Garret had shaken her up in more ways than one, and for the second time in her life, she felt lost and without any real direction. Or maybe she was always lost and without direction and didn't even know it. But still, it was odd how someone could be the center of your universe and then suddenly be completely gone. Poof. With Aiden she'd had friendship but lacked passion. With Garret she'd had the pure enjoyment of his company but lacked substance. Was it possible to have a best friend and passionate lover who made you laugh all day long? Someone who put you first? Addison leaned her head back against the seat and sighed. Too many questions.

"And no answers."

When the inside of the car started to get stuffy Addison finally opened the door and headed inside the gallery. She smiled when she heard Loudmouth being piped through the speakers.

Addison made a beeline for her father's office and poked her head through the doorway. "Dad, do you have a minute to talk?"

"Sure," he answered casually, but as soon as her father looked up and saw her face, he put his reading glasses down and stood up from where he sat behind his massive antique desk. "Sweetheart, what's wrong?"

Addison walked into the room and held up her naked ring finger.

"Oh . . . Addie," he said, using the childhood endearment that she'd balked against as a teenager. His use of it now was almost her undoing and she swallowed hard. "What happened?" He walked over and gave her a much-needed hug.

"I broke up with Garret," Addison replied with a muffled sob against his shoulder.

"Oh . . . sweetie." He hugged her harder and then backed up and gave her a sympathetic shake of his head. "I'm so sorry."

"Thank you, Dad." His hug immediately helped to calm Addison down. "Is Mom here?"

"No, she's recording back-to-back shows today. But you can bend my ear." He pointed to the leather sofa against the far wall. "Have a seat and tell me about it."

After sitting down, Addison explained Garret's reality-show nonsense. "Although he denied it, I really do think it was one of the main reasons he wanted to get married."

"Oh, Addison, I'm so sorry to hear that." He blew out a sigh that held a hint of anger. "I rather liked the fellow, but I have to admit that your mother complained that she thought Garret lacked depth. She wanted to talk to you about him, but I thought we should steer clear of your love life. And now I wish I had encouraged her to say something."

Addison scooted sideways on the smooth brown leather to face her father. "No, Dad. This was my own choice. I'm twenty-eight years old. I take full responsibility." She paused to swallow the hot emotion squeezing her throat. "I had so much fun with Garret that I overlooked his flaws. He could be very charming and always had me in stitches. He's not a bad guy . . . just a bit . . . I don't know . . . confused, I guess. It can be hard enough being Melinda Monroe's daughter, but even so, I had a normal childhood growing up in the suburbs. I can't imagine being the son of a rock star."

"You're being too kind." He reached over and patted

her hand. "Just like with Aiden. I don't care who you are. Bad behavior is simply bad behavior, no matter how you slice it or the reasons behind it. If Garret's motives for marrying you weren't pure, then as sad as you are right now, you're better off in the long run."

"Oh, believe me, I *know*. But that doesn't mean it doesn't hurt." Addison groaned. "But the media is going to jump on this just like with Aiden. There will be a lot of junk put out there that isn't remotely true."

Her father squeezed her hand. "I'm so sorry, Addison. You know I love your mother dearly, and don't get me wrong; I'm really proud of her. But damn if I don't sometimes wish that her show hadn't gotten so big that it makes her only daughter a target for this kind of rubbish." He rubbed a hand down his face. "Unfortunately, the media loves a scandal and the public somehow enjoys seeing a wealthy or famous person fall from grace. You're always getting caught in the crossfire. I know we should count our blessings, but sometimes I just hate it."

"I get where you're coming from, and it's okay, Dad. And you're right. I *am* lucky . . . well, except for the whole falling-in-love part," she added drolly. "And I am proud of Mom too."

"Your mother didn't set out to become famous, you know. All she wanted to do was help people, especially middle-class folks, manage their money and plan for the future. She simply wanted resources out there to help, advise. All it took was one segment on *Good Morning America* and a runaway bestseller and everything changed in a heartbeat."

"I know it's not easy that she's gone so much."

He gave her a solemn nod. "Yeah, to tell you the truth, I miss the days when I was a starving artist teaching at school and Mel was trying to convince publishers that self-help books on finance would sell. But when the economy was booming nobody wanted to hear her dire predictions of how the prosperity was a house of cards ready to cave in." He chuckled. "We were eating canned soup and peanut butter and jelly and . . . I don't know. Things were just so much . . ."

"Simpler?" Addison gently supplied.

"Yes, and all we had was loving each other. Now . . . sometimes we forget the value of that. Ah, I guess I'll always just be a hippie at heart . . . an old hippie," he added with a grin. "But here I go rambling on when we need to be talking about you."

Addison groaned. "Oh, I have to call and cancel so many things . . . the reception hall, the caterer . . . flowers." She smacked her hand to her forehead. "And that's just the beginning."

"Give me a list and I'll do it."

"Oh, Dad, no! This is my mess." Addison had to clench her teeth in an effort not to cry. "I'll clean it up." She hated the look of pain on her father's face and the concern she would cause her busy mother. Addison thought of Garret and the stark sorrow in his eyes. Should she try to patch things up?

She sank her fingers into the leather sofa. Maybe she should just do the damned show!

"No, I'm insisting." Her dad looked at her for a moment and then, as if knowing where her thoughts were going, said, "And I want you to get out of town. Away from the paparazzi and away from Garret Ruleman."

"Out of town? But where would I go?"

After frowning for a minute her father snapped his fingers. "You know what? I was just talking to your uncle Mitch this morning. I asked how he liked living in Cricket Creek, and he went on and on about how both he and your cousin Mia love it there. They need a Chicago fix once in a while, but he said he doesn't regret the laid-back way of life there one bit."

Addison could see where this was going. "Dad . . ."

"No. You should go there for an extended visit. You and Mia are close, and Mitch said that Mia's fiancé is on the road a lot, playing baseball."

"Oh yeah. Isn't he in the minor leagues?"

"Yes, and Mia can't go see him play too often because she's the promotions manager for the local baseball team. I just bet sweet little Mia would welcome your company."

"Seriously, you think I should head to a small town in . . . where is it?"

"Kentucky. Cricket Creek, Kentucky."

Addison leaned back against the leather. "Oh, I don't know. Where would I stay? I wouldn't want to impose on them."

"Mia lives in a condo overlooking the baseball complex and the Ohio River. I just bet there are some for short-term lease."

"And what will I do for money?" Addison tilted her head in question at her father. This was crazy . . . and yet it held a certain appeal.

"The last time I looked you had two weeks' paid vacation coming," he said, and when Addison still hesitated, he continued. "Look, I'll miss your pretty face and your mother will too, but getting away from LA just might be the ticket you need right now."

"I would probably fly under the radar there," Addison admitted, warming up slightly to the suggestion.

"And Uncle Mitch's wife owns a jewelry store in a lovely little mall called Wedding Row—I think Mitch called it. Maybe she needs some help in the shop?"

"I think I need to stay away from anything to do with weddings," Addison answered flatly.

"Hey, don't let either of these guys make you jaded. The right man will come along. You wait and see."

"Well, I'm not holding my breath." Addison rolled her eyes. "I'm taking a long break from men."

"So, are you going to do it?"

Addison pressed her lips together, thought for a moment, and then nodded. "A change in atmosphere for a while would probably do me some good." And, in truth, doing something on her own held a great deal of appeal as well. "But you have to promise me that you and Mom will come to visit if I stay longer than a couple of weeks."

"We wouldn't last that long before missing you too much not to visit. And I'd love to see Mitch and Mia. According to him Cricket Creek is a small town but has a lot to offer in the way of theater and local cuisine. You know how Uncle Mitch is."

Addison grinned. "Yeah, you're the hippie, and he's the suit and tie. You'd never know you guys were brothers."

"So, is it a deal?"

Addison thought about it for another moment, weighing whether another shake-up in her life was what she really needed. She suddenly felt a little surge of panic. This was going too fast and felt surreal. "No, wait. This is insane. Who would do my job?"

"You do a tremendous job and work hard, Addison, but there are lots of qualified people out of work. I can get by for a month or so and hold your position until you get back. The worst part is going to be missing you . . . well, and dealing with your mother not liking this without her input, but I feel it in my gut that this would do you a world of good, or I wouldn't suggest it."

"Are you sure?"

"Yes. And, hey, if you don't like it there you can come back after a couple of weeks. But give it a shot. And having you gone will be a good way to get your mother to take a much-needed break and come to visit."

"All right, then." Addison leaned over and hugged her father. When she pulled back she said, "Cancel everything but the trip to Hawaii. You and Mom need to take a second honeymoon for your thirtieth anniversary."

He arched an eyebrow. "I'll see what I can do to pull her away from work. But listen. You head home and start packing. I'll call Mitch and get this ball rolling. He and Mia are going to be thrilled. Do you want to fly?"

Addison frowned. "No, I'll want my car. I'll take my time driving, and that will give you a few days to get things set up."

"Perfect."

He put his hands on her shoulders. "You need to do what you want and not what others want or expect of you. You do that way too much. And as much as I hate to admit it, that includes working at Beauty and the Beat. Keep that in mind, okay?"

"I will." Addison gave her father a kiss on the cheek. "Oh, Dad. I love you so much. And I'm so sorry about this stupid mess I've created. I feel like I'm running away."

"You don't have anything to be sorry about. It's called life, and we all live and learn every single day. Your mom and I just want you to be happy. And you're not running away . . . just taking a break. Unless you want to do *Dancing with the Stars*? When your mother turned it down, it was offered to you."

Addison laughed. "You know my answer to *that*." She smiled. "You always make me feel better."

"That's what you do for people you love. If someone is bringing you down, they don't deserve to be in your life. Seriously, sometimes you're just too damned . . . nice. The next time someone treats you poorly, kick them right out of your life. Remember that, okay?"

"I will."

"Hey, try to unwind and get a good night's sleep before you start your adventure."

When Addison returned to her condo to pack, she wasn't quite sure what kind of adventure she'd find in a small town in Kentucky, a state she hadn't visited unless you count going to the Kentucky Derby a few times. But, seriously, at this point maybe she should think about having an *un*-adventure.

She smiled softly. She'd witnessed strength from her mother and compassion from her father and only hoped that she had absorbed a little from each parent. They loved her unconditionally, and for that she would be forever grateful. After a determined lift of her chin Addison squared her shoulders. "No more whining," she announced sternly. "Ah . . . and speaking of wine . . ." She searched her cabinet and found a bottle of merlot.

A few minutes later Addison sat down on the sofa and sipped the rich wine. Her mood was an odd combination of excitement and sadness mixed with a little bit of fear. It was an emotional cocktail that made her feel a bit off-kilter. She sipped and pondered about her life.

Her cell phone was sitting on the glass coffee table . . . silent. Addison stared at it for a moment and couldn't decide if she was relieved or disappointed that Garret hadn't called and tried to smooth things over. Not that it would change her mind at this point, but it stung a bit that she was so easily dismissed without a real fight. Was Garret at a bar right this minute, hitting on women, or home alone, missing her? But when Addison envisioned his sad face she leaned forward, set her glass down, and almost picked up the phone with the intention of calling him just to see if he was okay.

"Stop!" Addison said so loudly that her voice seemed to bounce off the walls and echo in the silence. "Garret's well-being is no longer my concern!" Glaring at the phone as if it were somehow to blame, she sat back against the sofa so fast that she bounced against the cushion. Addison wished she had a girlfriend to confide in, but she'd lost contact with her high school friends after the move to LA and her college friends were now scattered all over the country, many of them married with a child or two.

Not knowing whether to laugh or cry, she had the suspicion that laughter would dissolve into tears and so she simply sat there, looked around her condo, and frowned. While she paid rent, the building actually belonged to her mother and father. The furnishings were gorgeous but courtesy of an interior designer friend of her mother's and not a reflection of Addison's taste. But the decorating had been a birthday surprise, and her mother, who loved bold colors, gushed over the results while she tugged Addison in and out of every room. Addison didn't

have the heart to tell her mother that she would have
preferred something lighter, softer, with a few antiques
scattered here and there.

After another sip of wine, Addison picked up a jewel-
toned pillow, hugged the silky material to her chest, and
thought about, well . . . just about everything. She knew
that in spite of the breakup she had a nice life. Loving
parents, no financial worries, excellent health, and a
solid education, and she really did enjoy working at
Beauty and the Beat. On a daily basis life went smoothly.
In fact, the broken engagements were the only traumas
she really suffered and, like her father said, in truth
were for the best. She had an even, easygoing temperament and avoided confrontation. She rarely cursed,
drank socially but moderately, and her political views
were pretty much middle-of-the-road. She just simply
went with the flow. . . .

"Oh my God!" Addison suddenly tossed the pillow
aside and put a hand to her chest. "I'm not nice. . . . I'm
boring!" Oh, she listened, she laughed, and was enter-
tained by others, but who did she entertain? No wonder
Garret liked being with her: He wanted an audience and
she was perfect. No one felt passionate about her because she wasn't . . . exciting. And then another thought
hit her: "Oh my God. I bet I suck in bed!" When Garret
wanted to role-play one night Addison had simply laughed,
but now she wished she had put on the maid's outfit or
whatever it was he had suggested. She didn't even remember because she hadn't considered his request and
he'd never brought it up again.

*I'd likely fit right in in a sleepy little river town like
Cricket Creek, Kentucky,* she thought with a snort before
polishing off the rest of the wine in her glass. Seriously,
what kind of excitement happened in a town named after water and an insect? Uncle Mitch said it was lovely,
but she suddenly had her doubts. She pictured people
sitting on front porches, rocking in big rockers, drinking
sweet tea, and watching grass grow. She envisioned pot-

bellied men wearing overalls and boots while spitting tobacco and sipping on moonshine.

"I'm sure not going to find Prince Charming in Cricket Creek, Kentucky," she insisted, and decided she needed one more glass of merlot. Raising her glass she said, "Perfect. I'm done with men, anyway. Un-adventure, here I come."

3

Amarillo Sky

AFTER WIPING SWEAT FROM HIS BROW, REID REACHED for another bale of hay and tossed it onto the flat-bed trailer. Back in Lexington he'd gone to the gym on a regular basis, but this farmwork was kicking his butt. He flicked a glance at his sister, Sara, who stood there with her hands on her hips, staring at him. Then again, maybe it was frustration that was making him overheat.

"Stop ignoring me." Sara flipped her long brown braid over her shoulder and took a step closer to him.

Reid threw the next bale onto the trailer with more force than necessary. It landed with a thud, sending straw flying. Sopping up more sweat with his sleeve, he turned to face her. "Weddings, Sara? Are you kidding me? First you turn the family farm into Old MacDonald's for schoolkids, and now you want to host barn weddings? What's next? A circus?"

"You have a lot of nerve." Sara stepped closer and poked Reid in the chest. She was one of two people on earth who could get away with it. His mother was the other one. Reid braced himself for what was coming. "After back-to-back years of drought on top of the recession, we nearly lost everything. But *you* were off in Lexington, sitting in your fancy office."

"I have a degree in finance. I thought it was important to use it, just like you used your degree in teaching."

"Yeah, it was, until I was needed here!" Sara swung her arm in an arc. "Jeff put his music career on hold when times got tough. Braden came home from college, and I came back when the stress of it all gave Dad a heart attack and turned Mom into a worrywart. But oh no, *you*? You stayed in your . . . your ivory tower."

"I was working hard, earning a living," Reid responded tightly. "Sara, you gave up tenure, health benefits, and your retirement when you quit teaching third grade. Maybe not the smartest decision you could have made. This Old MacDonald's thing is making money, but not enough. And for how long? Jeff making it as a country singer is a long shot at best. And Braden? In my opinion he should have finished college! Look, profitable farms are run by huge corporations. The days of family farms are numbered. It's just the sad truth."

"Oh, really?" Sara flipped her braid so hard that this time it came all the way around to smack her in the opposite cheek. "Tell that to the people of Cricket Creek. This entire town was going under until we banded together and turned things around. Some things, no matter how high the mountain, are worth the climb. Maybe you just don't get it. Not everything has to add up nice and neat like your God almighty numbers." She kicked her toe in the dirt sending dust flying. "Don't you care, Reid?"

Guilt smacked Reid in the gut so hard that he took a physical step backward. "Numbers speak the truth, Sara. I saw Mom and Dad struggle year after year, working their fingers to the bone, only to barely keep their heads above water. The price of equipment soared. Interest rates were sky-high. Scientific methods in farming rapidly changed. And then the government swooped in with regulations that strangled family farms. Why would I want to live a life like that? Twelve-hour days but with very little profit? Uncertain future? No vacation?" Reid shook his head. "Look what it did to Dad! What's the damned point?"

Sara tapped her own chest. "Because farming is in our blood. It has been for generations and so has this land."

Reid sighed. "I understand. That's why most farmers work other jobs just to support and hold on to the farm. And most of them are Dad's age. It's no wonder his health suffered. Sara, I've done my research. Did you know that only about two percent of Americans still actually live on farms and that only about six percent of them are under the age of thirty-five?"

"Who cares?"

"You should! The writing is on the wall." He raised his arms skyward.

"You and your damned numbers!" Sara stomped her foot just like she used to do when they were kids. Under normal circumstances Reid would have laughed.

"Well, try this number on for size: Every week about three hundred and thirty family farmers leave their land for good. Every week, Sara."

"Don't you see? It's not just about producing the crops. It's about saving the beauty of the land." Sara swung her arm in an arc once more. "Do you want our farm to become a subdivision? A shopping mall? If we can't survive on farming alone, then let's at least save the beauty of the land and use it for the greater good." She lifted her chin a notch. "And my Old MacDonald business that you scoffed at? My teaching degree that you claim I'm not using?" When her voice cracked Reid's anger dissipated like summer rain on a hot sidewalk. "It's helping. I'm helping."

"Sara, I wasn't scoffing. Listen—"

"No, you listen! When I taught third grade, the field trip that my students liked the most was the visit to our farm. And Dad loved showing them around. I happen to believe that it's an important learning experience to know where food in the grocery store comes from and to appreciate the land. When other classes expressed interest, I printed up pamphlets and soon got requests from schools in neighboring counties. We have programs for kindergarten through fourth grade, and last year, the year I quit to do this full-time, we were sold out with a waiting list. Mom jumped on board and created the October pumpkin-patch fall festival. She's been providing homemade jams and jellies to Wine and Diner up in town with great feedback. With my help, she's going to teach some gardening and canning classes through the county-outreach program."

"All good ideas, but I looked at the books and it's still not enough, Sara."

"I know that!" She raised her hands skyward. "That's why I want to do the barn weddings, starting with my own as a prototype. We can take pictures and print up brochures. I'm going to talk to Jessica at Wine and Diner about doing some catering for more formal receptions, and Dad wants to do pig roasts."

"Formal receptions?" Reid pointed at the metal building. "Who would want to get married in there?"

"Dear Lord." Sara rolled her eyes. "Not in *there*. I want to redo the old wooden barn down by the lake. Since we don't raise cattle anymore, that whole area is up for grabs."

"And who would do the renovation?"

"I've talked to Jason Craig about it."

"Jason Craig?"

Sara nodded. "He went to school with Jeff. He did the addition and gazebo over at Wine and Diner. They do outdoor weddings in their courtyard but it's seasonal and only fits more intimate receptions. And having Wedding Row certainly helps."

"What in the world is Wedding Row?"

"That new strip of really pretty shops down by the stadium. Grammar's Bakery just put in a bakery specializing in cakes. I think Mabel's niece is going to run it.

There's a jewelry store, a tuxedo shop, a florist, and soon there will be a photographer. All we need is a bridal boutique, and Cricket Creek will be poised not only for local weddings but for couples looking for a destination wedding as well."

"Right . . . In a *barn*?"

"A beautiful renovated barn. I'll show you pictures. Some of them are just exquisite." Sara sighed. "There's just something wonderful about an earthy, rustic barn that's transformed into elegance. Then a lovely, romantic honeymoon in a bed-and-breakfast in town. Baseball games! We have shopping, theater . . . boating!"

"How could you manage to plan weddings along with everything else you're already doing? Sara, I know your heart is in the right place, but you're biting off more than you can chew." Reid wasn't one bit sold on the idea. "And the money for the renovation? Where will it come from? Will Jeff loan it to you after he becomes a rich superstar?"

"Don't be an ass."

"It's called being a realist. Doing the math. Where was the money coming from again?" He cupped his hand to his ear.

"Do you always have to be such a downer?"

"Meaning you don't know."

Sara shrugged slightly. "I have some savings."

She didn't mean . . . ? Reid braced his foot on a bale of hay and blew out a sigh. "Aw, Sara . . . damn."

"Hey, I've done some research. This could be a moneymaker, an investment for my future. I'm not as dumb as I look. Even though I look like you."

Reid finally smiled. "But a helluva lot prettier."

"Wow . . ." Sara put her hands her hips and tilted her head. "Did you just pay me a compliment?" Her braid slipped over her shoulder and she looked not much older than a teenager. In that moment Reid realized how much he'd missed his sister.

"Yeah, that *was* a compliment, since you're way older

than me." Reid hefted another bale of hay onto the flat-bed trailer. He grinned when she narrowed her eyes.

"Right, older by fifteen stinking minutes. I was just eager to get away from you kicking and poking me."

Reid laughed. "Yeah, I imagine you shoved me out of the way, saying, '*Me first!*'"

In fact, Sara had done that all throughout their child-hood, and he would give in more often than not—though he used to tease her mercilessly. But this barn-wedding thing was different. He didn't want to see Sara lose her hard-earned retirement savings. After seeing his clients lose retirement money in the stock market crash during the tough economic years, Reid was hesitant to encour-age anything remotely risky, especially when it involved his sister or his family. Even though he wouldn't admit it, Reid was glad to take a break from investment financing for a few months. Losing money instead of making money for clients had taken its toll. Granted, a bad econ-omy wasn't his fault, but damn ... it sucked. Lately his ivory tower felt more like a prison.

"There you go, getting all quiet on me again," Sara complained and looked at him expectantly. "I hope you're considering my idea. Maybe willing to go over some numbers with me?"

"The dreaded numbers?" Reid continued to work but glanced her way.

"Please?"

"I'll look over whatever you have to give to me," he offered, feeling a flash of guilt when she gave him a bright smile. Reid wasn't likely to warm up to the idea. Barns and weddings and Cricket Creek just didn't come together in his brain.

"Thanks, Reid! Dad will be over with the tractor in a little while. We have a group of first-graders due here in about an hour. You're welcome to tag along and see how the program works." She grinned. "Just remember that you'll be addressed as Farmer Reid."

"Maybe tomorrow. I promised Braden I'd help him

out in the cornfields, and then I still have some unpacking to do over at the cabin."

Sara nodded. "Okay, well, I have to get going." She stepped closer and gave Reid a hug. "I'm glad you're here. I've missed you, *baby* brother."

Reid hugged her back and felt a tug of emotion. "I've missed you too." He watched her walk away and then paused to gather his thoughts. You'd never know by looking around that the farm was in financial trouble. The grounds appeared fresh and vibrant. The neatly trimmed green grass of the front lawn was in gorgeous contrast to the three-story, classic white farmhouse. Bright, colorful flowers surrounded the base of the wraparound porch where Reid had spent many a long summer evening, playing board games with his siblings and then later cuddling with a girl on the porch swing or drinking some beer with friends. Jeff would often bring out his guitar and jam until his parents begged them to call it a night. Sunday evenings were often family gatherings after a huge chicken dinner. He thought of his mom's apple pie and homemade ice cream and sighed.

Reid gazed over at the house, shook his head, and smiled fondly at the memories. Oversized baskets of ferns hung from the ceiling and spun in the gentle morning breeze. One of his mother's seasonal flags, this one with spring flowers and yellow ducks, jutted out from a post and cheerfully flapped back and forth. Booker, the old hound who wasn't supposed to be a house dog but always managed to sneak inside, lazily lounged next to the front steps, watching for a barn cat so he could bark at it or, if he got up enough gumption, a squirrel to chase. Little John, their big but gentle giant of a dog, tried to get Booker riled up when he wasn't chasing chickens or running through the woods.

A tall sturdy oak tree gracefully stood to the left of the house, still sporting a tree house and a tire swing where Reid used to push baby brother Braden so high that he would laugh with delight and then plead for more as soon as Reid would stop. Reid grinned. Now that Sara was getting married, maybe his mom would finally get the grandchild she'd been wanting for the past few years. Maybe then she would stop telling Reid that he needed a girl in his life.

Reid scrubbed a hand down his face and felt a tug of emotion at the memories. There was no doubt that despite the hard work and sacrifice, farming was a good way of life. But those days were over. And while the Old MacDonald grade school program had merit, Reid just couldn't see the whole barn-wedding thing taking flight. He would just have to find a way to put an end to that nonsense before Sara sank her retirement into a pie-in-the-sky scheme.

4

More

ADDISON SMILED AS SHE DROVE DOWN MAIN STREET IN Cricket Creek, Kentucky. With antiques shops, a local bakery, and several cute boutiques, the quaint river town looked more colorful and vibrant than she had imagined. The six-day cross-country trip had been fun in a low-key, relaxing way. Other than Mia, her parents were the only people she had spoken with, usually at the end of the day when she'd reached her destination. She'd avoided calls and text messages from acquaintances, knowing they were more interested in the broken-engagement scoop than in showing real concern. She'd begun to realize that other than her parents, she didn't really have much keeping her in LA.

Addison had enjoyed stops at a few national treasures, but she was becoming road weary and was anxious to get out of her convertible and visit with Mia and Uncle Mitch. She had tried to avoid looking at tabloids or pop news shows, but did catch the tail end of an interview with Garret, where he'd hinted that there was some juicy reason for their breakup. But, of course, unlike with Aiden's cheating, there really wasn't. Since Addison wasn't exactly big news, she hoped that her broken engagement would blow over soon, especially with her remaining out of town and out of sight.

"Destination is on the right. You have arrived!" announced her GPS.

"Thank goodness!" She spotted Wine and Diner, the lovely-looking restaurant where she was supposed to meet Mia for a late lunch. After parking her car Addison pulled her cell phone out of her purse and called her cousin. "I'm here!" Addison laughed when Mia squealed with delight and then told her she was in a booth near the front window. "I'll be right in."

"Addison!" Mia slid from the bench seat and didn't even give Addison a chance to get all the way over to her table. Mia hugged her hard. "Oh, my gosh, it is so good to see you!"

Addison laughed and hugged her cousin back. "Yes, it's been way too long!" She stepped back. "Is Uncle Mitch here?"

Mia pulled a face and tugged Addison toward the table. "No, he actually had a meeting to attend, but he's looking forward to seeing you. Hopefully Uncle Paul and Aunt Mel will come for a visit while you're here. I've missed you guys."

After sliding into the booth Addison nodded. "Me too. I just hope my dad can drag Mom away from her work." She smiled at her cousin. "You look great, by the way," Addison said, and meant it. Mia was as perky and cute as ever.

"Thanks! Except for missing Cam I've never been happier."

"Well, it shows."

"And you're gorgeous as ever. You're looking more like your gorgeous mom every time I see you. I get such a kick out of watching her show. She sure doesn't pull any punches."

"Yeah, I might look like Mom, but I've got the laid-back temperament of my dad. I need to toughen up, but I just don't know how." Addison shrugged.

"Does your dad still have the ponytail?"

"He does." Addison grinned. "He has the whole Beau Bridges thing going on."

"I always thought Uncle Paul was supercool."

"He and Mom are so different—that's for sure—but I guess the whole opposites-attract thing works for them."

A moment later a waitress approached them. Addison thought her pink retro fifties outfit was fun.

"Hi there, Mia. It's nice to see your pretty face."

"Hi, Sunny. I'd like you to meet my cousin Addison Monroe."

"Nice to meet you, Addison." She handed them each a menu. "Can I get y'all somethin' to drink?"

"I'll have raspberry tea," Mia replied.

"Sounds refreshing. I'll have the same," Addison requested with a smile.

"Comin' right up, girls. I'll give you a few minutes to look over the menu. Chicken-fried steak, mashed potatoes, and green beans is the blue plate special, and French onion is the soup of the day. I'll bring your drinks in a jiffy."

"So, what's good here?" Addison glanced down at the menu.

"Unfortunately, everything. Just ask my expanding butt," Mia replied with a roll of her eyes. "This used to be an old-fashioned diner but Jessica Robinson—well, she's now Jessica McKenna, married to one of my bosses—took the restaurant over from her aunt a few years ago. Jessica took traditional diner fare and gave it an upscale twist. Oh, she was once a chef at Chicago Blue. You've eaten there, right?"

"Yes, I remember it."

"Dad and I used to eat there. It was a hot spot, but I heard business has fallen off since Jessica left. Anyway, the food here is scrumptious." She pointed over her shoulder. "Check out the desserts in the display case. I refuse to look at them."

"Are you kidding?" Addison groaned. "I feel like I've eaten my way across America. I should probably go light."

"Well, the soups and salads are great too. All made from scratch. Jessica's chicken salad is wonderful . . . it's the kind with grapes and walnuts."

"Oh, my stomach is rumbling just thinking about it." Addison opened the menu and chuckled. "Stone soup? Oh, and the fable behind it? How cute!" She closed her menu. "That's it. I don't have to look any further. I already know what I want."

After Sunny delivered the drinks they both ordered stone soup and chicken salad sandwiches.

"So, catch me up on things," Addison requested. "I think the last time I saw you was at your dad's wedding a couple of years ago. How are Uncle Mitch and Nicolina doing? She was such a beautiful bride. And are you and her daughter, Bella, close? She seemed sweet but with a feisty side."

"They're doing wonderful except that Nicolina's jewelry shop keeps her so busy that Dad has to sometimes kidnap his own wife."

"A far cry from the work-driven Uncle Mitch that I remember."

Mia smiled softly. "Yes, so true. Oh, and Bella is like a sister to me and she lives here now too. We're like one big happy family. And now you've arrived! I have to say that life is good."

"And how's your hot baseball player doing?"

Mia twirled her straw in a sad circle. "Oh, I am so proud of his success in the minor leagues, but, like I mentioned, I miss him so much." She brightened. "Hey, maybe we can hit the road in that sweet Mustang of yours and take in a few of his games?"

"I'd like that. I stayed a Cubs fan even after we moved to Los Angles. I love baseball."

Mia arched one eyebrow. "I could introduce you to some really cute Cougar players."

Addison shook her head. "I'm done with dudes for a while."

"Did you just say *dudes*?"

Addison had to grin. Mia was already making her feel better. "California has left its mark in more ways than one. If I start saying *hella* you can smack me."

"Well, before long you'll be saying *y'all* and *bless your heart*."

"I love a good Southern twang," Addison said, but then shook her head. "But I have to admit that the mere fact that I'm here is still sort of surreal. A week ago I was planning my wedding . . . again."

"Yeah, I got my invitation. Oh, Addison, I'm so sorry." Mia's smile faded and she shook her head. "You don't have to, but do you *want* to tell me about the whole Garret Ruleman thing? I saw some stuff on TV but I know it's not true. I won't breathe a word." She made a show of crossing her heart just like they had done when they were little. Before Uncle Mitch's first marriage fell apart they used to see each other on a regular basis. And then everything had changed.

"I don't mind talking about it."

"It might help."

Addison took a swallow of her cold tea and then began. "After Aiden cheated, I found myself mourning the loss of our friendship much more than the romantic side. I know now that something neither of us realized was missing. Something important called passion. But still, the whole thing tore me up and I fell into a blue funk." Addison sighed. "When I met Garret he brought laughter back into my life. He had me trying new and crazy adventures like skydiving, swimming with dolphins . . . even silly stuff like karaoke." Addison shrugged. "I simply adored being with him and assumed it was love. When he proposed it was a no-brainer, or so I thought." Addison looked across the table at Mia. "So, how, tell me—how do you know when it's the real deal?" Addison leaned forward with a hand to her chest. "Apparently I don't have a clue."

Mia frowned for a moment. "I don't know if I can really explain it but I guess it's the intensity of *everything*. Everything about being with Cam is just . . . more. I love him more, miss him more, and even get angrier than with anyone else I've ever known. I even get jealous from time to time, and I'm not that kind of person except with him. It's because I care about Cam more than I've ever felt about any other guy before."

Addison nibbled on her lip, thinking.

Mia grinned. "But do you want the easy answer?"

Addison nodded hard. "Please."

"The kiss." Mia closed her eyes and sighed.

"The kiss?" Addison sat back in her seat in disbelief. "Like, being a good kisser is the key to happiness?"

"Yeah . . . for real . . . it's how you *know*." Mia gave her a dreamy smile. "*The kiss*, especially the very first one, just blows you away. You can't stop thinking about it, reliving it over and over. At the risk of sounding corny, you just sort of . . . melt."

Addison looked at her while trying to recall if she ever felt like she was melting. *Nope. But really, come on . . .*

"Don't roll your eyes at me."

"I didn't!" Addison laughed, while Sunny refilled their tea and put down a basket of crackers.

"Internally, you did. But anyway, finish your Garret story. What really ended the engagement?"

By the time Addison finished telling Mia about the reality-show idea, Mia was shaking her head. "Yeah, two broken engagements in less than five years is too many," Addison lamented. After Sunny delivered the soup and sandwiches, Addison said, "I have enough wedding stuff to open my own store." Addison took a sip of her soup and pointed to the bowl with her spoon. "Oh, this is so good."

"Wow . . ." Mia raised her eyebrows. "Wow . . ." she repeated, and then smiled slowly. "You should totally do it."

"Do what?" Addison asked absently as she scooped up another bite of the savory broth.

"You should open up a bridal shop."

"I was kidding."

"I'm not," Mia said as she opened a pack of crackers. "No, seriously. Dad put in this gorgeous strip of shops down by the river called Wedding Row. The buildings are new but look like an extension of Main Street in Cricket Creek. Nicolina's jewelry shop is next door, along with a bakery specializing in wedding cakes. There are a tuxedo shop and florist and soon there will be a photographer, but Dad has been searching for someone to open a bridal boutique, without any luck." She lifted her palms toward Addison. "Voilà!"

"Mia . . ." Addison warned in a low tone, but there was no stopping her bubbly cousin.

"The shop is ready to go. I mean shelving, lighting, and everything. All it needs is inventory and someone to open it up."

"Mia, I'm only here for a visit."

"Yeah, so was I." Mia raised her hands skyward. "So was my father, and look how that turned out."

"But my family lives in LA," Addison protested, but a tiny bit of excitement blossomed in her stomach.

"They would visit. It would force your mom to take some time off." Mia took a drink of her tea and then tilted her head. "There aren't paparazzi here in Cricket Creek."

Addison took a bite of her sandwich and chewed slowly as she actually started to consider this crazy suggestion. "I do have a degree in business, but what do I know about running a bridal boutique?"

"Don't you help your father run his art gallery?"

"Yes."

"There you go. Same concept. Just different inventory."

"But would there really be that much demand for wedding dresses in a small town? I wouldn't know where to begin."

"I'll be your first customer. Cam has been bugging me

to set a date. Well, okay, next September after baseball season is over. I want to get married here at Wine and Diner, I think. There's a beautiful courtyard and gazebo. Cam and I met here, so it would be perfect. Granted, Cricket Creek is small, but we're within a few hours of Nashville, Tennessee; Lexington, Kentucky; and Cincinnati, Ohio. And those are just a few of the urban areas close enough to drive from. Weddings are big business these days. That's why Dad and Nicolina thought of Wedding Row. But you can think small and then grow. Hey, I rhymed."

Addison chuckled. "You are very persuasive. You know that? I bet you're good at your job."

"Well, I used to plan lots of charity balls back in Chicago. I had more skills than I gave myself credit for. . . . Wait. . . ." Mia paused and then gasped. "You could *plan* weddings too!"

"Well, I do have experience in *planning* a wedding," Addison said with dark humor. "Make that plural." She held up two fingers.

"I could help in the baseball off-season. Actually, with Cam gone so much I could find time to help you even now. We could have the boutique stocked and ready to open inside a month, maybe sooner. Dad wants to add a hotel and convention center down by the stadium, so that could eventually bring in out-of-town guests. The marina is going to expand too. This little town is continuing to grow by leaps and bounds. I even heard that they are expanding Whisper's Edge, the retirement community down by the riverfront. The owner, Tristan McMillan, teamed up with his mother, who just moved here and opened up a real estate office on the corner of Wedding Row, and it's doing well. As a matter of fact, Maggie McMillan is in charge of leasing the remaining space left in Wedding Row, so we'll get the key from her later. See? No one wants to leave Cricket Creek once they come here," Mia said before happily sliding a spoonful of soup into her mouth.

"Oh, Mia, I don't know. I mean, I don't have a place to live. . . ."

"Well, there are a couple of choices. You could lease a condo high-rise where I live. Dad checked and there is one available. But there are really cool lofts above the shops in Wedding Row. Nicolina used to live above her jewelry shop before she and Dad built their own house. She still uses it as an office. Maggie McMillan lives above her real estate agency as well. The lofts have a big open floor plan and view of the river, hardwood flooring, exposed brick walls, and beamed ceilings. The appliances are stainless steel and the countertops are granite."

"Your dad always did do things top-notch."

"They're pretty sweet."

Addison thought of having her own place, her own business. No cameras following her around. "Mia, my head is spinning."

"So you're giving it some thought?"

"Yes," Addison said and Mia's face lit up. "I'll take a look."

"Shut the front door!"

Addison tossed her head back and laughed. "Of course, I'd like to see the loft too."

"Yes!" Mia smacked her hands down on the table so hard that the ice jingled in the glasses. "This is awesome!"

"I know I'm just looking, but even so, I've never done something this spontaneous. I feel as if I'm jumping without a net. My heart is pounding so hard right now!"

"Doesn't it feel great?" With another laugh Mia stood up and danced in a circle with her nose up in the air.

"What in the world are you doing?"

"The Snoopy happy dance! Come on, get up and do it with me!"

"Mia! We're in public!" Addison reminded her cousin with a laugh.

"Oh, believe me, I've created much more commotion in this restaurant than a mere dance."

Sunny came over to check on them. "Hey, I know the chicken salad is good, but dang, girl."

"No, I just found out that my sweet cousin Addison is going to move here."

"Potentially," Addison reminded her.

"Oh, you will," Mia said firmly.

Sunny sat the pitcher of tea down on the table. "Well, now, Mia. That does call for celebration," Sunny said, and started doing the dance with Mia. Sunny added finger-poking moves toward the ceiling. "Join us, Addison!"

"You guys are seriously crazy." Addison looked around, but no one seemed to act as if dancing in a diner was out of the ordinary. With a grin she slid from the booth and started doing the happy dance with them.

"What are y'all drinkin'?" asked an elderly woman a couple of booths over. "Sunny, I'll have whatever they're havin'."

"Just tea, Violet," Mia answered with a laugh. "We're just high on life."

"You go, girl," Violet answered, and raised her water glass.

Laughing, they sat down and Sunny refilled their glasses.

"That's Violet, who owns Violet's Vintage Clothing down the street," Mia explained. "A totally sweet lady. I shop there all the time and she helps me run Heels for Meals, a charity we started for needy people in the area. Sunny, our waitress, helps out too, along with a few other ladies in town. I'll have you on board too."

"Wow," Addison said, "it sure seems like you're living a nice, fulfilling life here in Cricket Creek. I have to tell you I'm surprised that you and Uncle Mitch ended up in a small town in Kentucky. I remember being in awe of that huge house you used to live in."

"I know." Mia grinned. "Last week I never could have guessed that you'd be sitting across from me at Wine and Diner. Life is full of surprises, so get ready, girlfriend." She did a little snap of her fingers and a head bop, making Addison laugh.

"Yeah, I guess Dad was right. I needed a change of atmosphere."

Mia raised her glass. "Here's to fresh starts."

Addison touched her glass to Mia's. "Well." Addison grinned back at her cousin. "And there is one other perk of running a bridal boutique."

"And what's that?"

"I've sworn off men and marriage. Any guy coming into the shop will be someone's fiancé." She held up her left hand. "That should keep a ring off my finger."

"Maybe in the shop." Mia crumbled some crackers into her soup. "But I wouldn't be so sure. There are a lot of cute guys here in Cricket Creek. Not only baseball players, and, oh, those country boys in their Wrangler jeans can be pretty darned sexy. . . ." She paused and raised her eyebrows.

"What?" Addison thought about her image of potbellies in overalls.

Mia nodded toward the front door. "Don't look now, but one just walked in. Hmm, haven't seen *him* around here before."

"Mia . . ." Addison warned in a low voice. "I've sworn off men. Remember?"

"He might just change your mind. Don't be obvious, but look!"

"No way. I'm *not* looking."

"Oh yeah. He's heading to the stools at the counter, close enough so you can see him. Check him out," Mia urged in a stage whisper. "Yeah, baby . . ."

"I'm not interested," Addison insisted. She scooped up a bit of soup but turned her head to look nonetheless. The spoon paused halfway to her mouth. *Oh my . . .*

He was tall with brown hair kissed by the sun and just shy of needing a trim. A white cotton T-shirt tucked into jeans showcased his broad shoulders and bulging biceps. He walked slowly while looking down at his phone, and Addison wanted to but just *couldn't* look away. Sexy stubble shadowed a firm jaw and when he licked his bottom lip while reading, Addison felt as if she needed to fan her face. Both Aiden and Garret were handsome men, but this guy had a rugged edge instead of glossy perfection and damn if she didn't find it sexy as hell.

The waitress behind the counter greeted him. "Well, hey there. If it isn't Reid Greenfield! Long time, no see, Sugar Pie. What brings you back to Cricket Creek? Family visit?"

Addison watched Reid swing one long leg over the stool and sit a very fine butt down on the red vinyl.

"Hi, Myra. Sure is good to see you too. Yeah, I'm here to help out on the farm for a while," he answered in a soft Southern drawl that slid down Addison's spine like smooth Southern Comfort. "I'd like a glass of your sweet tea, if you don't mind, while I look over the menu."

"Your sweet, sexy self can have anything your little ole heart desires," Myra answered with a sassy sway of her hips.

"Is she really flirting with him?" Addison felt an odd stab of jealousy. "She's got to be old enough to be his mother," Addison grumbled, but kept her eyes on Reid.

Mia chuckled. "Oh, that's Myra for you. She's got that free-spirit, hippie thing going on like Uncle Paul and pretty much says whatever she wants. Even though she turned the restaurant over to her niece, Jessica, she still works from time to time, ever since Jess and Ty had a baby. She's a trip, for sure, but she's happily married to Owen Lawson, the groundskeeper at the baseball stadium and father-in-law to Noah Falcon, the hometown hero who built the stadium. As a matter of fact, Myra hired me as a waitress when I first arrived in town."

"You were a waitress?" Addison asked absently. Most of her brain was still focused on Reid.

"For, like, a minute, until I caused a fight that landed Cam in jail. I actually jumped on the back of a guy and pulled his ears until he cried uncle."

"That's nice," Addison said, but then blinked and finally tore her gaze from Reid. "Wait. What did you just say?"

Mia laughed. "It's a long story that I'll save for later. It gets better if I have a martini or two. Hey, speaking of martinis, we should go to Sully's Tavern later and have a couple after I show you around. Stay with me tonight and we can walk from my place. We have a lot to discuss!"

"Sounds like a plan," Addison agreed with a grin. It was difficult not to get pulled in by Mia's enthusiasm.

"Maybe Reid over there will show up and pull you onto the dance floor and do a little two-steppin'."

"I'm guessing that's nothing like Dubstepping."

Mia laughed. "No, thank goodness. And let me tell you, I'd rather be dancing the night away at Sully's than any amped-up big-city nightclub."

Addison would never have guessed that her globe-hopping cousin would have settled down in a small town. After taking another sneak peek at Reid she slipped the forgotten spoonful of soup into her mouth. While eating her lunch, she listened to her cousin chatter away about Cricket Creek, but snuck glances at Reid when Mia wasn't looking. She didn't even want to, but every time she heard his whiskey-smooth voice she felt compelled to glance his way.

"Still checking him out?" Mia asked with a wiggle of her eyebrows.

Addison felt heat creep into her cheeks. "I was . . . um checking out the desserts."

"I think indulging in something decadent and delicious is just what you need, Addison. I suggest you go for it."

Jump from the frying pan into the fire? "Tempting, I'll admit, but, no, thank you." She told herself not to look Reid's way again and gave Mia her full attention.

After paying the bill they lingered over coffee, taking notes and brainstorming until Mia looked at her watch. "Wow, it's getting late. I'd better call Maggie and arrange a showing. Are you ready to head over and take a look?"

"Sure," Addison said. The more they'd chatted, the more the idea started taking root in her brain. She would discuss the venture with her mother but Addison was starting to really get excited. "I can't wait to see it."

Just as they both stood up, Mia's phone rang. "Oh, it's my boss," Mia said. "I'll have to take this."

"No problem. We can go in my car. I'll head out and open the windows or maybe put the top down."

"Oh, that sounds fun! It's such a nice day." Mia nodded. "I won't be long."

Addison hitched her purse over her shoulder and started toward the exit. She glanced out the front window to admire the quaint view, and when she turned toward the door she ran smack into someone so hard that the lid popped off of his to-go cup, splashing tea down the front of his white T-shirt. It was Reid. "Oh, I'm so sorry!" Addison immediately felt heat in her cheeks. "I wasn't watching where I was going." She quickly grabbed some paper napkins from a table and handed them to him even though touching his chest held some serious appeal. "Sorry," she repeated with a wince.

"Totally my fault," Reid said as he looked down and dabbed at the brown splotches. Addison could see the outline of his pectoral muscles through the white cotton and wished she were doing the job for him. She inhaled sharply and caught the spicy masculine scent of his aftershave. "I was reading a text message, or I would have seen you coming." When he looked up and smiled at her, Addison noticed a cute dimple in his cheek. Up close she could see that his eyes were a very dark blue and for an embarrassing moment she simply stared at him, feeling warm and sort of befuddled. Living in LA, Addison was no stranger to handsome men, but she'd never had this sort of reaction to a perfect stranger. He held up the phone to show her the message. "Apparently picking up cupcakes is something I needed to be reminded of three times."

When she noticed the message was from a woman Addison felt her stomach drop. Silly . . . why should she care if he had a girlfriend?

"After you." Reid gestured toward the door, deftly tossing the wet napkins in the trash can a few feet away.

"Thank you." When he held the door open for her

Addison felt another unexpected little thrill at passing so close to him. When they were outside she knew she should keep walking to her car, but for some reason she lingered, searching for something else to say. *Nice to meet you? Have a nice day? Hope your shirt doesn't stain?* But before she could open her mouth his phone dinged, indicating another text message.

"I remember the cupcakes, Sara," Reid grumbled, reminding Addison that the message had been from a woman.

"Sorry again." Suddenly feeling foolish, Addison started walking toward the parking lot.

Reid looked up, and to Addison's surprise he fell in step beside her. "Make that four times my sister has reminded me." He held up four fingers and sighed. "She runs an educational program for kids on our farm, and someone is having a birthday." He chuckled. "And I am probably boring you to death with information you don't want to know."

Oh . . . his sister*!* Addison felt a little surge of joy and gave him a grin. "Did you text her back?"

"The first two times. Now it's just redundant," he grumbled good-naturedly as they walked toward the parking lot. "So, are you in town for a visit?"

"I thought I was, but my cousin Mia wants me to open a bridal boutique and plan weddings. Oddly enough, I'm actually considering it."

"Are you kidding me? You might be the answer to my prayers."

"Oh . . ." Addison said, and another stab of disappointment came from out of nowhere. "So, you're getting married?" Addison asked with false brightness as she dug inside her purse in search of her car keys. She suddenly wished Mia would hurry up, before she made a complete fool of herself. What in the world was she doing giving personal information to a stranger? What was up with getting flustered over a guy she didn't even know—especially since she had sworn off guys, anyway?

And where in the world were her keys?

5

Unanswered Prayers

"Um . . ." Reid began, but judging by the sudden frown on her pretty face he was quickly wearing out his welcome. Instead of introducing himself, Reid decided he should probably take a hike before she pulled mace out of the big purse she was frantically digging around in. Odd, but Reid usually avoided small talk and now he remembered why. After glancing back toward Wine and Diner, she stopped in back of a sweet red Mustang convertible with California plates. Taking in the details, he now noticed her designer bag and that she'd slipped a pair of Gucci sunglasses over her big brown eyes. And although she was casually dressed in jeans and a lightweight lavender sweater, her watch looked expensive and she wore a diamond tennis bracelet that glittered in the sunshine. *Great . . .* She probably really wasn't interested in talking to a country boy like him, anyway. Feeling foolish followed by a little bit irritated, he took a step backward. "Um, I should get going. Good luck with, you know . . . everything."

She glanced up and flipped her shiny black hair over her shoulder. She was really pretty, and Reid found himself wondering about her family heritage.

"So, when is the wedding?"

Wait . . . huh? "Wedding? What wedding?"

"Your wedding." She pushed her sunglasses up higher on her nose and waited for his answer. "Isn't that why I'm the answer to your prayers?" She tilted her head slightly and the breeze played with her hair, making it caress her face.

Reid looked at her while trying to form an answer, but all he could think about was that the answer to his prayers would be to reach over and brush the hair from her face . . . pull her into his arms and kiss her.

Kiss her? What in the hell was coming over him? Maybe he was spending too much time in the sun.

Luckily a honking horn startled him back into thinking somewhat straight, but he took another step backward so that she was out of reach, just to play it safe. "No, I'm not getting married." Reid shook his head as if the very idea was ludicrous. "I value my independence way too much," he added, but then realized he was once again giving her more information than she probably wanted to know. He cleared his throat and tried to sound businesslike. "No, my sister has this wild idea to turn one of our old barns into a reception hall and host weddings on our farm, beginning with her own." Reid shoved his fingers through his hair and shook his head. "It would mean sinking a lot of her savings into the venture and I'm not sure it's a sound idea. I'd be interested in hiring a consultant, hopefully to dissuade her from going through with it." When she remained silent he stuck out his hand. "By the way, I'm Reid Greenfield."

She took his hand and gave him a firm handshake. "Addison Monroe. It's nice to meet you, Reid."

Reid smiled, enjoying the feel of her small hand in his and hearing his name on her lips. There was something familiar about her, something that tugged at the back of his brain but he couldn't put his finger on it. "So, am I going to be your first customer?"

"Well, we're putting the cart before the horse. I'm

heading over with Mia to look at the shop, but as much as I'm interested, I'm not one hundred percent sure that I'm actually going to do the venture without more thought and research. Although I do have to say that Mia is very persuasive."

Reid dug his wallet out of his back pocket and fished out one of his business cards. He appreciated that Addison was taking the time to consider all aspects of a new business. Hopefully she'd be a good influence on his sister. "This has my e-mail and cell phone number on it. If you go through with the shop, I would appreciate if you'd at least give Sara real numbers as to what it would take to get involved in doing receptions and weddings. It's not that I'm totally against the idea; I just don't want to see her lose her hard-earned retirement. I'd be glad to show you the barn and surroundings and then get your opinion. But I want you to err on the side of caution."

Addison took the card. "I'm hardly an expert." She glanced at his business card. "And it appears that you have the credentials to advise your sister in business matters."

"Are you kidding? She won't listen to me—well, unless you count listening only to try to prove me wrong." Reid gave her a half-lopsided grin. "Of course, that's pretty hard to do."

She tilted her head and chuckled. "I'll keep you in mind. But like I said, I'm no expert. This whole thing came out of left field."

"Well, I'm sure you'll do your homework. After all, it's going to be your business. I just want you to play devil's advocate so she goes into this with her eyes wide open. I don't want the barn on our farm to become a money pit and eat up Sara's retirement."

"If I go through with this venture, I'll consider your offer."

"That's all I can ask. At any rate, it was nice to meet you, Addison. I wish you the best of luck," Reid added, and he was about to ask if she'd like to have dinner and talk it over but decided it might be too pushy. She had his card. If she was interested, she'd give him a call. So he turned and walked toward his pickup truck, oddly reluctant to leave her company. His hand was on the door handle when she called out to him.

"Reid?"

He turned around, finding her grinning over at him. "Yeah?" he asked, and couldn't believe that his pulse kicked up a notch just from seeing her smile.

"Don't forget the cupcakes!" Addison pointed to the Grammar's Bakery across the street.

Reid put the heel of his hand to his forehead, and she laughed. "I was going to pull across the street in front of the bakery," he said, but she only laughed harder.

"Sure you were. Your secret is safe with me."

"Thank you!" Reid shook his head as he headed across the street to the bakery. It really wasn't like him to forget to run an errand, especially since he'd been reminded four—well, now, make it five times—but in his defense, Addison had been quite a distraction. He was still thinking over why he was so drawn to someone he had just met when he reached the entrance to the bakery. The bell tinkled over the door as he walked in. *Ahhh,* he took a deep whiff of the fragrant aroma of brewed coffee and freshly baked goodies.

"Well, if it isn't Reid Greenfield," said Mabel Grammar, owner of the bakery. "I declare, I do think you're even better-lookin' than the last time I saw you. We sure grown 'em good here in Cricket Creek," she boasted. "Back home for good, I hope." She leaned over the counter and held her arms out. "Now get over here and give me some sugar."

"And you're lookin' mighty fine yourself." Reid walked over to the enticing display of Danish and cookies.

"You talkin' about me or the cookies? Although I do have some pretty nice buns," she added with a deep chuckle.

"Both." After giving Mabel a hug he asked, "What's your secret—Botox? Come on, Mabel, fess up."

"Ha! It's easy: just eat more doughnuts." She stuck a pose and fluttered her eyelashes. "Keeps the wrinkles in my round face filled in and my bum as big and round as Kim Kardashian's."

Reid laughed. Cricket Creek might have gone through some changes in recent years but some things stayed the same. "Well, it looks good on you," he said, wishing it was as easy to flirt with Addison as it was with Mabel. "I'm here to pick up two dozen cupcakes for Sara."

"Got them right here," Mable said, and pulled a box from a shelf. "Decorated with farm animals and vegetables, just like Sara ordered. I've heard nothing but good things about the Old MacDonald program. Good for Sara for teaching kids about farming. They need to know that not everything is computer generated or made in a factory."

"True," Reid said, and realized that he hadn't given his sister the acknowledgment that she deserved. He thought about the ivory-tower comment she made and wondered if he had grown out of touch with his family. But it was his job to help people invest and manage their money. How could he turn that off, especially when it came to his very own family?

"Anything else I can get you today?" Mabel asked.

"Oh, I can't resist your butter cookies. I'll take a dozen, and throw in a cheese Danish for the ride back home."

Mable reached for a white paper bag. "Coming right up." After he paid his bill, she said, "Don't be a stranger."

"I won't," Reid promised. After he walked back outside he looked down Main Street, noticing the improvements and new shops. Sara had been right. Cricket Creek had weathered some tough economic times, but beginning with Noah Falcon's return home to build the baseball stadium, the little town had refused to throw in the towel. But saving the family farm wasn't the same thing, and Reid was well aware that Sara was as stubborn as the day was long. Hopefully, Addison Monroe would take him up on his offer and talk some sense into his well-meaning sister.

With his hands full, Reid crossed the street at the light, nodding to greetings, waves, and honking horns from people he hadn't seen in a while. Although he enjoyed living in Lexington, he had to admit that seeing old friends and eating at his favorite spots felt pretty damned good.

As Reid drove home he thought he might head over to Sully's later on, drink a few beers, and maybe play some pool. He wouldn't have to twist Braden's arm too hard to talk his little brother into going with him. When he passed what he assumed was Wedding Row he slowed down and his thoughts turned back to Addison Monroe, wondering again why she seemed so familiar, and then it suddenly dawned on him. Addison Monroe must be the daughter of finance guru Melinda Monroe.

Reid smacked the steering wheel. "Wow . . ." he murmured, and shook his head in a bit of wonder. Reid had read all of Melinda's bestselling books and watched her show on a regular basis. Addison came off as much more mild mannered but was the spitting image of her famous mother. His smile widened and he wondered why he hadn't put two and two together sooner. Melinda Monroe wasn't a fan of spending money foolishly and would never suggest using retirement money for anything other than what it was intended for. Hopefully, that same way of thinking was drummed into Addison's head and would ultimately help convince Sara to drop the barn-renovation idea and find another way to generate extra income for the family farm.

Reid swerved slightly when he spotted Addison's red Mustang pulling into the parking lot in front of Wedding Row. It had been a while since he'd had such a strong pull of attraction to a woman, and damned if he didn't kind of like it. With the stress of being a financial adviser during tough economic times Reid had pulled back from much of a social life, including dating. He glanced in his rearview mirror and caught another glimpse of the flashy red convertible and grinned. For the first time in a long while he felt an urge to get back in the game. And he knew just where he was going to test the waters.

Reid didn't know how long he planned on staying in Cricket Creek, but he knew one thing for sure. In spite of the financial struggle at the farm, coming home for a spell was just what he needed. He turned on the radio and then suddenly remembered the cheese Danish, and the delicious treat called his name. "Oh yeah . . ." Reid said, and reached over for the bag. He sank his teeth into the sweet gooey goodness and moaned with appreciation as he chewed.

When Trace Adkins started singing "Ladies Love Country Boys," Reid chuckled. He wasn't sure if Addison Monroe would yell "Turn it up" if he started blaring Hank Jr., but he had to wonder if she could possibly fall for his Southern-boy drawl. She might be way up there out of his league, but, hey, it was worth a shot. Hopefully, after touring the property she would decide to open the bridal boutique and give him the chance to find out.

6

Say Yes to the Dress!

"HELLO, MIA!" MAGGIE SAID, AND STOOD UP FROM BE-hind her desk. Smiling, she walked toward the entrance. "And you must be Addison," Maggie added, extending her hand to the pretty young woman with amazing hair and expressive eyes. "I'm Maggie McMillan. I hear that you're interested in looking at the building intended for the bridal boutique."

"It's a spontaneous decision, but yes," Addison said with a fond glance at Mia.

"Take it from me: Those can be the best kind of decisions," Mia said with a smile at her cousin. When Addison raised her eyebrows, Mia added, "I'll explain over martinis at Sully's later tonight."

"I agree that you need to go with your gut," Maggie said. "Not long ago I told my son, Tristan, that life doesn't always have to make perfect sense. And it's true. I'd love to show the store to you!" Maggie picked up the key. "Do you ladies need a water or soda to take along?" After both gave a negative shake of their heads, Maggie nodded and gestured toward the door. "Then let's go have a look."

As Maggie led the way she smiled at the easy chatter between the cousins. When she had been their age, her life had been far different and she had had to put her own dreams on hold. Not that she regretted putting her son first, but now that Tristan was a successful, happy young man with a lovely fiancée, it was high time that she moved forward with her own aspirations. Her recent move from Cincinnati to Cricket Creek to help Tristan expand Whisper's Edge was just what she needed to jump-start the rest of her life.

"Wedding Row was such a wonderful concept, Mia," Maggie commented. "Your father and Nicolina did a fantastic job of blending the buildings into the surroundings." She waved her arm in an arc. "You would have thought this had been here for many years instead of being a new construction. From the gas streetlights to the cobblestone paving, these shops have the quaint feel of Cricket Creek."

"It's just lovely," Addison agreed as they rounded the corner to where the bridal shop was located. "Oh, Designs by Diamante! We'll have to stop in and see Nicolina soon," Addison said to Mia. "The necklace you sent me for Christmas was gorgeous. No wonder Uncle Mitch has to kidnap her from her work."

"Nicolina does lots of bridal jewelry," Mia said. "You could even put some of her pieces in your store."

"Excellent idea," Addison agreed.

Maggie hid her smile. Mia was doing much of the selling for her. "Addison, just so you know, there are plans to start a second phase called Riverside Row that will include a deli, an upscale pub, and several other restaurants. We also have interest from a high-end salon and day spa. Soon shopping on Wedding Row will be an all-day event and not just for brides."

"Oh, that would be wonderful," Mia said to Addison. "The only thing we're lacking is additional places to hold receptions. The convention center and hotel will solve that issue, but that's pretty far down the road. Dad has pulled way back from the full-throttle mode he used to be in all the time. But we can work on that later."

"Oh!" Addison said as they stood outside the bridal boutique. "The display window already has a gown in it!"

"I did that last week," Maggie said. "Pretty, isn't it?"

"Oh yes. Especially the lighting. I'm enchanted. Let's go inside!"

Mia gave her a nod. "Nice touch, Maggie."

"Well, I also have a bit of my own agenda at stake other than just securing the lease. I thought if we got a bridal boutique here in Cricket Creek it would speed up Tristan and Savannah getting married. They bought a beautiful farmhouse overlooking the river but have yet to set a wedding date. Tristan has just been so busy with the expansion of Whisper's Edge. But if I get Savannah in a dress we might just get the ball rolling."

Mia gave Addison a nudge with her elbow. "Well, there's another sale for you and another wedding to plan, and you haven't even opened the doors yet."

"You ladies are tag-teaming me," Addison said with a laugh. "But I have to admit that I'm feeling pretty darned excited. Maybe having planned my own two weddings will pay off in an odd twist of fate."

"You were married twice?" Maggie blurted out. "Sorry—not that it's my business. I was just surprised since you're so young."

"Nope, I was only engaged twice. Never made it down the aisle."

"Oh, well, I think you'd be splendid at running a bridal boutique." Maggie wasn't one to push but some instinct told her that something special was going on here. Maybe it was from years of showing homes, but she somehow could picture Addison owning a bridal boutique and doing quite well. She just had a lovely, serene way about her that would resonate with jittery brides. Maggie sighed inwardly. Not that she had ever been a bride, but she still got emotional at weddings and she really could not wait for Tristan to marry the lovely Savannah Perry. "It took my son a long time to find the perfect woman, so there's time for you, Addison. The right one just hasn't come along. But I'm looking forward to my son's wedding. I'd like nothing better than to be a grandma," Maggie said with a smile.

"A grandma? You don't look old enough, Maggie," Mia told her.

"You're too sweet," Maggie said as she opened the door with a flourish.

"Oh ..." Addison said with a look at Mia. "You're right—it's ready to go."

Maggie's heels clicked over the gleaming hardwood flooring as she walked over and flipped on the lights and waited for the exclamation. She wasn't disappointed. "The lighting over the racks against the wall will spotlight wedding dresses that will face the center rather than be crammed together. Overhead, the lights will be muted so as to give the dresses the attention they deserve."

"The chandelier in the center of the room is an elegant touch," Mia said.

Addison nodded. "The lighted display cases are so pretty. I can envision adding some antiques, some vintage jewelry and gowns along with the new."

Maggie walked over to the dressing rooms. "I know a woman living in Whisper's Edge who makes exquisite bridal veils."

"Oh, I love the idea of using local crafters." Addison turned to Mia. "A display case with Nicolina's jewelry would be fantastic."

Maggie put her hand on Addison's arm. "The concept behind having Wedding Row is for the shops to play off of and to promote each other. And if you decide to actually do some wedding planning we could add office space in the back." Maggie knew that talking as if it was already a done deal often worked, but in this case she didn't have to do much selling. Addison seemed quite taken with the whole thing and walked around with a sense of wonder on her pretty face.

"Oh, Mia, I . . . I think I want to do this!" She put a hand to her chest. "Funny that after two botched engagements, I would feel so drawn to opening a wedding boutique, but it just somehow feels right."

"Oh, Addison, I would adore it if you moved here, so, like Maggie, I have my own agenda, but my heart is pounding too." Mia smiled and pointed to the front window. "Just say yes to the dress!"

Addison laughed. "Yes!" She turned to Maggie. "As crazy as it seems I already know I want to lease the shop. I just need to go over the details with my mother to make sure this is doable for me."

"Excellent," Maggie said. "Do you want to go to the local bank? I can give you names."

"Actually, I have a trust fund that was set up for my education but I didn't have to use it because of scholarships. I also have stock in my parent's company that I could borrow against. My mother will have the answers to the best way for me to go about this. I'll talk to her and then we can get the paperwork in place."

"Her mother is Melinda Monroe," Mia explained. "You know, *Melinda Knows Money*?"

"Oh my gosh—I'm a big fan of your mother's," Maggie gushed, and it was true. "Now that you mention it, I can certainly see the resemblance! She shook her head. "I was a single mom and desperately needed help with my finances. Her books helped me save money for my son's education and plan for the future. When you talk to her, tell her I said thanks!"

"I will," Addison said with a warm smile. "Send me the paperwork and I'll get things moving in the right direction."

"Sounds good," Maggie said briskly. "Now, would you like to lease the flat upstairs as well? I certainly love mine. And makes for an easy commute to work," she added with a wink.

Addison smiled with pure delight. "Oh, I had forgotten about that! Yes!"

"You can park around the back of the building and

enter there, but you can also go up the back steps from the shop. Follow me," Maggie said. She loved the enthusiasm floating in the air. One of the things she relished about real estate was the joy of ownership or, in this case, the start of a new business. Maggie had never been just about the sale and liked to match clients to homes that they would be happy living in. Addison seemed sharp and savvy, not surprising, given who her mother and uncle were. When they reached the top of the stairs, Maggie switched on the lights.

"Oh my gosh—it's gorgeous!" Addison spun in a circle as if trying to take it all in at once, but then hurried over to the floor-to-ceiling windows. "Oh, would you look at the view of the river? There goes a barge," she said as if she'd just spotted the *Queen Mary*. "Oh, Mia, I can see the stadium to the left."

"I love the open feel," Mia said. "You could furnish it with a modern flair or with antiques."

"Or an eclectic mix," Addison agreed. "Wow, recessed lighting. Oh, and the kitchen is gleaming with stainless-steel appliances, but the exposed-brick wall to the left just warms everything up, don't you think?"

"Did you see the loft guest bedroom?" Maggie asked.

Addison put a hand over her mouth and Mia squealed with delight, making Maggie forget to be businesslike. She chuckled. You'd never know these two young women came from privilege. Mia was a sweetheart and Addison seemed so grounded. It was hard to believe that two men had let her get away.

"You don't like it at all, do you?" Maggie teased.

"I don't like it. I love it," Addison admitted, and then turned to Mia. "What was that dance we did in the diner?"

"The Snoopy happy dance."

"Let's do it again!" Addison said.

"Come on, Maggie. Join us!"

Maggie hesitated for a fraction but then giggled like a schoolgirl. "Oh, why not?" A moment later all three were dancing in the middle of the big open space.

"Time to go to Sully's and celebrate!" Mia announced. "Oh, and we need to come up with a name for your shop. Let's get the party started!"

Maggie laughed with the girls as she locked up the building. "Addison, I'll get the paperwork to you, and if you have any questions don't hesitate to call." She handed her a business card. "My cell phone is on there and I'll pick up just about anytime of the day. Congratulations! I can't wait to see the bridal boutique full of dresses!" She gave them both a hug and was still smiling after they left.

But as she closed up her office and headed up to her own loft apartment, she felt a stab of loneliness. She was so glad that she had made the decision to move to Cricket Creek to live near Tristan, but he was busy with the Whisper's Edge expansion and spent much of his downtime with his fiancée. Although she also kept busy trying to list other property and lease the remaining shops in Wedding Row, her nights were often spent alone. Now that summer was arriving, Maggie would also work with the Chamber of Commerce, helping to place visitors in rental properties, and although she absolutely adored having her own agency, her social life left, well, a whole lot to be desired. Savannah had encouraged her to join some of the activities at Whisper's Edge, but at fifty-three Maggie really didn't feel as if she fit in with that crowd just yet, as lovely as the ladies of the retirement home were to her.

Maggie sighed as she thought of the day last week when she had bought the wedding dress at Violet's Vintage Clothing with the intent of putting it in the display window. Violet, bless her heart, had thought that Maggie was getting married. "Not ever likely," Maggie said with another little sigh.

"Oh, just stop," she chastised her sorry self. It wasn't like her to let blue feelings get a grip on her, and she straightened her spine. But when she opened the fridge she didn't feel like cooking dinner. The freezer had a selection of frozen dinners, and she wrinkled her nose. "Yuck."

"What you need to do is get the hell out of here and go out on the town," she said out loud, as if hearing her own words would stiffen her resolve. Back in Cincinnati, she'd had her regular dining spots, hit an occasional happy hour where she would see friends, hobnob, and socialize. But it wasn't as easy in a small town. Even though she'd been born in Cricket Creek, she'd left in a bit of a local scandal and hadn't really kept in touch with anyone as a result. Coming home from freshman year of college pregnant would do that to you, especially when she had no idea who the father was. And it didn't help that her own father hadn't been supportive.

Maggie ground her teeth together. That was years ago. Tristan was a grown man, and her father was long gone. She thought about going up to Wine and Diner, where there was an elegant bar in the rear of the restaurant. She could sashay in there and maybe listen to the live music they had in the lounge most evenings. Have a glass of wine. Flirt.

What? Flirt? Did she even remember how? "Maybe I am ready for Whisper's Edge retirement community after all," she grumbled, and felt the sting of tears threatening. God, she knew she had so many blessings in her life, but she just needed something exciting to happen.

And she would kill for a hot, steamy kiss.

"Not likely to happen," she grumbled again, and then decided she just might head over to Sully's and buy Mia and Addison a martini. Not only would she be networking and could write it off, but it would get her out for the evening. Maggie snapped her fingers. "Yeah, that's the ticket," she said, and tried to pump herself up. Just when she'd talked herself into it, her phone rang on her business line.

"Maggie McMillan," she answered in her best business voice.

"Hello, Maggie. This is, um, Rick. I mean, Richard ... Rule. I'm interested in renting a vacation home for a week or so. Do you have anything available?"

7

Rules of the Game

"WELL, I HAVE A FEW SUGGESTIONS," RESPONDED THE pleasant voice of Maggie McMillan. "Several bed-and-breakfasts, a newly remodeled lodge located near the marina, or I have a very nice secluded log cabin down by the river. I also have some furnished condos that we usually rent by the month, but I happen to know at least one is available by the week. It's within walking distance to the baseball stadium and has a river view."

"Interesting," Rick said. The sound of her low-pitched, sultry tone was somehow soothing—a good thing, since he was in a helluva bad mood. "Can you tell me some details about the cabin?"

"Sure, just give me a minute to get to my desk and pull up the information."

Finding out that his own publicist had started a rumor that Rick had been having an affair with his son's fiancée would put anybody in a foul mood. When he'd confronted his now former publicist, the jackass had said that Rick needed to ramp up his bad-boy image if he wanted to have a shot at another world tour. To make matters worse, Garret refused to deny the accusations, since he'd landed a role on a *Big Brother*–knockoff reality show and wanted to boost the ratings.

Rick had been fond of Addison Monroe and wanted to assure her that he wasn't a part of this fiasco. But Garret refused to give him Addison's phone number, so Rick had decided he would track Addison down and personally apologize for whatever damage he'd done to her reputation—if she wanted, he could even make a public statement denying everything. The tabloids were going to have a field day with this sordid lie. Rick couldn't believe that Garret wouldn't do the right thing and squash the rumors and it made Rick furious. Unfortunately, firing his publicist led to the man spitefully mouthing off to the media that rock star Rick Ruleman was going off the deep end.

Screw the world tour, and shame on Garret.

Unfortunately, Addison had disappeared a week ago and no one seemed to know where she was hiding out, not that Rick could blame her. Rick had his manager do some serious digging and he'd turned up a Facebook post by Addison's cousin Mia Monroe saying that she was superthrilled to have her cousin in town for a visit. Mia lived in Cricket Creek, Kentucky. Bingo.

"Mr. Rule?" asked the pleasant voice.

"Yes?"

"You're in luck! The log cabin is indeed available weekly. It's spacious, with cathedral ceilings, a stone fireplace, and lovely furnishings. The wraparound porch has a river view and there's a hot tub to relax in. In a word, it's gorgeous."

"Sounds like it."

"Oh yes, and you have the privacy of the wooded location, but the drive up into Cricket Creek is fairly short, so you have the best of both worlds. I can send you the information along with pictures. If you like it, I can hold it for you. I'd just need a credit-card deposit and some information."

Damn . . . he didn't want her to know his real identity.

If word got out he was heading to Cricket Creek, he'd blow Addison's cover and have paparazzi crawling all over the place. He'd have to wait until tomorrow and have his manager book it for him. He gave her Phil's e-mail address. "Thanks. I'll check it out and get back to you."

"Sure thing. Let me know if I can be of any other help."

"I will. Thanks a lot."

After ending the call Rick leaned back in his leather office chair and blew out a long sigh. He ran his hand over his scruffy signature beard and then shoved his fingers through his shoulder-length hair, artfully cut to frame his face. He had a small gold hoop earring in one ear and wore black leather almost every day. More often than not he had a young, busty blonde on his arm whenever he went out on the town, which was just about every night.

Rick pinched the bridge of his nose with his thumb and index finger. Living the life of a rock legend was damned tiring. He'd been ready to head out for the night when a picture of him and Addison embracing flashed across the television screen. Rick remembered when the embrace happened . . . on the night his son had announced his engagement to Addison. But clearly some hotshot pop-news reporter had dug it up to throw fuel onto the rumor that Rick was responsible for his son's broken engagement.

Rick sighed again and looked down at the big combat boots he almost always wore. They were heavy. The buttery-soft black leather pants were clingy and hot. His beard itched. And his long-ass choppy hair was ridiculous. But the long hair, bearded face, and leather were part of his brand, his style. Who he was . . .

Or was it?

"Hell, no."

Was it ever?

Rick clenched and unclenched his fists, thinking, brooding. Wondering how his life had come to . . . this. Pretending until he didn't even know who the hell he truly was anymore. He started humming the slow, soulful *original* version of his first breakout hit single, "Jagged Edge." But his record label had wanted hard rock, and at eighteen who was he to argue? After "Jagged Edge" went platinum, his future was set. He'd had to work harder at a style of music that didn't come as naturally and often felt as if he were playing a role instead of living his life. But money and fame were difficult to turn down.

Was Garret's flippant, unconcerned attitude about life a result of being Rick Ruleman's son? The answer was easy: of course. How in the hell could Rick expect his son to be responsible when he himself still lived off of his glory days, refusing to grow up? What had Garret's mother called it when she'd shouted that she'd wanted a divorce? Oh yeah: the Peter Pan syndrome. He'd laughed in her face and walked out the door, never really thinking she'd have the nerve to divorce him or go for sole custody of five-year-old Garret. But she did, calling him an absentee husband and father. And he didn't fight it because he knew she was right. But instead of letting Becca know that he was devastated, Rick had acted as if he didn't care.

But he did care then and he cared now. . . . He just sucked at life.

Rick looked down at the combat boots. And so he played the role of badass rock star, but now that he was in his midfifties he was stretching it a bit. Thinking he needed a stiff drink, he pushed to his feet and headed for the liquor cabinet in the dining room. Except for drinking to excess now and then he had at least stayed away from drugs and preached against them. He did have that to be proud of. He'd seen too many of his friends go down that sorry-ass path to ever become a user. And to his knowledge Garret never touched the shit either.

After pouring two fingers of bourbon over cracked ice, Rick plopped down on the sofa in the great room. He took a deep swallow, letting the smooth, cold bourbon turn to fire in his belly and numb his brain. He leaned back, holding the crystal glass loosely in his fingers, willing his body to relax. It was early. He could still go out, but the thought held little appeal. He suddenly decided that for once he'd turn in early, get a good night's rest. In the morning he'd head to Cricket Creek, Kentucky, to do some damage control.

And then the doorbell rang.

Irritated at the interruption he headed for the front door, thinking it would likely be Frank, who knew the code to open the front gate. But when he opened the door it was Caitlyn. Caitlyn . . . Hell, he didn't even remember the last name of the twentysomething starlet who was his latest arm candy. Caitlyn was wild and insatiable in bed . . . making it damned difficult for a fifty-five-year-old to keep up with her. Before Rick could think of a plausible reason to send her packing, she pulled her skintight, super-short red dress up and over her head.

And stood there completely naked.

"Now!" was all she said, and when Rick failed to move she walked over on her impossibly high heels, pushed him up against the wall, and kissed him.

Rick resisted for a moment, easing her away from him. "Caitlyn . . ." he began, but she put a fingertip to his lips.

"Shh, no talking," she demanded, and cupped his cock through the leather. "Ohhh, not ready, huh? I'll have to take care of that little problem." She gave him a slow smile as she unbuttoned his shirt and raked her nails down his chest just hard enough to almost cause pain.

He felt his cock respond. "Baby, I was born ready," he said automatically.

"Me too." She planted her high-heel-clad feet apart and then guided his hand between her thighs. "See, babe? Do me right here against the wall. I want it hard and fast." She reached for the snap on his pants, undid the zipper, and boldly reached for him.

"God, you're big. So sexy," she purred, but Rick wondered if it was true. Yeah, he worked out, ran, lifted, but he was twenty-five years older than her. . . . Was he really sexy, or was it who he was that made him sexy to her? Would she give him the time of day if he wasn't famous?

No. *Hell, no.* The answer was like cold water on his ardor.

"Caitlyn . . ."

"What don't you understand about not talking?" she asked, and then covered his mouth with a deep, hungry kiss. She pushed her big breasts into his chest and moved slowly up and down, letting her nipples tease and taunt. With a groan, Rick gave in, cupping her bare ass, pushing her against the wall. "Yeah, here, and then take me in front of the fireplace," she pleaded. "Over and over again. First, I want to straddle you and ride you hard. Then I'm going to get on my hands and knees while you give it to me from behind, going as deep and fast as you can."

Knowing the floor would play havoc on his knees, Rick shook his head. "No, baby. I want you in my bed." He took her hand and led her across the room, but when a shaft of setting sunlight illuminated her face she suddenly looked so very . . . *young.* Rick swallowed hard. This was wrong.

He stopped in his tracks.

"Caitlyn, I think you should go."

When she reached for his cock again Rick pushed her hand away. She pulled a pout. "Really?"

"Yeah, really," Rick repeated this time with an edge to his voice. And in that moment he knew without a shadow of a doubt that he had to get his sorry-ass excuse for a life under control. "And you should think more highly of yourself." He picked up her dress and tossed it to her. "I'm sorry."

"Is this some kind of role-play? Because — "

"No, Caitlyn. As a matter of fact, I'm tired of playing a role. It's time to get real."

"What's wrong with you? Are you tripping on something?"

"I don't and never will do any of that crap." Rick all but pushed a sputtering and protesting Caitlyn out the door. "Seriously, better yourself."

He headed to the bathroom and stared at himself in the mirror. "Time for a makeover, beginning with the beard."

8

Honky-Tonk Heaven

"SULLY'S IS FUN!" ADDISON TOOK ANOTHER SWALLOW OF her martini, called a Redneck Sunset. She and Mia sat at a high-top table near the back of the bar by flat-screen televisions showing a variety of sporting events. The event getting the most attention was two men in a cage grappling with each other until one tapped out. "How's your Honky-Tonk Heaven?"

"Delish," Mia replied with a chuckle. "It tastes a little bit like a Washington Apple but less tart. Even though Pete pokes fun at posh restaurants with fancy martini names, he's an amazing mixologist. He knows the importance of chilling the glasses, and you'll never see any shards of ice floating in one of his martinis."

"Excellent."

"It was Pete's son, Clint, who actually came up with the funny names, but don't be fooled. He only uses top-shelf liquor."

"I can tell." Addison nodded with appreciation and then lifted her glass. "And it packs quite a punch but tastes good enough to be dangerous."

"Hey, if we get hammered we can walk to my condo from here, so no worries. We're celebrating, remember?"

Addison felt another tingle of excitement. "I can't really believe I'm opening a bridal shop, of all things. Everything is happening so fast! But Mom crunched the numbers with me and she thinks the shop will do well." She tapped her toes to the country music blaring from the jukebox and looked around. She'd never been fond of going to clubs, much to Garret's dismay. Unlike happy hours Addison was used to at piano lounges, where subtle music played in the background and hushed conversations buzzed at a low hum, accented by the muted tinkle of glasses, this bar was loud and hopping. Two couples played a lively game of pool at the far end of the bar. Darts were being tossed in the corner and an old-fashioned pinball machine dinged and flashed with enthusiasm. Music, laughter, shouted greetings, and friendly wagers mingled together in a loud blend of fun.

"Tonight is trivia night." Mia picked up a sheet of paper lined and numbered for answers. "Want to play?"

"I have a lot of nerdy, useless knowledge," Addison admitted with a grin. "We should put it to good use."

"Let's do it!" Mia picked up the pencil and turned the sheet of paper over. "For now, let's brainstorm names for your shop." She tapped the pencil against her cheek. "How about the name Happily Ever After?"

Addison snorted.

"Now . . . now. A bridal-shop owner can't have that jaded attitude," Mia warned in a low tone, but gave Addison a sympathetic smile and then raised her eyebrows. "Any other suggestions?"

"Wedding Bell Blues?"

"Addison . . ."

"Okay, *okay*." Addison took another sip of Redneck Sunset and then nibbled on the inside of her cheek. "I don't know. How about Wear White Anyway?"

Mia laughed.

"Third Time's the Charm?"

Mia chuckled again but then sobered. "Listen, your prince will come along someday. Maybe when you least expect it. Trust me, if it happened to me, it can happen to you."

"Mia, I already told you. I'm taking a break from men."

"Really? Are you sure?"

"Absolutely."

"Too bad, because guess who just walked in."

"Adam Levine? Because I'd make him an exception to my new rule."

"No, not quite. But that hot guy from Wine and Diner just came in, looking pretty fly in faded jeans and a blue button-down shirt."

"Reid Greenfield?" Addison's pulse quickened, and it was hard not to turn around for a look. "Oh, I forgot to tell you that I met him while you were on the phone."

"You did? So he talked to you?"

"Well . . ." Addison rolled her eyes. "Yeah, after I ran into him, spilling tea all over his white T-shirt. Not my finest moment."

Mia laughed. "Well, I spilled ice water onto Cam's lap the first time we met, so believe it or not, this could be the start of something good."

"Mia . . ." Addison warned in a low voice.

Mia raised her hands upward in surrender.

"I'm not starting anything with anybody."

"I know . . ." she said glumly. "Oh . . . he is coming closer, at the tub of iced beer behind you."

"Again, I'm not interested in starting *anything* except for a business," Addison insisted, even though the urge to turn around got stronger when she heard Reid's smooth, sexy voice asking for a Kentucky Ale. The fact that Reid was standing fairly close made her skin feel warm and tingly. "But as a matter of fact, Reid *was* interested in me. In hiring me as a consultant, that is."

Mia took a sip of her Honky-Tonk Heaven. "Really? For a wedding?" She pulled a pout. "Is he getting married?"

"No, actually, he wants me to dissuade his sister from renovating a barn on their property to use for wedding receptions. He doesn't think it's a good way to invest her retirement money."

Mia shook her head. "Well, Reid might just be wrong. Barn weddings used to be popular only among farmers, but it's recently come back in vogue. I've been doing research for my own wedding and barn weddings are pretty cool. I even pinned a couple to my wedding wish board in Pinterest."

"So you like the concept?"

"Yeah, I like intertwining something rustic and earthy with elegance. It's not like it's something new, but barn weddings are gaining mainstream popularity. It has the earthy appeal that everyone's going for these days. And weddings are big bucks. She might be on to something lucrative, and you should talk to her about it."

"But Reid wants me to talk her *out* of it."

Mia tapped the table with her fingernail. "But as a consultant it would be up to you to change his mind if your research proves otherwise."

Addison didn't think that would go over too well, since he was pretty much dead set against his sister taking a risk, but she nodded. She'd definitely want to do a lot of research and look at the property and numbers before presenting her case to him. "I suppose so."

"Well, guess what. Reid is heading over here right now."

"He is?" Addison swallowed hard and suddenly felt a flutter of nervous anticipation. A moment later he was standing at their table, smiling. Addison felt her cheeks grow warm and the flutter remained. "Well, hello, Reid," she managed, a bit embarrassed that her voice sounded breathy.

"Hi, Addison," he said in that slow Southern way, and nodded to Mia and offered his hand. "I'm Reid Greenfield. I don't think we've met."

"Mia Monroe." Mia smiled. "Nice to meet you, Reid. Would you like to join us?"

Addison narrowed her eyes slightly at her cousin, who gave her a look of pure innocence.

"Sure, I'll join you for a drink. Would you ladies like a refill?"

Knowing she shouldn't have another martini, Addison felt her head nod up and down, anyway.

"Mia?" Reid asked, but Mia's phone beeped.

"Oh my gosh," Mia said as she looked down at a text message. "Cam's game got canceled and he has tomorrow off. He's coming home for the night! He said he'll be home in an hour or so." Mia bounced up and down in her chair.

"Oh, Mia, that's awesome!" Addison exclaimed, but then frowned. "Oh, hey, listen. I'll stay somewhere else tonight."

"No!" Mia protested. Her bouncing stopped. "I can't let you do that."

"I insist. Didn't you say that there's a furnished condo up for grabs? Let's go move my stuff from your guestroom now before Cam arrives."

"Addison, I don't want you spending your first night here alone. We can hang out together. I want you to meet Cam."

"Mia, how long has it been since you've seen your fiancé?"

"Ten days, three hours, and five minutes," she said with a small smile.

"Exactly."

"I'll get Addison home safely," Reid offered, causing both women to look his way. "If you'd like to stay, that is." He gestured toward the paper. "I'm pretty good at trivia."

Before Addison could answer, Mia said, "I'll get the keys from the front desk before they close. Do you have spare car keys?"

"Yes, but—"

"Super. Give them to me and I'll put the instruction packet and keys in your car, in case you wind up staying here late. I'm pretty sure the condo will be on the ground floor. They keep a few of those open for families who come in to visit baseball players." Without giving Addison a chance to protest Mia held out her hand for the keys. "Cam will most likely have to leave in the afternoon, but let's get together for breakfast. Not too early, though."

Knowing it was pointless to argue and not really sure that she wanted to anyway, Addison put her spare key in Mia's palm.

"Great, I'll see you in the morning. Nice to meet you, Reid," Mia said as she scrambled from her seat. "Take good care of my cuz, okay?" She hurried toward the door without looking back.

"Did you just get railroaded into this?" Reid asked with a slight grin.

"No . . . I . . . well, kinda," she admitted, but gestured toward a stool. "But since you're so good at trivia, have a seat."

"I might have embellished that statement a little," he admitted as he sat down.

"That's okay. I probably have enough useless knowledge for the both of us."

"I doubt that there's anything useless about you . . . I mean, your knowledge," he added, and then raised the bottle to his lips. Addison tried not to be a bit fascinated at the strong column of his throat as he swallowed, or the fact that the first three buttons of his blue shirt were undone, giving Addison an enticing view of tanned skin and a peek at dark chest hair. Most California men shaved their chest and Addison found the masculine sight sexy as hell.

"So what should our team name be?" Addison asked, and picked up the pencil. "We have to turn our answers in with a team name."

"How about City Girl and Country Boy?" Reid suggested with a grin that caused a cute dimple to dent his left cheek. When he leaned back a little his shirt gaped open wider, making Addison wonder what he looked like shirtless. She remembered how his tea-stained T-shirt had clung to his chest and decided he would look pretty amazing. "Don't like the idea?" he asked when she failed to respond—well, at least not in a verbal way.

"Oh, um, no, it's a good name." Feeling her cheeks grow warm she dipped her head and wrote the name down and tried to cool off with the last sip of her drink.

"Oh, I forgot to order you a refill. What are you drinking?"

"A Redneck Sunset."

Reid laughed, and just like his voice, his laughter was deep and smooth, and Addison decided that she liked the sound. "I'll go up to the main bar and get you another one. It's too busy to wait for a server."

"Thanks," Addison said. She pushed the glass his way just as he reached for it. Their fingers briefly brushed together in an accidental way, but Addison felt a warm awareness. What was it about Reid that made her feel like a lovestruck teenager? She watched him walk across the room, drawing female attention, and when a woman walked over and embraced him Addison felt a flash of jealousy. She wanted to slap her hand off Reid's forearm, and suddenly felt foolish. She decided that she was suffering from some sort of postengagement-breakup syndrome that was making her react this way. And then she remembered what Mia had said in answer to how you knew when love was the real deal.

The kiss.

What would it be like to kiss Reid?

Would it feel different from when she kissed Garret? Garret had been a good kisser. She'd always enjoyed kissing him. Really, could a mere kiss be anything mindblowing?

Addison decided that for the sake of curiosity she needed to find out.

A text message from Mia said that she was in the process of moving Addison's suitcases into condo 129 and the keys would be in her car. Addison smiled at the message. There was no way she was going to intrude on Mia's night with Cam. The dreamy look on Mia's sweet face told the story. Her cousin was deeply in love and it showed. Addison wondered if her moment of realization that she was truly, deeply, madly in love would ever come.

"From This Moment!" she said with a snap of her fingers.

"From this moment ... what ... my little city girl?" Reid asked as he leaned in close and placed another Redneck Sunset in front of her. Deep in thought, Addison turned in surprise as he straightened. Their lips came just shy of brushing together. The moment was brief, but her heated response lingered.

Feeling a little bit rattled, Addison waved a hand through the air, nearly knocking over her martini. "Oh, I'm just thinking of names for my shop. I kind of like From This Moment," she said a bit shyly.

"Like the Shania Twain song?"

Addison frowned. "I'm not sure ... Wait. I think I know the song you're talking about."

"Not a country music fan?"

"No, you're wrong. I love all kinds of music, country included. But that's from a while ago, right? Still, I bet I know it. Can you hum a little bit?"

"I'd sing it, but all of that talent went to my brother Jeff. I think they have it on the jukebox. Pete Sully is a big Shania fan."

"Oh, will you play it?"

"If you dance with me."

"Oh ..." Addison opened her mouth to decline dancing, but yes came tumbling out.

"Great, I'll go select it now. It might be a while before they play it."

Addison nodded mutely and then took a sip of her Redneck Sunset. As she watched Reid walk over and put coins into the jukebox she reminded herself that she was taking a break from men. But the devil on her shoulder whispered that this was just one night.

One dance.

One kiss.

Addison was simply having fun. What was the harm? She'd give herself tonight to kick back and forget about her mistakes. Tonight she'd simply go with the flow. No big deal. End of story. And Mia had a big imagination where kissing was concerned. Seriously, a kiss was just a kiss....

Right?

9

This Kiss, This Kiss

WHILE REID PUNCHED IN THE NUMBERS FOR SHANIA Twain's "From This Moment On," he wondered what in the hell had gotten into him. Seriously, what in the world had compelled him to ask Addison to dance, of all things? He'd Googled her name after meeting her, and she was indeed Melinda Monroe's daughter. That was intimidating enough, but he'd also read that Addison had been engaged to movie star Aiden Anderson and most recently to the son of rock star Rick Ruleman. He was sure there was more, but he'd read enough to make him back off, no matter how much he was attracted to her.

The city girl–country boy team name suddenly took on even more meaning. Not to mention that Addison must take a flippant attitude toward engagement and marriage. Not surprising, given her LA roots. He and Addison Monroe were worlds apart. He needed to remember that little detail and back it the hell down instead of spending the evening with her. Now that he wasn't standing right next to her, looking into her incredible eyes, some of his good sense returned. What the hell had he been thinking?

As a matter of fact, if he hadn't already promised to get her home safely he would already be trying to think up an excuse to leave. But he was a man of his word. His only problem was that as soon as he got around her, his good sense seemed to take a giant leap out the window. Just like when he walked in the door of Sully's. He'd spotted Addison right away and told himself to stay away from her. But damned if his feet didn't walk him right over to her table, not even knowing what he was going to say. Reid sighed. While the leap felt pretty damned good in an exciting kind of way, he had a feeling that the landing was going to hurt like hell. Addison Monroe was not the kind of girl he should be flirting with, plain and simple.

As Reid walked back toward the table, he told himself to just play the trivia game that was about to begin and keep his cool. Hopefully, the song would be pre-empted by the start of the game and his offer to dance would go unnoticed. He would walk her home as promised and then go about his business. He might even nix hiring her as a consultant and try to talk some sense into Sara on his own.

But when Pete Sully picked up the mic and the questions started, Reid scooted his stool closer to Addison so that they could put their heads together as they answered. As promised, Addison easily blew through the first three questions. Reid was impressed, especially since the category was one-hit wonders.

"Oh, I know this. . . . Let me think."

"How in the world do you know who sang 'Afternoon Delight'?"

"Shh . . . it's on the tip of my tongue."

Reid almost groaned when he listened to another snippet of the song. Afternoon delight? The tip of her tongue? Why did everything suddenly have sexual overtones? She put her hand over his and squeezed. "You know? For real?"

"Starland Vocal Band," Addison whispered as she wrote the answer on their sheet.

"Unbelievable."

"Not really. My dad's art gallery is called Beauty and the Beat. I picked up his love of art and music a long time ago. I love everything from classic rock to classical, and for some reason my brain hangs on to trivia. But Dad and I both enjoy obscure bands or songs. He's always looking for new talent." Addison grinned. "He's kind of an old hippie with long hair pulled back in a ponytail, totally the opposite of my mother. But they somehow make it work."

"My mom and dad are a little bit the same way. They butt heads all the time but still have a strong marriage." Reid decided not to mention that he was well aware of who her mother was, since she didn't mention it herself. He guessed she was trying to distance herself from the recent gossip.

"Hard to find that kind of commitment these days," Addison said, and he wondered if she was talking about her broken engagements.

"Who sang 'Gonna Fly Now'?" Pete asked the crowed and played a few bars. "I'll accept two different answers."

"The theme from *Rocky*," Reid said, and looked at Addison. "Yo, Addison, do you know the answer?"

She giggled at his really bad Rocky impression and then frowned, tapping the pencil to her bottom lip, making Reid wish he were the pencil. She had a great mouth, nice shape with a full bottom lip. "Oh . . . um it won an Academy Award, I think."

"You know that?"

"Yeah, but it's not the answer to the question. Wait. . . ." She closed her eyes and tilted her head back in thought. Damned if seeing her like that didn't do funny things to Reid's gut. She seemed so sweet, so pretty, it was getting difficult to remember that she had a famous mom and ran in circles that Reid would never feel comfortable in. He wondered how long she'd stay in Cricket Creek before getting bored and returning to LA and her jet-set lifestyle. Probably not long. "Oh . . ." She opened her eyes and put her hand on Reid's forearm. "Bill some-body. Bill . . . Bill Conti! I think. I'm not certain but I'll write it down."

"Here's the last question in this category. Listen closely," Pete said and played a few bars. "Name the song."

" 'Are You Gonna Kiss Me or Not,' " Reid whispered.

"What?" Her eyes widened. "I . . . um . . . I don't know."

"No, I'm sure of this one."

She arched one eyebrow. "Really? You're that confi-dent, huh?"

"Yeah, trust me," Reid said, and then had to hold back a chuckle when he suddenly realized she didn't know that was the title to the song. "Absolutely positive."

"Well, aren't you just so sure of yourself?"

"Not usually, but this time I am. Write it down," he whispered in her ear.

"Oh, it's the title to the song," she sputtered, and quickly wrote it down. She gave his shoulder a playful shove, and he laughed.

"Want another Redneck Sunset?"

"If I have another I might be howling at the moon."

"Then I'll be right back with one while we're in be-tween categories. We just might win this thing."

Reid returned with another beer and Addison's mar-tini in time for the next round. He was pretty good at sports trivia and held his own. Addison killed it in the romantic-comedy movie category, and they laughed through the random-question speed round, spitting out answers at each other left and right. They were laughing and breathless at the lightning-fast questions, but he felt as if they did well. Reid couldn't remember when he'd had this much fun.

"Time to bring me your answers," Pete boomed into the mic. "We'll play some music while we tally the scores. But don't leave, because tonight's winner will get dinner for two at Wine and Diner and two tickets to a Cricket Creek Cougars baseball game."

"Nice prize," Addison commented, just before Shania

Twain started crooning "From This Moment On." "Oh, *that* song . . . I do think I've found my name."

"Well, then, we should dance," Reid offered, in spite of his earlier misgivings at getting involved with her. Suddenly everything ceased to matter except for having her in his arms.

"That would be nice." She smiled shyly at Reid and he found his hand reaching out to hers. He led her to the dance floor in front of the stage where live bands played on the weekends. Other couples were heading to the dance floor too. He pulled her close, holding one small delicate hand in his and swayed to the music.

Addison was of average height and in heels fit just right for a slow dance. He inhaled her sweet floral scent laced with something sensual just beneath the surface. When her hair brushed against his cheek it felt as soft as he'd imagined. Reid couldn't remember the last time he'd danced with a woman, most likely at a wedding, and he'd forgotten how intimate and sexy it felt, especially with someone he was already attracted to. The palm of his hand rested against her back. He could feel the warmth of her skin beneath the soft, stretchy fabric, and when he pulled her slightly closer she didn't resist. A delicate, feminine quality about her brought out a protective instinct that came out of nowhere. And yet he sensed strength, determination, and so when the song ended and he suddenly felt her breath hitch, he was confused. Pulling back he looked into her brown eyes and noticed the sheen of unshed tears.

"Are you okay?"

She pressed her lips together and gave him a jerky nod. "I think I need a breath of fresh air."

Reid nodded and led her toward the back door that opened to a deck overlooking the river. It was popular during the summer, but the cool nights kept people inside and tonight was no exception. "Is something wrong, Addison? Did I do something to upset you?"

She swallowed hard and cleared her throat. "No, the song . . . just . . . got to me."

"Somebody from your past?" he asked, trying to ignore the disappointment that she might still care for someone.

Addison lifted one shoulder slightly and stared out over the river. "In a way, yes." She frowned and then shook her head. "I'm sorry, Reid. I was having a wonderful time. We should go back in there. I just had a little pity party. Stupid. I blame it on the three Redneck Sunsets." She tried to smile but it wobbled at the corners. "It's so pretty out here. Just look at the moon . . ." she said, and Reid knew it was an attempt to change the subject.

Reid wasn't having it. He stepped closer. "I'm so sorry. I would never have played that song if I'd known it was going to upset you."

She put a hand on his chest and then pulled it back as if she'd touched something too hot. "No, it's not your fault. I guess I just wonder . . . No, never mind." She looked down at the ground.

Reid tilted her chin up. "Wonder what?"

She hesitated. "If my moment will ever come," she answered so softly that he barely heard her. Then, without really thinking, he dipped his head and kissed her.

The gentle touch of his mouth on hers was meant to soothe, but instead of pulling back like he'd intended, Reid pulled her closer. When her lips parted he deepened the kiss, threading his fingers in her amazing hair. She clung to his shoulders and kissed him back. Her lips were soft, compliant, and the gentle tangle of their tongues was sultry, a slowly building heat that promised so much more.

And he wanted it. Wanted her.

Reid licked her full bottom lip, nibbled at it, and then captured her mouth for more. The cool breeze blew her hair forward around their faces, as if hiding their intimate kiss from the world. He felt her relax, melt against him, as if giving in to something she didn't want but couldn't resist. Reid knew the feeling.

But the sound of voices, music, finally filtered into his brain. They were in public. He needed to pull back . . . and he did, but with reluctance. "Wow," he said, inhaling a deep breath. He looked down at her to see if the reaction was only on his end, but she tilted her head to the side and frowned slightly, as if thinking. She licked her bottom lip but remained silent. Reid wasn't sure how to take it, but Addison suddenly smiled slowly.

"Yeah . . . *wow*."

Reid felt relief followed by a crazy sense of joy. He chuckled softly and was wondering if he could steal another kiss when he heard "City Girl and Country Boy" announced over the speakers. "I think we just won," he said.

"Woo-hoo!" she said, and laughed when he took her hand. He tugged her toward the door but then stopped before entering.

"Are you okay?"

"Yeah, better. Thank you for kissing some sense into me."

"Anytime," Reid offered, and then pushed open the door before stepping back for her to enter before him. They hurried over to Pete and claimed the prize, bowing to the applause before heading back to their table. "Can I get you anything else? A drink, something to eat, maybe?"

"Actually, it's getting a bit late and I should get the keys and get settled in the condo."

Reid felt a flicker of disappointment. "Okay, sure. But do you want some food to go? Have you eaten since lunch?"

Addison winced. "No . . ."

Reid nodded. "Hey, I'll go up to the bar and settle the tab. I'm going to order a couple of club sandwiches to go. They're pretty good. That way you'll have something for later. I know I'm sure getting hungry."

"Let me pay for mine."

Reid shook his head firmly. "This is Cricket Creek. We do things the old-fashioned way. Now, mayo or mustard?"

She smiled. "A little of both, and hold the onion, please."

"You got it." He tapped the table with his hand. "I'll be right back." Reid placed the order and paid the tab, thinking that this night had gone differently than he expected. When Braden had softball practice and couldn't join him Reid had almost stayed back at his cabin with a six-pack and a baseball game. But he'd felt restless and decided a night out was just what he needed. A slow dance and a hot kiss hadn't been on the agenda, and he wondered if his intense attraction to Addison wasn't from the mere fact that it had been such a long time since he held a woman in his arms. Yeah, that had to be it.

Reid also reminded himself that he was back in Cricket Creek to help his family's financial problems. He needed to stick to his plan of attack and then head back to his career in Lexington. Getting involved with a woman, especially someone like Addison, who was fresh out of a failed relationship, would be just plain stupid.

But when he returned to the table and she gave him a sweet, shy smile, his resolve melted like sugar in hot tea. He wanted to kiss her again. "My truck is parked out in the side lot," he said.

"Oh, are you okay to drive? We can walk."

"I didn't even finish my third beer, so I'm fine."

"Just making sure." She nodded and fell in step beside him.

Reid held the door open for her, and damned if he didn't have the urge to hold her hand as they walked toward his truck. He couldn't remember the last time he'd longed to hold a girl's hand. Reid refrained but just barely. Instead he fished inside his pocket for his keys. The lights blinked when he pushed the unlock button.

"Nice truck."

"Thanks." Reid grinned. She probably didn't ride in trucks much or maybe at all. "Even though I've lived in the city for the past few years I just can't give up owning a truck. Guess I'll always be a country boy."

"Nothing wrong with that."

He opened the door for her. "So, will you always be a city girl?" Reid asked the question lightly, but she didn't grin.

She lowered her gaze for a brief moment and then back at him. "I'm not really sure; I only knew that I was in dire need of a change in more ways than one."

Reid wasn't quite sure what to make of her answer, but on the short drive to the high-rise, they laughed about the trivia game and he made an effort not to get personal again.

"There's my car."

Reid nodded and pulled into the vacant spot next to her Mustang.

"Thanks for the ride."

"Oh no. I'm going to see you safely to your door."

"I don't think there's much of a crime wave in Cricket Creek."

"Indulge me," Reid responded with a grin.

To his relief she nodded and he came around to open the door for her. The step down from the truck must have been bigger than she anticipated, and she tumbled forward right into his arms. He caught her around the rib cage and helped her until her feet touched the ground.

"You'd never know that my middle name was Grace," she joked, but her cheeks glowed pink, and, damn, but he wanted to kiss her again.

"You missed the step and the handle. Guess you're not used to pickup trucks, city girl." Reid's hands lingered around her for a moment longer, reluctant to let go, but he did.

After she retrieved the packet Mia left, she looked at the map and fished out the keys, saying, "Oh, it's right over there."

Reid followed her to the front door. "I guess I don't have to whip out my gun and search for intruders."

"You have a gun?"

"No, I'm not packing." At her frown he explained, "Slang for carrying a gun."

Addison flipped on the light and chuckled. "Oh, well, I don't think you have to worry. Thanks again for the ride."

Reid nodded, trying to think of another reason to stay, but came up blank. "Well, then, I guess it's good night."

"Good night, Reid. I had fun."

"Me too." He squashed the urge to ask her out, but just barely. "Oh . . ." He reached in his pocket and handed her the dinner voucher and baseball tickets. "You did most of the work. Enjoy."

She hesitated, frowned slightly, and, if he wasn't mistaken, there was a flicker of disappointment. "Um, thanks . . ."

Reid nodded and then turned and walked away. A moment later he heard the door click shut. He inhaled a deep breath and let it out, reminding himself of the many reasons not to turn back around.

10

Rumor Has It

ADDISON TOLD HERSELF NOT TO BE DISAPPOINTED THAT Reid gave her the tickets and voucher instead of suggesting that they go together. "It's for the best. You're just getting over another broken engagement," she sternly reminded herself. "Forget about Reid Greenfield."

Impossible.

"No, it's not! Watch me."

Addison decided that she'd explore the condo. Watch some television. Unpack her things. Call her mother again.

Cry.

What? Why did sudden, unexpected emotion well up in her throat? Maybe because she'd shared a slow dance and a steamy kiss with a guy and he wasn't remotely interested in going a step farther. What was it about her, anyway? Oh yeah, she was . . . boring. Maybe his wow comment about the kiss meant "Wow, that was lame."

Addison dropped her purse onto the nearby table and sighed. The lyrics of the song came floating back to her. "From this moment . . . life has begun." She started humming the song. Would anyone ever live for her happiness? Love her like that? Addison inhaled a deep breath and blew it out. *What does that even feel like? Will I go through life and never really know?*

Addison remembered Mia's explanation about the real deal and closed her eyes, reliving the kiss. Neither Aiden nor Garret had ever made her feel like . . . that. Was Reid just an expert kisser? Addison rubbed her temples and sighed. Maybe she was just emotionally stunted. After all, how could she already be thinking about someone else? But after meeting Reid, Garret seemed like a fuzzy memory.

"Oh, boy . . ."

After a night of having fun, tension slowly started to creep up her neck. The martini buzz had faded, leaving behind a slight headache. . . . Oh, right; she hadn't eaten, and Reid had forgotten to give her one of the sandwiches. With a groan, Addison headed for the galley kitchen right off the main room, separated by a breakfast bar with three stools in front. She vaguely registered that the condo was nice enough with an open floor plan. But her good mood was busted.

Addison did manage a smile when she spotted a hot pink sticky note stuck to the refrigerator door: *I put some random things in the fridge, but come up and have breakfast before Cam has to get on the road. Love ya, Mia.*

With hope in her heart for something substantial to eat, she opened the fridge and spotted bottled water, a bottle of Chardonnay, three different kinds of beer, a couple of apples, Diet Coke, sliced veggies and a little jar of ranch dip. Bummer. On the counter sat a box of Wheat Thins and a bag of honey mustard pretzels. Nice, but not what she wanted. She wanted the damn sandwich.

Well, what she really wanted was another kiss from Reid. Addison groaned. "That's not true. I'll just order a pizza, I guess," she grumbled, but then thought that a salad would be healthier. But then she fisted her hands on her hips. So what? She thought about all of the times when she ate salad instead of what she really craved. She was a pleaser and pleased everyone but herself. The closest she'd come to defiance was refusing to do the reality show with Garret, and look where that got her. Dumped.

Addison lifted her chin. Well, that was about to change. The next thing that came down the pike that she wanted . . . she was going to grab it with both fists and . . . well, she wasn't quite sure, but it was a start. A new beginning. She smiled. From this moment she was going to live life to the fullest. "Perfect name for the boutique."

Addison grabbed a bottle of water and decided to head to her bedroom and change into some sweats. After taking a gulp of cold water, she walked down the hallway, pausing to check out the half bath before walking into the bedroom. Cream-colored walls, a queen-sized bed and a flat-screen television. Again, nice enough, and she smiled when she spotted her suitcases perched in the corner like little soldiers. She toed off her shoes and was about to open the big, bulging suitcases when she thought she heard the doorbell ringing. She took another swig of water and headed that way, thinking it must be Mia bringing Cam down to meet her after all. "Here's hoping she also brought dinner. . . ."

Addison swung the door open and there stood Reid, holding up the bag of sandwiches. Well, she'd been right about the dinner part. She blinked at him in surprise and squeezed the plastic bottle so hard she put a dent in it.

"I was ten minutes down the road when I remembered your sandwich. I thought you might want it."

"Th-thank you."

The next thing that came down the pike that she wanted she was going grab it with both fists. . . .

Addison reached out and took the bag from him. He turned to go. *No* . . . "Reid?" When he turned around she held up the bag. "Aren't you going to join me?"

"Oh yeah, if you want me to."

"I just asked."

Reid grinned. "Okay, then. I'll take that as a yes."

After he walked in Addison put the bag and her dented water bottle on the table and turned back to face him. She looked at him for a moment, gathering her courage.

"Are you okay?"

She nodded and took a step closer to him. Since she'd taken off her shoes he stood several inches taller than her, making her plan a little bit harder to pull off. She swallowed; took a deep breath. Her pulse pounded.

She couldn't do it.

"Can I get you something to drink?"

"Do you have a beer?"

"Three bottles of random brews. I don't remember, except one is Blue Moon."

"I'll take either of the other two."

Addison nodded but stood rooted to the spot, trying to gather her nerve, but after a moment she turned toward the kitchen. She took one more step but then did a 180, and, ignoring her knocking knees, which made her walk a bit funny, she quickly closed the gap between them. Coming up on tiptoes, she grabbed the front of his shirt, fisted her hands in the material, and tugged, well, a little too hard.

A button or two went flying and, caught off guard, wide-eyed Reid tumbled forward. With a surprised grunt Reid smacked into Addison with enough force to send her off balance in a backward little tiptoed trot. Because her knees were basically Jell-O she stumbled, trying, without any luck, to stop, and instead gained momentum while taking Reid right along with her. They did an interesting kind of backward tango. Reid, apparently trying to help the situation, or perhaps trying to fling her off, swerved sideways, swinging them away from the glass-topped coffee table. Addison hit the arm of the sofa and fell backward, tugging Reid with her. She landed on the cushions with a little bounce, her hands still fisted in his shirt.

She looked into his surprised face, mere inches from

hers. His mouth was within reaching distance if she just raised her head. "S-sorry."

"What were you trying to do?"

"Um . . ." Okay, she was invested, so she decided to see this thing through. "This . . ." She raised her head, pressed her mouth to his, and kissed him. He braced his hands against the wide leather cushions of the sectional sofa and quickly got with the program, kissing her back with sweet, sizzling passion. Addison loved the sensation of having the entire length of his hard body pressed to hers, and she wrapped her arms around him, feeling the ripple of muscle in his back. She moved one hand up into his hair, threading her fingers through the softness at the nape of his neck. Taking the lead, she retreated, licked, nibbled until he made a noise in his throat and pushed her back into the cushions, kissing her with a deep hunger that had her wanting more and more.

Finally, Reid rolled her to the side, pinning her between the sofa and his body. He came up on one elbow, resting his head in his hand. "Did you get what you wanted?" With raised eyebrows, he traced his fingertip over her moist bottom lip.

"Yeah . . ."

"Next time?"

All she could do was nod.

"All you have to do is ask."

Addison swallowed when he traced the fingertip from her bottom lip over her chin and oh so slowly down her neck, and stopped just when he reached the swell of her breasts. "Kiss me." Her throaty response wasn't a question but a demand.

Reid readily complied, lowering his head and capturing her mouth and kissing her slowly, thoroughly. Addison splayed one hand on his nearly exposed chest, feeling his warm skin, silky chest hair, and his deliciously defined ab muscles. She explored each intriguing contour until she came to his belt buckle blocking where she wanted to go. She teased back and forth, dipping below the leather, smiling when she felt his muscles clench in response.

Addison had never really taken the initiative during sex, but she felt a sense of feminine power, taking the lead.

He moaned and shifted and the big bulge beneath the worn denim told Addison that this was quickly going way beyond a stolen kiss. She knew it was time to stop, but when Reid slid his hand beneath her sweater, touching her bare skin, arousal trumped reason. His thumb rubbed back and forth just beneath her bra, causing a hot tingle that turned into a sweet, deep, aching need that only he could soothe.

God, she wanted his mouth on her breasts, his hands between her thighs. She arched her back, offering him more. She gasped when his hot mouth found her neck, kissing, nuzzling, while his callused thumb moved back and forth, upward over the silk and lace, teasing, promising. . . .

"Addison?" The whiskey-rough sound of her name on his lips washed over her like a caress, a question, and a plea at the same time.

Addison tried to think, to grasp on to reason. Reid was little more than a stranger, a possible client. She simply didn't do this sort of thing, but spontaneity was beginning to have its perks.

"Reid . . ." Her husky voice was an invitation, and he accepted with the deft unclasping of her bra. The rest of her sentence dissolved into a moan when he cupped one breast, rubbing his thumb over her eager nipple. Any remaining shreds of resistance were smothered by a bone-melting, mind-blowing kiss.

Strong, sure fingers unsnapped her jeans and slid the zipper down. He parted the denim and slipped his hand inside the gap, toying with the lace of her thong. Her belly quivered and she arched her hips, urging him to pull her pants downward. Still kissing her, he started to tug.

And then he stopped.

It took a moment for Addison's sex-addled brain to

register that Reid had gone very still. He removed his hand from her pants and the only sound in the room was their heavy breathing. Addison frowned and in a panic wondered what she'd done to turn him off like a faucet. Wait. . . . Oh God . . . Okay, no, she'd had a bikini wax.

"R-Reid?"

She heard his audible swallow. "Hey, I'm sorry. I let things get, um, out of control."

Really? Because she'd been the one who had almost ripped his shirt off and then kissed him. Her heart started to thump. She didn't like where this was going.

"It was wrong of me to take advantage of you."

"Advantage of me?"

Reid ran a hand down his face. "Yeah. Look, when my sister broke up with her boyfriend, not the guy she's marrying, but another guy she was serious with . . . she . . ."

When he paused Addison urged him on. "She?"

"Well, went a little wild for a minute. You know, to get over him."

"So you think that's what I was doing? Using you?"

"Maybe. I don't know, but I don't want to be that guy."

"Oh." Mortification started at her toes and worked its way up to her cheeks. What did she say now? Thanks? Embarrassment didn't even begin to cover what she was feeling, and even though she supposed—no, knew—that he was just being a really good guy, she was humiliated, and it transformed into being super-pissed. Not that she was about to let him know it. Digging deep for a steady voice she said, "Well, then, I'm starving. Let's eat those sandwiches. Whadayasay?" She kept her tone light and forced a smile.

"Okay, sure," he answered a bit uncertainly, but she felt the sudden tenseness in his shoulders relax just a little bit. "Look, if you'd rather that I'd leave . . ."

"No," Addison protested, trying to ignore her state of undress and the humiliation in her cheeks. "You're right. I was just, you know, acting out because of, you know, my situation. You just happened to be the guy within reach.

Lucky for me you're a gentleman. Must be that Southern upbringing." God, she was talking way too much.

"I'll take that beer now."

"Sure," Addison replied, wanting so badly to zip up her pants. "You're kind of blocking my way," she said, and swallowed hard when he had to lean and brace his arm across her in order to get the leverage to push up off of the sofa. She got an eyeful of his very fine chest before he put a knee on the cushion and stood up. When he turned his back Addison quickly zipped up and fastened her jeans before sitting up. He turned back around just in time to see her fumbling with her bra, without any success. Great . . .

"Need some help?" he asked uncertainly.

"No!" she answered more sharply than intended, but damned if she couldn't get the bra to hook to save her life.

"Stand up," Reid gently requested, and for some reason it brought tears to her eyes. Maybe he was right. Maybe acting out was what she was doing. She obeyed and turned around only so he wouldn't see the emotion threatening to spill down her cheeks. When he slid his hands beneath her sweater she inhaled sharply and she hoped he didn't notice. His fingers brushed against her skin, and damned if her body didn't betray her with goose bumps. She could feel his warm breath on her neck and oh, how she wanted to tilt her head to the side and have him kiss her neck, cup her breasts while she leaned back against him.

But she'd suffered enough humiliation for one night, and so when he hooked her bra she tugged her sweater back into place and walked toward the kitchen, pretending that the past fifteen minutes of hot making out never happened. She really wanted him to leave, but pride dictated otherwise.

Addison brought Reid a Kentucky Ale and herself a bottle of water. He reached into the paper bag, pulled out a sandwich and looked at the wrapper. "I think this one is light mayo and mustard, no onion," he said. If she wasn't mistaken he felt a bit unnerved as well.

"Thanks," Addison said with careful politeness. She put the bottle of beer in front of him, trying really hard not to notice the three missing buttons on his shirt and his half-exposed chest. She removed the sandwich from the wrapper and started eating without really tasting it. "Oh, this is good." Addison nodded with fake appreciation and took another bite. "Mmm. Really good."

Reid nodded, chewing.

Addison chatted while they ate, and after they were finished she walked him to the door. After she closed the door she tried to remember the conversation but failed. She frowned, thinking it had something to do with baseball and one-hit wonders. She really didn't know. "Wow . . ." She put a hand to her mouth and shook her head, not really sure if she should laugh or cry.

She walked on wooden legs into the bedroom, retrieved her toiletries from her smallest suitcase, and headed to the bathroom to get ready for bed. As she brushed her teeth she looked at herself in the mirror and shook her head, wondering what in the world had gotten into her. Was Reid right? Was she getting over her broken engagement by going wild?

She spit into the sink, rinsed her mouth, and sighed. She didn't really know, but one thing was for certain: Rebound or not, in her twenty-eight years of living, no other kiss had ever made her melt the way Reid's did.

After locating a soft cotton sleep shirt Addison slipped beneath the covers, hoping to fall right to sleep. Of course, when she closed her eyes all she could see was Reid's face. Pissed, she punched the pillow, tossed and turned for a while before groaning. Sleep wasn't going to happen. She leaned over and reached for the remote, wondering if her life could possibly get any crazier. With a sigh, she turned on the television, hoping to find a boring movie that would lull her to sleep.

When the screen came to life Addison gasped. There

she was, embracing Rick Ruleman. She turned up the volume and listened with growing horror while some "reporter" speculated whether the rumor was true that Addison Monroe, daughter of finance guru Melinda Monroe, was having an affair with her ex-fiancé's father, Rick Ruleman, promptly ending her engagement. Garret, who said he was headlining a new reality show about his life called *House Rules*, declined comment while being hounded with questions by paparazzi but pulled a sad face that hinted that the rumor was true. Rick Ruleman was unavailable for comment, as was his publicist, who was rumored to have been fired. Addison Monroe was also missing in action, leading to further speculation that she and Rick were hiding out together.

What?

Addison shook her head and sighed, wondering how Garret could be such a selfish ass. She also wondered if he had started the rumor, but, then again, she wouldn't put is past Rick Ruleman's camp to start something that would perpetuate the aging rock star's bad-boy image. What better than an affair with his son's fiancée? After all, Addison had never seen Rick without a blond bombshell on his arm, most of them young enough to be his daughter. "Disgusting," she grumbled through gritted teeth.

Since it was still early enough in LA for her to call, Addison muted the TV, reached for her phone, and called her mother.

"Oh, honey," her mother answered, letting Addison know that her parents had already heard the rumors. "I'm so sorry."

Addison leaned back against the propped up pillows. "Mom, what should I do? Some sort of damage control?"

"Your father and I talked about this. We think it's best that you keep quiet and let the rumors die down."

Addison clutched the phone tighter. "Not likely with Garret's stupid show. I'm sure he wants to bump up the ratings and this is the perfect vehicle."

"Admittedly, it will take a while. Are you going to call him and tell him to back the hell off? I mean, Garret knows this isn't true."

"My guess is that both father and son are using this for their own purposes and I don't think I'll get help from either camp. And, Mom, I hope this doesn't adversely affect your ratings. I'm so sorry about all of this," she said, and felt tears coming on.

Her mother sighed. "Listen. The only fault you shoulder in this is being too trusting. We've talked to Mitch about the wedding boutique and I happen to agree that it's a great idea. Go full steam ahead and I'll work out the financial details."

"Mom, I want to do this on my own, with my own money."

She chuckled. "That's my girl. Luckily, you've invested well. You'll have to liquidate some stock and pay taxes on that as income."

"Yes, but most likely I'll show a loss for the first year in business and offset some of that income."

"True, and your uncle Mitch offered the first three months lease-free."

"No . . . no favors."

"It's not a favor but an incentive he would have offered to anybody. He was getting desperate to open the bridal boutique, which was supposed to be the flagship of Wedding Row. In fact, he and Nicolina were getting ready to reluctantly open it on their own and find someone to manage it if they didn't lease it out soon. Seems like you arrived at just the right time. So, see, life has a way of working out."

Addison managed a smile. "I just take a few crazy twists and turns along the way."

"Keeps you on your toes," she joked. "Listen, sweetie, you should pretty much fly under the radar there in Cricket Creek. This thing with Garret will die down. Sometimes denial after something like this only convinces some people of your guilt."

"Wow, this sucks. I'd like to punch both of them."

"Well, look at the bright side. You aren't engaged to Garret any longer. Throw yourself into this boutique, Addison. As much as your father and I will miss you, maybe getting you away from this kind of thing is for the best. Who knows who you might meet in that cute little town? Someone with substance."

"I'm off the market, Mom."

"Like I said, throw yourself into this boutique and have fun with Mia. I love you, sweetie. This other nonsense will die down before you know it. I promise."

Addison pressed her lips together and after clearing her throat said, "I'll take your advice. I love you too. Give Dad a hug for me."

"We'll come for a visit as soon as I can get away."

After Addison hung up the phone she sat there for a few minutes. Her mood became a strange mixture of emotions, and she put her face in her hands when she recalled grabbing Reid by his shirt. But oddly enough, Addison acknowledged that her spontaneous kiss was a step in the right direction. She was finally taking her life by the horns, doing what she wanted, moving forward, and pursuing a dream of her own.

And she wasn't about to look back.

11

Lean on Me

AT THE SOUND OF THE BELL DINGING MAGGIE LOOKED UP from the stack of paperwork piled high on her desk. She thought perhaps it might be Addison, but a tall dark-haired man entered the office instead. Aviator sunglasses shaded his eyes and he walked with a kind of feline grace that made her sit up and take notice. He wore khaki pants and a deep green oxford shirt—nothing out of the ordinary—but he wore it well. "May I help you?"

"Maggie McMillan?" His deep, slightly raspy voice was damned sexy, and when he removed his sunglasses his light blue eyes had her forgetting to answer. She nodded absently. *Wait. What did he ask?* "I'm here to pick up the keys to the cabin down by the river."

"Oh . . ." Maggie stood up and stuck out her hand. "Yes. Richard Rule?"

He grasped her hand and shook it firmly. "Nice to meet you, Maggie."

Maggie smiled, trying to ignore the little tingle resulting from the handshake. "I have the keys here somewhere. The pictures I sent don't even begin to do the cabin justice."

"I'm looking forward to seeing it."

Wow, he had a nice smile. "Um, as I mentioned, it's very nicely appointed, with a big deck overlooking the river. There's a hot tub and a gas grill."

"Perfect."

For a moment those eyes held her captive. For another moment she pictured him lounging in the hot tub.

"Good . . . um . . ." Flustered, Maggie looked down and found her notes. "Oh, you've rented it for two weeks with the option for longer?" She glanced back up at him. "Sorry for being so scatterbrained. I'm a bit swamped."

"I'm actually here two days early, so don't feel so unprepared. I hope I can go ahead and get settled, but if not I can stay somewhere else for a couple of days."

Maggie nodded. "The cabin is empty so I don't see why you can't get in today. You can follow me out to the property, since it's off the beaten path. I'd like to make sure everything is in order, since you're here early."

"I'd appreciate that. Are you free now, or should I come back later?"

"Oh no. Now is fine. I'll just grab my car keys and you can follow me."

"Good deal." For some reason his smile sent another flutter through her usually steady pulse. Maggie rarely got rattled and yet she found herself looking at his left hand in search of a wedding band. There was none.

"Here we go," Maggie said briskly, and showed him the packet. "It was right here on my desk all along."

"Busy time for you?"

"I recently moved here from Cincinnati and opened my own agency," she answered with a measure of pride. "I'm helping my son develop some property, along with all of the other hats I find myself wearing, including leasing several shops in town."

He fell into step beside her. "So the answer is yes. Listen, I can probably find my way. Like I said, I'm early."

She gave him a wave of her hand. "Oh no, I want to be sure the cabin is ready, and like I said, it is hard to find, nestled in the woods and off a couple of dirt roads. If it's too remote for your liking I have other rentals I can put you in. I want you to be satisfied," she added, and for some reason felt the need to blush. "With the cabin."

"If you insist, I won't argue," Richard said as he held the front door open for her.

Maggie had to pass by him closely. The man smelled as good as he looked, sending her already heightened reaction to him up another notch. Except for a hint of stubble darkening his face he had a clean-cut, business-man look to him, and she guessed by the fine lines around his eyes he was somewhere around her age. His sleeves were rolled up, revealing tanned forearms suggesting time spent outdoors and, wow, she spotted an unexpected scripted tattoo peeking out from beneath the green sleeve. She wasn't sure what it said, since he lowered his arm, but it hinted at a bad-boy edge that went with the slight rasp in his voice. *Intriguing* . . .

Maggie locked the door and then gave him what she hoped was an all-business bright smile. She pointed to her silver SUV. "Follow me."

He slipped his aviators back on. "And if I lose you?"

"I won't let that happen," Maggie assured him, but when he grinned she hoped that she didn't sound like she was flirting. "But to be on the safe side," Maggie said in a brisk tone, handing him the packet and pointing to the card stapled to the top, "here's my number."

"Thanks," he said, flashing that smile that made her feel warm all over. He walked toward his rental, a sedan of some sort, but Maggie wondered if he usually drove something sleek and fast. When she slid behind the wheel in her SUV she wanted to check her appearance in the visor mirror but didn't want him to see her primping. Maggie preferred soft pastels and floral patterns even though she usually wore dark blue and black for business. Today, however, she had opted for a buttercup yellow sweater set and cream-colored capri pants in celebration of the recent warmer weather. She did reach up and fluff her layered honey blond haircut that she'd been growing out. She'd even been thinking about going a shade lighter.

Maggie grinned. Lately her life was all about change. And now that she was in her fifties she started thinking about everything she'd put on hold while raising Tristan. Not that she regretted one single minute of putting her son first, but now that he'd found Savannah and was well on his way into adulthood, Maggie had started feeling restless. She looked in the rearview mirror and thought about her reaction to Richard Rule and wondered if it wasn't time to jump into . . . what? Dating? How did one go about dating at this stage of the game?

"Oh, stop," Maggie chided herself as she turned off the main road and onto a one-lane, bumpy gravel path leading to the cabin. She told herself that she needed to concentrate on her new business and not on some frivolous notion that she needed to flirt or date, for heaven's sake. And as far as Richard Rule was concerned, the man was sexy, for sure, but just visiting. *Wait. . . . Sexy?* Maggie chuckled. When was the last time she'd even thought of a man in those terms? "Whew," she breathed as she reached over and turned on the air-conditioning. "Hot flash," she grumbled, but suddenly wondered if the heat in her face wasn't due to the man following closely behind her. Telling herself to get a grip, she flipped on the classic country station she liked and drowned out her wayward thoughts by singing along with Waylon Jennings.

But when Maggie pulled up to the cabin she took a quick moment to swipe on some coral lipstick before getting out of her vehicle. She was just dropping the tube back into her purse when Richard approached her door and opened it for her. She stepped out, and when her wedge heel hit a jagged rock her ankle turned sideways. "Oh!" Pain shot up her leg and she braced her hand on Richard's arm.

"Maggie, are you okay?"

"Yes, just turned my ankle a little bit. I'm okay," she assured him, but when she put weight on it she winced.

"Let's get you inside and see if we can round up some ice to keep the swelling down."

Feeling silly, Maggie shook her head. "Oh, I'm sure I'm fine. I just need to walk it off."

"This isn't a baseball game—you don't have to be brave," he said with a smile. "If it hurts, let me know."

Maggie nodded but gritted her teeth as she walked toward the front fieldstone steps, trying very hard not to limp. Tears sprang to her eyes. She wasn't a wimp when it came to pain, but her doggone ankle throbbed. The eight or so steps leading to the wraparound porch looked like Mount Everest. She put her hand on the cool metal railing and swallowed hard. *Oh, boy . . .*

"Maggie, let me carry you up."

"Oh, don't be silly." Maggie waved him off, but when she put her weight on her foot she gave him a sideways glance. "Maybe I could just lean on you a little?"

"Just let me pick you up." Rick could tell that Maggie's ankle really did hurt and even leaning on him wasn't going to get her up the steps without putting her through more discomfort.

"No!"

"Do I have to flex a muscle?" he teased. Carrying her would be so much easier and, to be honest, he wanted to. She was just a cute little thing, all perky and smiles, but her smoky voice hinted at a sensual side beneath her prim-and-proper sweater set. He was used to women flaunting themselves but he somehow found her demure but feminine outfit way sexier. "Seriously, don't you think I'm capable of carrying you up a few steps?"

"It's not that—"

"Good." Rick tossed the packet to the top of the steps, slid his arm around her waist, and scooped her up into his arms.

"Richard, put me down!"

"I will when we reach the porch. Put your arms around my neck."

She hesitated but complied, making Rick smile. He was used to women falling all over him instead of backing away, and he found it refreshing. Challenging. Rick guessed her to be somewhere near his age, maybe a few years younger, and it was suddenly a bit of a blow to his ego when it dawned on him that she didn't know he was Rick Ruleman, rock star, and so she wasn't falling all over him.

Then again if Maggie was attracted to him it would be because she liked him for who he was rather than what he did for a living. Rick knew one thing: *He* was attracted to *her*.

"There. All in one piece," Rick said when they reached the landing.

"Thank you ever so much," she said. "But you can put me down now."

"Do I have to?"

"Are you flirting with me?"

"I'm trying. Is it working?"

Her answer was a throaty laugh. "You're charming—let's put it that way. But please put me down."

"Okay, but keep the weight off of your foot," he cautioned. She smelled nice, like spring flowers with some sort of sultry undertone . . . subtle but sexy.

"I promise," she said. Her mouth was close to his ear and her warm breath brushed up against his neck. If he turned his head their mouths would be mere inches apart. Of course, kissing her would be an inappropriate, bonehead move . . . funny, but that wouldn't have stopped Rick Ruleman.

Rick bent forward and gently allowed her feet to touch the ground. "Easy, now." Rick kept his arm around her waist to keep her steady. When she nodded he reached down for the packet and retrieved the key. He pushed open the door before sliding his arm back around beneath her shoulders. "Lean against me," he said, but when she did a little hopping limp he shook his head and stopped.

"What are you doing?"

"Checking it out. The pictures didn't do this place justice. It reminds me of my ... I mean, of a ski lodge in the mountains." Cathedral ceilings made the cabin seem massive and a gorgeous fieldstone fireplace was the focal point of the great room.

"Well, former big leaguer Ty McKenna owns this place, but with coaching the Cougars and with his wife running a restaurant they barely have any downtime to enjoy it. Speaking of ... Wait until you see the gourmet kitchen. It runs the width of the cabin in the back and overlooks the river."

"I'm impressed."

Maggie nodded. "They built this as a weekend retreat, but they've recently talked about listing it. Until they can make a decision they opted to rent it out." She pointed to the left. "The master bedroom is over there with a walk-in closet and a garden bath." She pointed upward. "The loft upstairs has three additional bedrooms and two more full baths. There's a hot tub on a back deck that goes the entire width of the cabin and is accessible from the master bedroom." She grimaced. "I wish I could walk around and show it all to you."

Rick pointed to the sectional sofa in the middle of the great room. "Do you think you can make it over there?"

"Since everything seems to be in order, why don't you just assist me back to my car?"

"Because, Maggie, I want to get some ice on it to keep the swelling down."

"I'll do that when I get home," she stubbornly insisted.

"Take it from someone who has sprained ankles multiple times. Icing early makes all the difference in the world. You'll thank me tomorrow."

Maggie closed her eyes and inhaled. "I feel like such a clumsy dork."

Rick grinned down at her. "But a very cute clumsy dork."

"Gee, thanks." Maggie rolled her eyes but blushed, and before she could protest he scooped her up once more and carried her over to the sofa. "Do you always get your way?" she asked. Rick wondered if the breathless quality of her voice was from surprise or something more.

"No," he answered quickly. Although to the rest of the world it probably seemed like he'd led a charmed life. "But indulge me, okay?" He gently set her down on the deep brown sofa and then sat by her, taking her injured foot into his hand. Cupping his hand around her heel, he shook his head. He hated that she winced when he removed her sandal. "Well, it's swollen." He looked up and their eyes met. "I'm sorry this happened. I should have noticed the rock."

Maggie frowned. "Hey, in no way, shape or form is this remotely your fault."

Rick nodded slowly. Of course he knew she was right, but he suddenly wondered how many people had been hurt by him in his lifetime. He'd been living a lie for such a long-ass time he no longer knew the truth. Without the beard, long hair, and leather, Rick felt exposed. Vulnerable.

"Seriously, Richard." Maggie leaned forward and placed her small hand on his arm.

"I know. I just feel bad, I guess."

"Don't. Hey, trust me—I'm pretty darned resilient." She pointed to her ankle and then waved a dismissive hand. "I'll be right as rain in a couple of days."

"Maybe," Rick said, and then gently placed a jewel-toned pillow beneath her leg, propping up her ankle. "But until then I'll be checking up on you, so don't even try to fight it."

When she opened her mouth Rick raised one finger.

"No protesting! Just sit here and let me get that ice."

"But—"

"Nope!" When he cut her off again she laughed.

"Okay . . . okay!" She lifted her hands in surrender.

"That's more like it." Rick could tell that Maggie wasn't used to anyone pampering her. Well, *that* was about to change. As he walked into the amazing kitchen in search of ice he reminded himself that he was only here for a couple of weeks or so while he regrouped and attempted to approach Addison with an explanation and apology. Getting romantically involved with Maggie would be a bad idea, but they could become friends. *No harm in that, right?* Rick frowned. Had he ever been just friends with a woman before? The answer would be a big, fat no. With a sigh he decided that he'd better keep things strictly business between them. He didn't want to lie to her about his identity, and, after all, he was here in hiding to straighten out his sorry-ass life, not complicate it. The reminder put a sudden damper on his good mood.

But when Rick entered the room with the plastic bag of crushed ice Maggie looked up and smiled, slicing through his gloom like a ray of warm sunshine. Keeping his distance wasn't going to be easy.

12

Reality Bites

REID LOOKED UP AT THE STRIPED AWNING ABOVE ADDI-son's bridal shop and read, "From This Moment." The scripted name reminded Reid of the dance they'd shared together at Sully's. He inhaled sharply, trying to chase away the memory of having Addison in his arms. He was here on business, not pleasure, and he'd best re-member that little fact. Although Addison's grand open-ing wasn't for a couple of weeks, Reid knew that she was already taking orders for dresses and was available for consultation. He knew this because Sara had already spoken with Addison about the whole barn-wedding idea that Sara just wouldn't let go.

Reid flexed his fingers, trying to maintain his cool, but it irked him that instead of dissuading his sister, accord-ing to Sara, Addison was actually on board with the hare-brained idea. Someone like Addison had money to burn and no worries about her future, but his sister didn't have that luxury. If Addison's fancy little boutique went under she could move on to the next pet project, giving her mother a nice little tax write-off.

Reid rolled his shoulders, trying to regain his compo-

sure before confronting Addison. He'd deliberately left
his dusty work clothes on, including his boots, to drive
home the fact that he and his sister were hardworking
farmers rather than a rich girl playing with Mama's
money. He'd probably arrived after hours, but the lights
were on in the boutique and with luck the front door
would still be open.

After their make-out session, Addison had filled his
thoughts for nearly two weeks. He'd vowed to take it
slow but Reid didn't think he could last much longer before seeing her again. He'd had every intention of asking
her out for dinner, until while he was checking out at the
grocery store he'd seen Addison's picture on the cover of
one of those tabloids. She'd been kissing Rick Ruleman.
Unable not to, Reid had picked the magazine up and
read the article detailing how Addison had an affair with
the rock legend, ending her engagement to Rick's son,
Garret, who was reported to be heartbroken.

Sara had warned Reid that those papers were full of
crap, but the picture was pretty damning. No wonder Addison was hiding out in Cricket Creek. Her mother was
probably embarrassed as hell. Looked like he'd been
right about Addison being pretty wild and not his type at
all.

After another deep breath, Reid pushed open the
deep red door and entered the shop. He clumped across
the gleaming hardwood floor, feeling a little bit like Pig-
pen in the Charlie Brown comics. Soft music played
through hidden speakers, and the air smelled like vanilla
and flowers. Wedding gowns were artfully displayed on
both sides of the middle of the big open room. Overhead
lighting glinted off white fabric, making the details spar-
kle. Lighted display cases showcased jewelry and beaded
purses. Antiques, white linen—all created an air of elegance. He would have been impressed that she'd pulled
this together so quickly if he hadn't been so pissed.

Reid looked around, trying to see where Addison was
hiding, but wondered if she wasn't upstairs and had for-

gotten to lock the front door. Sara had told him that Addison had moved from the condo to the loft apartment. He felt a flash of concern and then squashed it, reminding himself that she wasn't the sweet and innocent little thing that she'd pretended to be.

And then he saw her.

With her back to him, Addison struggled with a big box, tugging it into the room from what appeared to be a storage area. She wore jeans and a plain pink T-shirt. Her long dark hair was pulled into a ponytail, and if he wasn't mistaken she was barefoot. He wondered why she didn't seem to hear him but then noticed earphones. She paused and bobbed her head and shoulders to the beat and then did a cute little wiggle thing while snapping her fingers. Lifting her arms she hummed for a minute, sang a word here and there. She did a shimmy to the left and then to the right. She bobbed and weaved, started singing again as if she couldn't help herself. Reid grinned but then reminded himself that nothing about her was amusing. Still dancing but a little bit more subdued she opened the flaps on the top of the box. "Addison?" he called out, but she must have had the music turned up pretty loud because she didn't respond.

"Oh!" her soft, throaty exclamation of delight teased his senses and he smiled, forgetting for a moment how pissed he was at her, and he stood rooted to the spot. She lifted up a wedding veil and examined it tenderly, cooing over the pearls and details. She stood in the soft lighting, looking so damned pretty that his blood stirred. She bent forward and pulled out some tissue paper, letting it flutter to the floor, and then examined another veil, handling it with care before putting it on a linen-covered display table. "Oh, pink rosebuds!" she said with a sense of wonder that for some reason Reid found super-sweet but somehow sexy. He decided it was time to make his presence known.

He started clumping across the room toward her. "Addison?" he said, but she started bopping her head again before bending back into the box. Finally he walked closer and tapped her on the back.

"Eeeek!" She quickly stood up and then stumbled backward, tripping over the edge of a round Oriental rug and she fell, landing on her butt with a grunt. The veil she clutched went flying upward and fluttered to the floor with a light *clink*.

"Oh, crap. Are you okay?" Reid towered over her while she blinked up at him.

"How did *you* get in here?" She tugged the earbuds out and gave him a decidedly unfriendly stare.

When she ignored his outstretched hand he crossed his arms across his chest. "The front door was open." He tilted his head in that direction.

"Well, we're closed," she said shortly. "I thought I'd locked it."

Reid understood her anger. She'd thrown herself at him and he'd responded, but he hadn't called her since that night. For a second he felt like an ass. Then he remembered the picture of her kissing a long-haired, leather-clad rock star.

"Well?"

Reid looked down at her. "I need to talk to you." Her feet were indeed bare. Peach-tinted toenails seemed to beg for his touch. "You're barefoot," he said without thinking. Her delicate feet looked even more feminine next to his big clunky boots.

"I have a blister from my shoes," she explained, but then shook her head as if clearing it. "What do you want, Reid?"

I want to know why you were kissing Rick Ruleman.

"Well?" Her chin came up in defiance but then she seemed to catch herself. When she put her palms on the floor and pushed upward he saw her wince, and some of his anger faded.

"Are you okay?" He held his hand out but she ignored it once more.

"Just . . . sore. I've been doing a lot of bending and

lifting." She sliced her hand through the air. "As you can imagine."

Reid nodded and he knew the polite thing to do would to be to tell her how great the shop looked, but he didn't. "About this thing with my sister . . ."

"I'm sorry, Reid, but I did my research and Sara is onto something. Barn weddings are popular. With Wedding Row in place she would really develop a thriving business. I had to be honest."

"Honest?" He all but growled the word, making her eyebrows shoot up. "Do you even know the meaning of the word? Look, I know you just do what you want . . . take what you want."

"Excuse me?" Her eyes widened, but he kept on talking.

"And this shop is a fun little distraction while you hide out here in Cricket Creek from your . . . indiscretions."

"Indiscretions? Who even says that?"

"You know what I mean."

"Really?" she asked flatly. "Enlighten me."

"Let's not go there. But listen. My sister doesn't have money to play around with, unlike you. I asked you to discourage her from sinking her retirement into this little game, and you had to go and do the direct opposite. Were you trying to get back at me? Is that it?"

Addison blinked at him.

Reid knew he was being an ass but he was fueled by anger and jealousy. "Well?"

"You seem to already have all of the answers," she answered tightly, but her voice shook.

"No, I don't. That's why I'm here." For the first time Reid noticed slight shadows beneath her eyes. What was keeping her up at night? Guilt?

Addison gave him a level stare and then swallowed hard. "For the record, I don't owe you *any* explanations. And I'm not about to defend myself. But here are the facts: If you're referring to my supposed affair with Rick

Ruleman, that was fabricated either by his camp to fuel his bad-boy image or by Garret to get big ratings for his reality show. A show I would have no part of because I value my privacy and my reputation. The picture that keeps showing up of me seeming to kiss Rick was taken at my engagement party to his son. It was completely innocent. *And* the funds to open this shop came from my own personal investments. I have a degree in business and I've been taught well by my mother, who I'm sure you're familiar with, since you seem to have been digging into my personal life. I know a thing or two about money."

Oh . . . shit. "Addison . . ."

She held up her index finger. "Oh no, please allow me to finish. And as for your sister's risk in hosting wedding receptions?" She tapped her chest. "I am prepared to be an investor in the renovation of the barn. In fact, I have talked to several of the shop owners in Wedding Row and they were all interested in helping to get this off the ground. Here's another fun fact: Sara's own wedding is going to be virtually free because we're taking the opportunity to showcase our shops. The gown, the cake, catering, tuxedoes, flowers . . . you name it. Jason Craig was even willing to throw in most of his labor for renovating the barn in exchange for having his wedding to Madison Robinson on your farm. It's called bartering, and, according to Sara, I understand farmers still do a lot of that."

Addison walked over to a desk and picked up a sheet of paper. She tapped the side of her cheek. "Let's see. I have Mia Monroe's wedding on the list. I assure you that it will be quite an affair. Maggie McMillan, the real estate lady in the corner shop, said that her son, Tristan, and Savannah Perry are interested as well. She even offered to add a link on her Web site to help book weddings with out-of-town clients. All of this, and we haven't even advertised. It's all just word of mouth." She tilted her head to the side. "Was there anything else you wanted to know? I'm kind of busy."

Speechless, Reid looked at her. Although he towered over her even more than usual in his work boots with her being barefoot, he suddenly felt very small.

"Nothing more? Super." She pointed to the door. "Oh, and just a simple a word of advice: Don't believe everything you read and don't listen to gossip. I'm just sayin'." She abruptly turned her back on him and reached into the box of veils.

Reid stood there for a moment, wondering what in the hell to do. *Sorry* wouldn't even begin to cut it. He thought the best thing to do would be to simply leave, but when he saw the slight hitch of her shoulders Reid thought she might be crying. Shit.

Reid simply could not stand to see a woman cry. His mother knew it and so did Sara and they weren't above using tears to their advantage, but this was different. He had made Addison cry. He had to make her stop. After clearing his throat he said, "Addison?"

She went very still but failed to turn around.

"Listen . . ."

Addison whirled around so fast that her ponytail looked like a helicopter blade. "No, *you* listen." She pointed at him, lest there be no mistake. "You think you know all about me, don't you, Reid Greenfield? That I'm a spoiled, rich socialite born with a silver spoon in my mouth. Well, I'm not!" She patted her chest so hard that Reid winced. "I grew up in a middle-class suburban neighborhood outside of Chicago. My dad was an art teacher at the local high school, and my mother tried without much success to sell her books on finance. They struggled. In fact, my mother is a Seminole Indian raised on a reservation in Florida, and my dad is the son of a plumber."

"Addison, I—"

"My mother didn't set out to become famous, only to help real people manage their money. She certainly saw plenty of poverty. They are two of the most humble, grounded people I know." She swallowed hard, but, thank

God, held her tears in check. Reid quit trying to stop her. Raising her hands she said, "I went to college on an academic scholarship and got engaged to my best friend *before* he became famous. Aiden and I weren't meant to get married, but that doesn't mean I wasn't deeply hurt when he cheated on me. I lost his friendship out of the whole mess and had to weather the gossip and mean accusations. And Garret? Yeah, I rebounded with Garret, who made me laugh like crazy and brought me out of my nerdy shell and helped me fit into a society that I never felt comfortable around. Yeah, he's a big kid, selfish and spoiled and terribly insecure. But I didn't cheat on him with his father. I've never cheated on anyone or anything, despite what everyone is saying about me behind my back and to the media. You can believe me or not believe me . . . I really don't give a damn what people believe anymore. Especially you." She pointed at him again.

"Why especially me?"

"Because . . . because you're a judgmental jerk with your head so far up your ass you can't see daylight."

Reid almost laughed. Curse words coming out of her mouth just seemed funny. But he didn't laugh because, unfortunately, she was right. With her hands fisted on her hips, she angled her head at him and glared, even as her eyes glittered with unshed tears.

"Now get out of my store before . . . before I . . . pick you up and . . . toss you to the curb," she sputtered. She stomped her foot, apparently forgetting she was barefoot, and winced.

Reid jammed his thumb over his shoulder. "You want to grab a cold beer? I think you could use one. I know I'm dusty, but I can fit in at Sully's."

"Are you serious? You've got to be kidding me."

"No, I'm serious." He gave her a slight shrug. "But you'd have to wear shoes."

She looked down at her feet and then back up at him. She took a couple of steps closer and then tilted her head up.

Reid held his breath.

"I wouldn't drink a beer with you if you were the last man on earth."

He shoved his hands in his pockets and rocked back on his heels. "Okay, I guess I deserve that."

"You think?"

Reid nodded slowly. "Yeah."

"Well, and I hate to tell you, but I'll be a frequent visitor on your farm. Renovations to the barn will begin soon, and I'm going to be consulting with Sara whether you like it or not. I would appreciate if you'd stay out of my way."

"I will."

"Good."

"But, Addison?"

She arched an eyebrow.

"I'm sorry. I was way out of line. And I'm really impressed with the shop."

She remained still and silent, unrelenting, and yet there was a vulnerable set to her mouth that hit Reid in the gut. He knew he'd been dead-ass wrong, and he'd screwed up his chance with a beautiful, funny, smart woman. The urge to pull her into his arms and hug her tightly was so damned strong but he was pretty sure he'd get a knee where he didn't want it, and so he nodded once more and turned around and walked out of the store.

13

Defying Gravity

ADDISON IGNORED THE THUMPING OF HER HEART AS SHE pulled her Mustang into the front driveway of the Greenfield farmhouse. If she ran into Reid she'd smile politely and give him the cold shoulder. Of course, seeing him actually made her body warm instead of cold but she'd never let him know it. She supposed, however, that Reid had gotten the message after her tirade last night. Afterward she'd felt a little bit embarrassed, especially when she realized much later while lying in bed that he must have seen her dancing and singing along with CeeLo Green. Why did it have to be *that* song? She gripped the steering wheel and shook her head. "Because that's the way my life goes, apparently."

At least the Sunday afternoon sunshine felt good on her cheeks. Although the upcoming grand opening of From This Moment sent a nervous flutter through her stomach, getting away for a while and taking in the country scenery felt amazingly freeing. She reminded herself that beautiful inventory filled every nook and cranny of the shop and that for all intents and purposes she was ready to open. She'd hired a local seamstress, and for now she'd concentrate on the paperwork and wedding planning. If the consulting end of the business accelerated, she'd hire an assistant to help her out. Mia promised to do what she could, but her job at the baseball stadium picked up with the beginning of the season, and coupled with watching Cam play baseball, she wouldn't be around much.

Stepping out of the car, Addison smiled at the picture-perfect farmhouse appearing before her, serene and welcoming. Abundant flowers provided a burst of color against the white background. Wicker furniture and fat baskets of ferns on the front porch called for lazy afternoons of sipping on sweet tea. A big oak tree graced the front lawn, reaching up to the sky with open arms. A tire swing hung from a thick branch, making Addison imagine laughing children—but definitely not an adorable young Reid—being pushed high in the air. The top of a tall silo peeked over the house, as if watching over it. Addison's smile deepened. This was a slice of Americana, a postcard into the past, and she admired Sara for doing all she could to preserve her family farm.

Addison inhaled the country air, fragrant with cut grass, sweet flowers, freshly turned earth, and a hint of hay. The late-spring day felt almost hot, but thankfully lacked the steamy summer humidity hovering right around the corner. Still, Addison was glad she'd worn cool white shorts and a short-sleeve light blue blouse. A thin gold belt and plaid Sperry Top-Siders gave the casual attire a touch of class with a businesslike edge.

Smile still in place, she started toward the sidewalk leading to the front steps. But out of the corner of her eye she spotted something big and furry galloping in her direction. At first Addison thought it was a fat little pony. *No ... Oh God, it ... Is it a wolf?* She stood, rooted to the spot as the animal raced across the yard and straight for her. Would it attack? Bite? She took a shaky step backward, wondering whether to bolt for the front steps or dive into her car. Before she could decide, the big ball of brown fur ran around her in a circle as if closing in for the kill. His deep bark struck terror in her heart. A scream bubbled up in Addison's throat but fear squeezed her vocal cords. Mind racing, adrenaline pumping, she wondered if there was anything in her purse that the dog would like to eat, like maybe a T-bone steak, so she could run like hell. But she could only think of chewing gum and didn't suppose that would do the trick unless the dog wanted minty-fresh breath.

After another deep bark the huge dog skidded to a stop and then pounced. The big paws came up on her shoulders, making Addison stagger backward and wonder if she should fight or play dead. The big furry head leaned in . . .

And licked her.

He happily lapped one cheek and then the other. Letting out her held breath, Addison giggled first from repressed hysteria and then from absolute relief that the big animal was actually a gentle giant.

"Little John, down!"

Little John paused in his licking but his paws remained. He looked at Addison as if asking permission for one last lick. He took her giggle as a yes.

"I said *down*!" Another command came from across the yard.

Addison looked over Little John's massive shoulder and spotted Reid standing next to the metal barn across from the house. He had a tool of some kind in his hand and he was *holy cow* . . . shirtless. His jeans had a rip across each knee and a hole in one thigh, but it was his chest that captured her undivided attention.

Little John gave Addison's chin a sly, quick lick before pushing away from her shoulders. Although the threat of being eaten alive no longer applied, when she brushed a lock of hair from her face she wasn't surprised to notice a tremble in her fingers. She was used to dogs, but little yappy things, not big brutes . . . even though Little John turned out to be a lovable brute.

Reid quickly closed the distance from across the yard and gave Little John a shake of his head. "You know better." When he shook his finger at Little John, the big dog hung his head. "I'm sorry. He's harmless, but I hope he didn't scare you."

"No," Addison scoffed. "I didn't see my life flash before my eyes or anything else like that."

Reid chuckled and seemed to relax a little bit. When he reached up and shoved damp hair off his forehead the movement caused a delicious ripple of muscle. A slight sheen of sweat made his tanned skin glisten. Just the right amount of tawny chest hair narrowed into an enticing line that disappeared beneath his jeans. With no belt, the worn denim hung low on his waist, and in spite of how irritated Addison felt toward him she couldn't help but notice how sexy he looked without a shirt.

"Sorry. I'm a dirty mess." He tilted his head toward the barn. "I was fixing the quad."

"The quad?"

"Four-wheeler. I was told to take you out to the old barn but it wouldn't start."

"Wait. . . . What? You? Where's Sara?"

"With Mom. They went out to the barn after church to start taking notes. I had orders to take you to them when you arrived."

"Oh . . . uh . . . thanks, but I'll walk."

"It's two miles."

"I'll drive."

"You'd have to go through the narrow path in the woods. It's not drivable in a car."

"How did Sara get there?"

"On a quad with my mother."

Addison's eyes widened. "Really?"

"And Mom was driving. We're outdoorsy people, in case you didn't notice."

Oh, she noticed everything about him.

"Look, I tried to tell them that you wouldn't want to ride with me but they weren't having it."

"Isn't there someone else?"

Reid shrugged, causing his pecs to do a delicious little dance. "Dad and Braden just left for a Cougars game. Sorry about your luck, but I'm all you've got."

"Why would Sara not wait for me?"

Reid took a step closer, crowding her space, making her want to touch him. *No!* She would not touch him.

"You really want to know?"

"Yes."

He hesitated. "Matchmaking."

"What?" Addison said so loud that Little John gave her a curious look. "Like, between me and you?" She pointed to herself and then to Reid, just to make sure she heard him right.

"Sara was singing your praises at breakfast, and my mother kept giving me *the look*."

"The look?"

"The *I-want-grandchildren* look."

Addison fisted her hands on her hips. "Did you let your mother know that I . . . um . . . ?" How could she put it delicately?

"Despise me? Yes."

"And?"

When Reid took another step closer it was all Addison could do not to put distance between them, but she didn't want him to know the effect he was having on her, standing there all tanned skin and honed muscles, and so she stood her ground. "She said that your anger was a shield of armor to guard you against getting hurt again. She said that deep down you want to kiss me."

"How could she know that? Wait. I mean, she's sure got it all wrong."

He gave her a lopsided grin. "I might have added that last part."

Addison inhaled sharply, trying to clear the unwanted attraction to him out of her head. Reid's unexpected charm after what had transpired between them hacked away at her anger, but she reminded herself that overlooking bad behavior landed her in the middle of regret over and over. She also reminded herself that she was taking a much-needed break from men, period. But she did need to get out there to take a look at the barn.

"You're not afraid, are you?"

"Of what?" Her chin came up and she gave him a challenging look. Of letting down her guard? *Hell, yeah.*

"Of—"

"You?" She thought about poking him in the chest, something she'd never done before until being around him. She also never interrupted and rarely raised her voice. She had certainly never grabbed a guy by the shirt and planted a kiss on him. Addison suddenly thought about Mia's explanation that when it's the real deal everything is just . . . more intense. *No!* Hardheaded, judgmental Reid Greenfield was not *the one!* "I'm not afraid of being around you. Oh, and about that . . . that grabbing and kissing you thing? That was a lapse of judgment, a moment of total insanity that will not be repeated. Ever."

"Um, I was merely trying to ask if you're afraid of riding through the woods on the back of the quad, city girl."

"Oh." She felt heat creep into her cheeks and then bristled. "Of course not," she answered, wishing she were wearing something more rugged and less preppy. "Country boy."

"Just making sure."

"Hey, I've been skydiving. Bungee jumped off of a bridge. Scuba diving." She paused, trying to think of something impressive. "Oh, and . . . swam with dolphins."

"Just dolphins and not sharks?"

Okay, she knew that Reid was having fun with this. "Let's just say I think I can handle riding on a four-wheeler." Addison wondered why she needed to prove her bravery to him, anyway.

He raised his eyebrows. "Okay, then," he said casually, but there was a sudden gleam in his eye that had her swallowing hard.

Addison just might have drawn a line in the sand; judging by his grin, she guessed he'd just used reverse psychology on her. Damn . . . the truth of the matter was that she wasn't really a very brave person when it came to things like this. Riding on a roller coaster was bad enough and those things she'd boasted about doing had scared her to death. But, really, how scary could riding through the woods on a four-wheeler be? "Let's get going." So she was going to have to put her arms around his bare torso. So what?

"I'm going to borrow one of Braden's shirts. I got grease on mine. I'll be back in a minute."

She watched him walk into the house and then sighed. "Oh, thank God . . ." Addison sat down on the top of the front steps to wait for him. Little John followed and lay down next to her. She looked down at the big, friendly mutt and patted his head. "Well, Little John. What did I just get myself into?"

A little while later Reid appeared wearing a clean white T-shirt. "Sorry I took a few minutes. I decided that I needed to do you a favor and take a really quick shower."

Addison had the sudden image of naked Reid with sudsy water sluicing over his skin.

"Are you ready?"

Since her vocal cords took another vacation she nodded. He offered his hand and she grasped it, trying to ignore the little tingle that happened every time the man barely touched her. He tugged her to a standing position, pulling her way too close for her comfort. He smelled freshly showered with a hint of spicy aftershave. Addison had the urge to run her fingers through his damp hair just to feel the wet silk between her fingertips. That thought had her taking a quick step backward, nearly stepping on Little John.

"Hey." Reid shoved his fingers through his hair and gave her a serious look. "I want to apologize again for my behavior at your shop. And, look, I know it's no excuse, but I watched my clients lose thousands of dollars of hard-earned retirement money when the market crashed. My sister was one of them. Finally, the stocks are coming back. The last thing I wanted to happen is for Sara to lose that money again."

"I told you that we have that covered. The risk will be minimal, Reid."

"I know, and I should back off." He blew out a sigh and Addison was surprised when he continued. "I was against my brother Jeff heading to Nashville to pursue singing. I mean, the odds were stacked against him, right? I encouraged Braden to finish school." He shook his head. "The truth is that Jeff's a talented musician who deserves to get his chance. Braden loves farming, so college wasn't where he belonged. I should keep my damned mouth shut and let people pursue their dreams." He swung his arm in an arc. "I love this place as much as the rest of my family. Even more than I thought after I came back. In truth, fear of losing it was what kept me away for all these years. And I feel guilty ... about all of it. But mostly about holding my brothers back. Now here I am, attempting to do the same thing with Sara." He gave her a resigned smile. "So I am officially backing down. If this doesn't take off"—he shrugged—"that's part of going after a dream. But Sara deserves her chance too."

Addison felt her anger toward him melting. "Don't be so hard on yourself. It's evident that you care."

Reid inhaled a deep breath and blew it out. "There's one more thing I want to confess." He paused and then gave her a crooked grin. "Part of my jackass behavior stemmed from ... jealousy."

"Jealousy?"

"Seeing that picture of you kissing Rick Ruleman."

Addison's heart thumped. "Really?" she finally asked softly.

"I know I have no right. You're getting over a broken engagement and trying to start your own business. I get it that you don't like or trust men right now. I don't want to take advantage of you being vulnerable. I was being honest about that even though I know it pissed you off."

Addison raised her eyebrows. "I hear a great big *but* in that big speech of yours."

Reid took a step closer and tucked a finger beneath her chin. "But I can't get you off of my mind."

"You can't charm your way back into my good graces."

"I'm simply telling the truth."

"You know what?"

"What?"

Addison fisted her hands, steeling herself against the pull of attraction to him. "Nothing. Let's get going." She started walking toward the four-wheeler.

"I want to kiss you."

Addison stopped in her tracks. "Too bad," she said casually, but her heart thudded when she heard him approach. He came up behind her.

"I think you're afraid."

"Oh, don't even try playing that card. It won't work. Besides, why would I be afraid of a kiss? I just don't want to."

"Okay."

"Don't say *okay* like that," she sputtered.

"Like what?" Reid stepped around to face her.

"In that tone like you don't believe me. It's infuriating."

He nodded silently and with raised eyebrows.

"Stop!"

Reid raised his arms akimbo. "What now?"

"That was a silent *okay* and you damned well know it."

"If you say so," he answered airily.

With a little high-pitched, embarrassing growl that she tried to disguise as a sneeze she stomped in her Sperrys over to the four-wheeler. She wanted to shove him. She wanted to smack him! But most of all she wanted to kiss him, and it pissed her off. Royally.

Reid was making her whole "stay away from men" vow go to hell in a handbasket and she had to get her life back on track. Getting involved with him would totally derail everything. No, she would not do it.

"Here. You have to wear this." He said, and handed her a helmet.

"I need a helmet? What kind of crazy trail is this, anyway?"

"It's just a precaution," he said in a tone hinting otherwise.

"How come you're not wearing one?"

"I have a hard head."

Addison swallowed. "I . . . I might have a tiny confession to make of my own."

"What might that be?"

"I'm a big scaredy-cat when it comes to things fast and dangerous."

"Ah . . ." Reid's eyes seemed to smolder as he strapped the helmet beneath her chin. "So you prefer slow and easy?"

Addison nodded, waiting for him to reassure her, but he only grinned. "So you'll go slow, right?"

Reid looped one long leg over the seat and sat down, motioning for her to do the same. "Hell, no. Wrap your arms around me and hold on tight," he said over his shoulder.

Before she could protest, Reid took off down the middle of the yard, causing dust to fly. Barking, Little John followed them down a well-worn path in between corn fields. Another dog followed, too, but quickly gave up. She didn't blame him.

Addison squealed when Reid made a sharp turn that took them into the woods. She held on for dear life, but it soon became obvious that he knew the woods like the back of his hand. And maybe it was because he was in such control or because holding on to him was worth the risk, but suddenly instead of being scared Addison laughed and enjoyed the exhilarating ride. When Reid drove through a creek, making water splash up her bare legs, she yelled but then giggled.

"You're crazy," she shouted when they seemed to defy gravity, climbing up a steep hill. Reid only laughed in response. Clinging to him, she felt the ripple of muscle and the heat of his skin through his T-shirt. She squeezed her thighs around his hips a bit harder, telling herself it was for safety's sake. By the time they reached an open field Addison was breathless for more reasons than one. When a weathered barn came into view he did a doughnut that had her begging for mercy and then skidded to a stop.

Weak from laughter and excitement Addison remained glued to his back for a long moment.

Reid looked over his shoulder. "You can let go now," he said with a chuckle.

Addison peeled herself off of him and scooted back but Reid had to assist her in removing the helmet since her fingers only managed to fumble with the straps.

"Too much for you, City Girl?"

Addison shook her hair free. "I think you just wanted me to have to cling to you, country boy."

"Guilty," he admitted, and Addison thought he was going to lean in and kiss her. But a woman shouted, stopping him.

"Reid William Greenfield! Just what in the world do you think you're doing, driving like a madman?"

Addison looked when a tiny woman stomped over and fisted her hands on her slim hips. She wore a blue baseball cap with a blond ponytail stuck out the back.

"Have you taken leave of your senses?" the woman demanded, and then looked at Sara, who also glared at Reid.

"Sorry, Mom, but Addison said that she wanted me to go as fast as I could."

"I don't believe you for one minute," she said, and then extended her hand to Addison. "I'm Susan Greenfield and I apologize for my son."

Addison grasped her small hand with its surprisingly strong grip. "No need. He was trying to scare me but I foiled his evil plan. I actually enjoyed it, much to his sorrow."

Susan sighed and put a hand to her chest. "Thank goodness, or he'd be in a heap of trouble."

"Yeah, epic fail, even though he tried his best," Addison added, not letting Reid off the hook with his mother. She leaned close to Reid and whispered, "Touché."

Addison hurried forward with Sara while Reid got a dressing-down from his feisty little mother.

"Well played," Sara said and gave Addison a high five.

14

The Look of Love

REID SHOVED HIS HANDS IN HIS POCKETS, PRETENDING indifference while he followed the chattering women around the barn. In reality he listened intently, taking mental notes. As promised, he'd take a step back, but Reid wouldn't be able or willing to watch his sister take a financial hit without speaking up. Part of the problem stemmed from his lack of knowledge about weddings in general. He'd attended his share of friends' and family's nuptials but never paid much attention to the details.

One thing that did floor Reid was the money spent on one single day. Apparently couples spent twenty, thirty . . . fifty grand or more for a wedding nowadays. Reid shook his head. With a higher than fifty percent divorce rate, spending that kind of cash wasn't worth the risk. Right?

Reid listened to the dreamy tone of Sara's voice when she chatted with Addison about colors, dresses, cakes, and music. He just didn't get it. And when he calculated what he could do with investing that kind of cash, he shook his head.

Reid also acknowledged that while his parents' marriage seemed as solid as a rock, weathering everything

from raising four headstrong children to financial difficulty, Reid had witnessed a couple of nasty divorces in-
volving his friends. He quickly made the decision that he
would have to be absolutely sure before even coming
close to tying the knot.

But when Reid's gaze fell upon Addison the sudden
thought that she'd make a beautiful bride landed in his
brain with a solid *thud*. He envisioned Addison walking
down the aisle while he waited ... and then mentally
shook himself. What in the world had suddenly come
over him? Weddings were a waste of money. Marriage
was a high risk. And children? He'd never even given
being a father much more than a passing thought.

Just then, his mother tipped her head to the side and
laughed at something Addison said. His mother turned,
caught Reid's eye, and gave him ... *the look*. Reid was
about ready to roll his eyes at his matchmaking mother
when she raised her wrist and looked at her watch.

"Oh dear. I have to get going and get that apple pie in
the oven."

"Apple pie tonight?" Reid asked hopefully. Sundays
usually meant pot roast or fried chicken and some sort
of heavenly dessert.

Susan gave him an apologetic look. "Oh, Reid. Sorry,
but your dad and I are going over to the Whimsy's for
horseshoes and dinner after he gets back from the baseball game. And Braden has a date with Ronnie, the cute
little redhead who works at Ava Whimsy's toy store on
Main Street. I know my apple pie is your favorite. I'll
save you a piece if there's any left over."

"Not likely," Reid said glumly. "What about you,
Sara?"

"Oh, I've got to meet Cody for dinner at his mom's
soon," Sara announced. "But, Addison, you're welcome
to stay and take more notes. I'll scan these and send
them to you and we can get together some evening when
you get the chance. I'll also meet with Jason this week
and get more numbers to you."

"Sounds good," Addison said. "I might walk around a little bit longer. I have to admit that as much as I'm looking forward to the grand opening of From This Moment, I'm enjoying a breather."

"Reid, I did put a pot roast on low in the oven over at your cabin before Sara and I came over here," his mother added innocently. "There's plenty if Addison wants to join you." Her little shrug didn't fool Reid. His mom and Sara had planned this way in advance. "Well, I must be off. It was so lovely to finally meet you, Addison. I can't wait to see your shop. I hear it's just beautiful. Just what Cricket Creek needed for our brides-to-be, and I still need a mother of the bride dress. All I've seen are those fussy beaded things that would weigh me down."

Addison smiled. "I hear you on that! I'll have a nice selection in the store in time for the grand opening."

"You ready, Mom?" Sara asked. Yep, his sister had joined the matchmaking ranks of Cricket Creek. Why was he always being double-teamed?

"Yes, let's get a move on." Sara nodded and hurried over to the four-wheeler, waving cheerfully. A setup. Reid was sure he was right. Not that he really minded spending the rest of the day with Addison, but he turned to her with feigned chagrin. "See what I mean?"

"Matchmaking? You really think so?"

"Trust me, it runs rampant in Cricket Creek. So beware."

"Oh, don't worry. I might soon be *planning* weddings but not my own. Nope, done with that." She made a show of dusting her hands. "And by the tone of your voice a wedding won't be in your future anytime soon. Should we high-five on that one?"

"Sure."

When Addison held up her hand Reid smacked it. But she couldn't quite hide the edge of sadness that crept into her voice even though she smiled. "Look. I know you have your reservations about this venture but this is a lovely setting for weddings, especially with the river in the background. We'll transform this barn into something elegant but rustic—chandeliers and champagne, but with weathered wood. You know?"

Reid didn't know but nodded.

"We'll have those fields of wildflowers in the spring. Wildflowers are my favorite. No one plants them; they just come to life. Won't they make for some romantic pictures? And amazing fall color with the surrounding woods. We need a gazebo for the vows and a back deck overlooking the water. Poured concrete for the floor or hardwood?" She didn't seem to be actually consulting him. "It will take some work but this old barn has good bones." She turned to face Reid. "You might consider hosting family reunions as well. Pig roasts, things like that. This really is a wonderful piece of land, Reid."

"I can't argue with that part." It was difficult not to enjoy her enthusiasm.

"Would you mind opening up the barn? I'd like to see the inside."

"It will be dusty with cobwebs and God knows what else, city girl."

"I'll be just fine, country boy."

"Don't say I didn't warn you." Reid walked over, unlatched the rusty hinge, and tugged the door open. Dust motes danced in the sudden sunshine slicing through the shaded interior. "You sure you want to venture inside?"

"Of course." Addison walked inside and immediately sneezed.

"You want to go farther?"

"Hey, I've breathed the LA smog for years. A little dust is nothing."

"Good point." He followed her inside and watched her as she walked around, looking at everything with a sense of awe.

"The layout is perfect with the high, beamed ceilings. Oh, Reid, it's beautiful in here."

"This old barn?"

She nodded. "I've always loved old buildings, antiques. There's just so much history. My father would be snapping pictures like crazy."

"He's a photographer?"

"Oh yeah, especially nature and rustic pieces of history like this barn. If walls could talk . . ."

"Well, it would be mostly mooing and neighing, I'd say. Maybe an occasional squawk."

Addison laughed. "Yeah, but weren't there barn dances and things like that? Bluegrass music? Stolen kisses in the hayloft?" She fell quiet and turned away.

The word *kiss* coming out of her mouth was all it took for Reid to close the gap between them. "Hey . . ." He put gentle hands on her shoulders and eased her around to face him. Her appreciation of the beauty of the land, the wildflowers, and the old barn seemed to go way beyond making money. He was seeing Addison in a different light and was drawn to her more than just physically. When she tilted her head Reid realized he'd forgotten to complete his sentence. "Let's give those walls something to talk about," he said before pulling her into his arms. Her eyes widened but she didn't protest. Reid only meant to give her a playful kiss, but as soon as his lips met hers he pulled her closer, kissed her deeper. She'd looked so prim and preppy in her pleated shorts and boat shoes, but those tanned legs and full breasts reminded him of her sensual side—the part he saw when she'd kissed him at the condo. And oh, how he longed to have those legs wrapped around his waist. He wanted that sexy, throaty voice calling out his name while he made sweet love to her all afternoon long.

Reid knew he should step back, break the kiss, but instead he cradled her head in his palms and kept on kissing her. Maybe it was human nature that the more he knew he should stay away the more he wanted her. Maybe it was because he thought she needed a real man instead of those idiots she was engaged to . . . Reid didn't know why he couldn't keep his distance; he knew only that since he'd met Addison she was never far from his thoughts.

Reid was giving the hayloft some serious consideration when he heard a rustling sound. The noise could be one of several things, but Reid knew for sure that they weren't alone. He reluctantly pulled his mouth from hers. Looking around, he spotted the culprit. Several of them. "Addison?"

"Hmmm?" she asked in a soft, dreamy tone that had him wanting to kiss her again.

"I think we should go."

"Why?" She tilted her head. "Are you sorry you kissed me?"

Reid rubbed his thumb over her bottom lip. "I'm surprised that you let me, but no, I'm not sorry I kissed you, Addison." He decided to leave it at that ... for now. "There are ... ah, some critters in here." He thought that *critters* sounded less frightening than *rodents and reptiles*, and he'd just spotted both.

"Critters?" Addison's eyes widened. "What kind of critters? A bug or something?"

"The kind you might not like."

"Are you messing with me? Yeah, you are." She gave his arm a playful punch. "Oh ... you're *not*?" She lowered her voice to a whisper.

"Sorry." Reid shook his head. "Now, before you get scared, let me tell you that it's a black snake and it's harmless."

"S-snake?"

"Harmless. It wants the mouse, not us."

"Mouse!"

"Mice, actually."

She swallowed hard. "So, what do we do? Run for it?" Her eyes were big in her pretty face.

"Well, it's over near the door. Most likely came in when I opened it, knowing there would be lunch in here."

With her hands clutching Reid's shoulders she slowly turned her head to look. "Oh, dear Lord. It's really long. Oh, and it just moved," she whispered. "Do you think it sees us?"

"Addison, I'm actually starting to get hungry and we should check on Mom's pot roast. It will most likely slither away when we approach it."

"There are two things I don't like about what you just said: *most likely* and *slither*. Seriously, how can you think about eating at a time like this?"

When Reid laughed the snake moved, raising its head.

"Shhh!" she whispered. "Did you forget that I'm a big scaredy-cat? Spiders, snakes, and mice are on the top of the list."

Reid held his chuckle but his shoulders moved up and down.

"You're having fun with this, aren't you?"

"No!" he said in such a fake tone that Addison narrowed her eyes at him. "Okay, maybe a little bit."

"So, what are we going to do?"

"I'm going to kneel down and I want you to climb on my back. You're about to get a piggyback ride."

"No, that's silly," Addison whispered, but then the snake slithered farther into the barn and there was a scurrying sound over in the corner. "Okay, you convinced me."

Reid knelt down and tilted his body forward, thinking he probably should have been more specific with his wish: He wanted her legs wrapped around him, just not quite like this. Still, when she climbed onto his back he liked it.

"Hold on tight."

"That's the second time you've said that to me," she whispered in his ear, and then wrapped her arms around his neck. "Is this going to be another wild ride?"

"To quote Jason Aldean, 'It's the only way I know,'" Reid answered, and then bolted toward the door. Just as he expected, when the snake felt the vibration of his running, it slithered farther into the barn, away from them. He tried not to bounce her around too much, but when he realized that she was laughing he played it up a little bit and ran around in the grass in front of the barn until he was laughing too hard to keep going. After coming to a stop he stood there for a moment, holding on to her legs and enjoying having her clinging to him. One of her shoes hung halfway off her foot, and for some reason he thought it was funny and started laughing harder.

It was a moment before he caught his breath enough to speak. "I think it's safe to put you down now," he said, and reluctantly loosened his grip. She slid down his back until her feet touched the ground.

"Thanks. I feel like such a weenie."

Reid turned around to face her. "But a very cute weenie." With her flushed face and tousled hair she looked fresh-out-of-bed sexy. Reid wanted to kiss her again but took a step back to put distance between them, and followed it with an awkward pause.

"Um, thanks for coming to my rescue."

Reid looked at her and, knowing he shouldn't, said, "Would you like to come over to my place for dinner? The pot roast is probably about ready."

"I . . . I should get back to the shop."

"But you said you needed a breather."

She hesitated. "I want to but shouldn't."

Reid inhaled a deep breath and blew it out. "Well, I would say that you're safe with me but that would be a lie. I'll be honest with you, Addison. I haven't felt this kind of attraction in a long time. The more I fight it, the more I want to be with you."

"And that's why I should stay away."

"Really? Maybe not. Maybe you shouldn't let those jackasses from your past rule your future. They don't deserve the power." He lifted one shoulder. "Forget about what you should or shouldn't do and do what you want to do."

She gave him a low chuckle. "That's what I was doing

when I grabbed you and kissed you." She took a step closer. "Look, you deserve better. You shouldn't be an experiment . . . a fling or my rebound guy. Using you to get over Garret would be wrong."

"Not if I'm a willing participant," he joked, because he really didn't think he was any of those things to her, but she shook her head.

"I won't do that to you."

"Wait." He paused for a moment. "Addison, what did you mean by *experiment*?"

She blushed and looked away. "Nothing . . ."

"No, I want to know."

"Wild horses couldn't drag it out of me," she said firmly.

Intriguing. "Okay, I'll drop it. For now, anyway."

"So, what's your story, Reid?" she asked softly.

Reid glanced away, looking at the old barn, the trees, the beauty that he'd missed while living away for so many years. Addison had been so open with him about her past. He wanted to do the same, but it was hard to put into words, especially since he'd kept his feelings hidden from his family for such a long time. The gentle touch of her hand on his forearm had him looking into her eyes.

He sighed. "When the economy tanked and my clients lost so much money I took it hard personally, when deep down I knew it was something out of my control, my hands. I did the best I could and worked overtime trying to find ways for them to recoup the losses. I withdrew, kept to myself. Rarely dated. I wasn't about to take another risk with my money, my clients, or my life. When the drought just about took my parents' farm I was so frustrated with them for holding on to this land when the writing was on the wall. To make matters worse, Braden quit school, Sara quit her job, and Jeff headed off to Nashville. I thought they'd all gone bat-shit crazy."

"But if you love something enough you do whatever it takes to hold on to it," Addison said, and then her gaze fell to her shoes. "Some things are worth fighting for."

"Yeah," Reid said, but he knew she wasn't thinking about the farm and it suddenly pissed him off that two jerks had taken away her confidence. And here he was basically offering to be her no-strings-attached booty call. She deserved better. Yeah, dinner at his cabin would be a bad idea.

Finally she looked back up at him. "I am pretty hungry and I just bet your mom is an amazing cook."

Damn. "Yeah, she is."

"Good. Then I'm accepting your offer," Addison said, and looked at him long enough to let him know she wasn't just talking about dinner.

"Addison . . . look—"

"No, wait. Let me stop you. This physical attraction we've got going on is mutual." She came closer and tapped his chest. "So *you* can be my rebound guy and *I'll* be your introduction back into dating. Since we've laid the ground rules up front, no one will get hurt. I think it's a great idea. All of the fun and none of the heartache."

No . . . this was not where he wanted this to go! "I don't really think—"

"Reid, you admitted that you overthink, so squash it. And, yeah, I'm a pleaser, but this way I don't have to worry about pleasing anyone but myself." After patting her chest she took a step back and stuck out her hand. "Deal?"

Reid looked at her small hand and was about to decline, but the vulnerable set to her mouth and those dark, expressive eyes sucked him in. He told himself that it was because he didn't want another guy to hurt her and that he could somehow protect her from that. But the fact that Reid wanted to drag Addison into his arms and hug her hit him like a sucker punch to the gut. He turned into a big ball of sappy mush whenever he was around her. He needed to be careful or he'd be the one to fall in love.

Reid grasped her small hand and squeezed, feeling better when she smiled. He wouldn't let her know about his growing feelings for her, complicating her life when she needed to get it straightened out. Addison wasn't the cheating Hollywood socialite he had accused her of being. Her only fault that he could see was being too sweet and way too trusting of the wrong people. This way he could protect her from any other ass who even thought of doing her wrong or spreading ugly rumors.

"Oh, I'm getting a text message," she said, and reached inside her pocket. "It's Mia. She's got the evening free and wants to help me in the shop." She looked up. "I have so much to do. I should go," she said softly.

Reid nodded, disappointed but somewhat relieved. Addison needed to sleep on this proposal she'd come up with to make sure it was what she truly wanted. He understood where she was coming from. The attraction between them couldn't be denied, but she didn't want to give Reid the power to hurt her. Still, this had the potential to blow up in his face. What in the hell had he been thinking?

15

Sweet Dreams Are Made of This

"ARE YOU KIDDING ME?" MIA PUT HER WINEGLASS DOWN on the coffee table and shook her head at Addison. "Seriously, Reid Greenfield is going to be your . . . *rebound guy*? Explain again how this really bad idea is supposed to work."

"It's pretty simple." Addison leaned back on the sofa that she'd bought at a consignment shop a few days ago. Her apartment was filling up with secondhand furniture and rustic antiques and she loved it. "I'm like his practice person for getting back into dating and he's my rebound guy to help me get over Garret. It's brilliant, don't you think?"

"No, it's a really poorly thought-out plan. Someone will get hurt, Addison. And you've been hurt enough. What happened to your no-men vow? I like that a whole lot better than this silly scenario."

Addison shrugged. "This is going to be way more fun." She raised her hands skyward. "No worries!"

"Yeah, until you fall for him. Then what happens to your little plan?"

"No way. I won't fall for him." Addison made a cutoff

motion toward her neck. "Not gonna happen, no way, no how."

"Right, and your over-the-top denial translates into 'You're already into him and trying to convince yourself otherwise.'"

"No . . ."

"I don't get it. I thought you two were butting heads. Why would you hang out with a guy you don't even get along with?"

Addison picked up a slice of the pizza they'd ordered after adding the finishing touches to an ad they were putting in the local paper. "To keep me out of trouble." She plucked a piece of pepperoni from her slice and popped it into her mouth.

"That's the dumbest thing I've ever heard. Not only that, but I think you've got it all wrong. This is going to get you into trouble, not keep you out of it. And for the record, I think it's wrong for you to treat Reid as if he's your secret stash of ice cream. A guilty pleasure."

"Maybe . . ."

"Oh . . . shifty eyes. What aren't you telling me?"

After swallowing another slice of pepperoni Addison sighed. "Do you promise not to breathe a word of what I'm going to confess?"

"Cross my heart."

Addison delayed her confession by taking a healthy bite of her pizza crust.

"You still eat your pizza the same way you did when we were kids," Mia said with a chuckle.

Nodding, Addison took her time chewing and then washed it down with a swallow of wine.

"Addie! You're killing me."

Addison closed her eyes and inhaled a deep breath. "I'm afraid that I might be, well, boring."

"Boring? I don't know one person who would find you boring."

Addison opened her eyes. "Don't laugh."

"I won't."

"Well," she said in a hushed tone, "especially in bed."

Mia laughed.

"Mia!"

"I'm sorry." Mia took a sip of wine and set her glass back down. "But that's just absurd."

"Maybe that's why guys bail on me. Because I'm not . . . you know. Good."

"So you're going to use Reid as an experiment? See if you rock his world?"

"Oh, it sounds so crass saying it out loud. Yeah, kinda. But look. We're not in love or have any agenda so I'll be able to judge from . . . you know, his reaction."

"You're joking, right? Please say yes."

Addison winced.

"My God, you're serious?"

"Look at my track record." Addison raised her palms upward. "Aiden turned to another woman. I sure didn't satisfy him, now, did I? And Garret? I mean, I thought it was pretty good but apparently I was wrong. He left me for a television show."

Mia scooted around to face her. "You're forgetting the L word."

Addison gasped. "You think I'm a *lesbian*?"

"No, Addison. Not that there's anything wrong with that."

"Lust?"

"I guess I have to spell it out for you." Mia shoved Addison's knee. "L-o-v-e, you dolt."

"Oh, come on. You don't have to be in love to have great sex."

"True, but amazing, mind-blowing sex is with someone you love. Like I said, don't you think it's wrong to use Reid like that, anyway?"

"No, it would just be sort of a by-product of our . . . arrangement. He's dipping his toe back into the dating pool and I'm keeping away from getting engaged. He'll be like . . . like my romance bodyguard."

"Oh, for Pete's sake." Mia reached for her wine.

"I'm not buying into this, Addie. Not one little bit, but I can tell that you're dead set on doing this. Like that time when we were kids and you said you could slide down the banister of that monster staircase without falling off. "You were wrong and got a broken arm to show for it."

"No chance of broken bones here."

"No, just a broken heart." Mia sighed. "And you can't put a cast on a broken heart."

"I'm not going to get emotionally invested. Reid might be going back to Lexington, for all I know. He's just here to help his family get back on track financially. I know all of this going in. I won't be blindsided like in the past."

"I just think you're asking for trouble."

"Well, the other perk is that if I'm seen with Reid, it will help squelch the ugly rumor that I'm having an affair with Rick Ruleman."

Mia dabbed at her mouth with her napkin. "True, but I still don't like it. If you ask me you're coming up with some pretty elaborate plans when all you really want to do is spend time with Reid," Mia pointed out.

"I just need to keep my guard up and this seemed like an easy way to do it."

Mia looked at her for a long moment and then reached over and squeezed her hand. "All right, I've had my say in the matter. I'll drop it and hope for the best. But you know I'm always here for you."

"I know. Thank you, Mia."

"So, are your parents coming into town for the grand opening?"

Addison shook her head. "No, I just talked to Mom about it yesterday and as much as she wants to come she thinks it could hit the gossip sites and bring attention to me and where I'm living."

Mia patted Addison's knee. "Oh, that just sucks, but I think they're right. Well, the Cougars will be out of town next weekend so I'll be able to help out."

"You don't want to visit Cam?"

"He's playing too far away to drive, but I hope to get to Nashville to see him play next weekend."

"It's got to be hard to be apart so much. My dad has to do the same thing with my mom's schedule."

Mia nodded. "It is, but making it to the major leagues is Cam's dream. I could have quit my job and traveled with him but he knows how much I like it and didn't even ask." Her eyes filled with tears. "That doesn't mean it doesn't suck sometimes." She swiped at her tears with her paper napkin. "Oh, Addison, it's good to have you here. And I just know that From This Moment is going to be a huge success. Take it from me: Life picks up when you feel good about your accomplishments. After that, the rest just falls into place."

Addison nodded because she knew Mia was right. "I'm nervous, for sure, but already feeling some of that positive emotion you're talking about."

"Addie, you deserve to be happy. And I'll tell you one thing: If I ever see Garret or Rick Ruleman I'll give them a piece of my mind. And I can get pretty darned feisty when I want to." She lifted both fists and glared.

Addison laughed. "I know! But I don't think we have to worry about either of them showing up here." She grinned. "And if they do I have my romance bodyguard."

Mia laughed with her. "Well, I will say this. Reid sure is hot. I don't really think he'd have to work too hard to get back into the dating game, especially in a small town where eligible bachelors are golden. We have the hottie baseball players but they come and go. A local boy is a prime target."

Addison nodded. "Yeah, well, I think Reid just wants to play it cool for a while," she said breezily, but the thought of Reid with another woman slid to the pit of her stomach and mixed with her pizza. "Flex his flirting muscles, you know?"

"No, I think the two of you are playing with fire, but I promised to shut up about it so I will. But listen, if you need someone to talk to about Reid or anything, I'm here for you. We were like sisters when we were kids and I feel like that all over again. Ah, and speaking of . . . I want you to be my maid of honor."

Addison put her hand to her mouth. "Oh, Mia, I'd be thrilled!"

Mia smiled and then leaned in for a hug. "I'm so happy you said yes! Well, I'd better get going. I've got an early Monday morning meeting with Noah Falcon."

Addison nodded and stood up. "Yeah, I'd better get some sleep too. I have a shipment of wedding dresses coming in tomorrow. You need to try some of them on."

"Oh, that will be fun! I'll call you tomorrow."

Addison walked Mia to the door. "Thanks for everything you've done for me. Get home safe."

Mia hugged her again. "I will."

Addison wrapped up the remaining slices of the pizza and then decided she'd drink the rest of her wine while taking a bubble bath. She lit a few fat vanilla-scented candles and turned on some soft music while the deep garden tub filled with water. While she missed her parents, her flat had already started to feel like home. And as she soaked in the fragrant bubbles, Addison relaxed to the point of almost dozing.

She mentally ticked off things she needed to get done tomorrow and for the grand opening, but then her thoughts drifted to Reid. What would it be like to make love to him? She closed her eyes and imagined having him sharing the big tub with her . . . washing her back, massaging her neck and then caressing her breasts with his big work-roughened hands. He'd look so masculine with bubbles clinging to his bare chest. . . . God, it would feel amazing to slide her wet soapy body against his.

Addison swallowed hard. What if she called him? Invited him over? Did she have the nerve?

"No," Addison grumbled out loud. Unless . . . she could come up with a really good reason for Reid to come over. Addison racked her brain but everything she came up with sounded flimsy, and so she sighed and gave up on the whole idea.

But later, when she slid beneath the cool sheets and fluffy comforter, Reid drifted back into her thoughts and stubbornly stayed there.

Addison sighed and closed her eyes. She imagined Reid's hands caressing her body, his mouth tasting her skin. Maybe she'd get lucky, if only in her dreams. . . .

16

Little Boy Blue and the Man on the Moon

RICK TOOK THE FORK IN THE TRAIL LEADING UP A HILL, pushing his body even harder than the day before. After nearly two weeks of living in the cabin he felt physically and mentally better, stronger and fresher than he had in too many years to count. Inhaling the river-scented air, he ran down the well-worn path through the woods, most likely used by kids riding four-wheelers and dirt bikes. With summer just around the corner, he would soon get up earlier to avoid the heat. Breathing hard, he paused to take his shirt off and mop the sweat from his brow and then slowed to a jog for his cool-down.

With his two weeks nearly up Rick reminded himself to head up into town to extend the lease for the rest of the summer months. Although his initial reason to come to Cricket Creek had been to apologize to Addison, living in the log cabin was bringing him a sense of peace that he hadn't felt in a long time. He had first option but he didn't want to risk losing the cabin to someone else. He'd even considered buying the place but wasn't quite sure, so he planned on talking to Maggie McMillan about the possibility. And he would take the opportunity to finally face Addison Monroe. He'd pulled into the parking lot of Wedding Row a couple of times but he'd been hesitant to get out, worried that he might be recognized and not wanting to blow his cover or bring unwanted attention to Addison, who was also avoiding the spotlight. He certainly didn't want to do anything to put a damper on the grand opening of her lovely shop. The irony didn't escape him that Addison was opening a bridal boutique, of all things. She had spunk and a sense of humor. He'd always liked Addison and the news of the breakup saddened Rick in too many ways to count.

Hours, no, make that *days* of soul-searching revealed more than Rick wanted to see and a lot in his lifestyle that he planned on changing. Becca, his ex-wife, had moved on a long time ago, remarried, and had two more children but often had a hard time raising rebellious Garret. She'd complained that Garret was a chip off of the old block, self-centered, refusing to grow up. Rick knew he'd been a "Cat's in the Cradle" father and he now felt such loss. And, in truth, he was ashamed. Garret was a damned good musician, given a hard time simply for being Rick's son. But what had Rick done about it?

Nothing . . . telling himself at the time that Garret needed to find his own way in life and not ride on Rick's coattails, when in fact being his son had resulted in the opposite, robbing Garret of the chance to follow his dream. What would have happened if Rick had taken Garret under his wing and helped launch his son's career? Then again, Rick wondered if deep down he'd wanted Garret to fail rather than be sucked into a lifestyle that many couldn't handle. Maybe even including himself. He loved his son and longed to have him back in his life.

Rick scrubbed a hand down his sweaty face and sighed. This past week he'd poured his sorrow into songwriting, bringing himself back to his bluegrass and blues roots. He'd always wanted his music to have more heart and soul and less head banging, but even in recent years

introducing new material while on tour was met with the
disapproval of fans who only wanted the old stuff, and so
Rick eventually stopped trying.

During the past few days he'd downloaded several
self-help, inspirational books and read each one. The sad
but darkly funny truth was that he didn't need to change,
but to go back to who he was before fame consumed his
life.

Rick paused to look out over the river, letting the
peace of the water wash over him. In all fairness, he'd
tried to put the songs he loved on his early albums but
his record label refused. He'd had success as a rock star
and he was stuck. In addition, he soon became a franchise, with dozens of employees depending on continued
success to put food on the table, and in order to do that
he'd had to spend most of the time touring . . . away from
Becca and Garret. Everyone saw the glitz and glamour
but didn't know the pressure, the grueling hours, and the
loneliness of being on the road. Tour buses and hotel
rooms were a poor substitute for being home. He wasn't
quite as selfish as Becca liked to believe when she went
after a huge divorce settlement, not that Rick cared
about the damned money.

"Enough about the past," Rick muttered as he
skipped a rock across the water. All of the books
preached to move on, go forward, and forgive people,
including himself. He planned on doing all of those
things. It just wasn't easy facing that he'd recently been
on the fast road to becoming an old, faded version of his
youth, clinging to something that was long gone and he'd
never really wanted in the first place. But regret caused
bitterness and the last thing he wanted to become was a
bitter old man.

When his stomach rumbled, Rick tossed his damp
shirt over his shoulder and headed back toward the
cabin. When he spotted an SUV parked in front his pulse
raced, thinking he'd been found. Then he spotted Maggie
McMillan stepping out of the driver's side, and he smiled.

Maggie wore navy blue slacks and a matching blazer, typical business attire for a real estate agent, but when she leaned back onto the SUV the blazer hiked upward, revealing a very nice butt. He found the straitlaced attire covering womanly curves damned sexy, and for a moment stood there and fantasized about what kind of lacy lingerie she wore beneath the suit. Rick shook his head, wondering if his reaction stemmed from the fact that this was the longest he'd gone without being with a woman in as far back as he could remember.

In truth, keeping up with Caitlyn had been like participating in a triathlon, often leaving Rick more worn-out than satisfied. What would it be like to be with a warm and willing woman who wanted to make love slow and easy instead of hard and fast? Someone who was more into touching than toys?

Someone who cared?

Instead of a hot-spot restaurant and a loud nightclub, what would it be like to stay in and make dinner together, share a bottle of excellent wine, and watch a movie while cuddling together on the sofa with a big bowl of popcorn? What would it be like to have a real, meaningful conversation about a subject that mattered?

Rick longed to find out.

With that thought in mind, Rick walked over to where Maggie looked down at some paperwork. She had her back to him and when she tilted her head, her hair slid to the side, revealing a delicate slice of her neck. There wasn't anything sexy about the movement, just sweetly feminine. "Good morning, Maggie."

"Oh!" When Maggie whipped around papers went flying in the breeze. "Oh no!" She chased after them but a sudden stiff gust of wind sent the papers skyward. They started fluttering downward, but just when Maggie got close the wind did its thing and sent the papers away just out of her reach, as if playing a teasing game of tag.

Rick decided he should help but when she started laughing he joined her in the fruitless effort. She finally pounced on one sheet and he jumped up to catch another, but another gust of wind sent the rest floating toward the river. "Here," Rick said with a sheepish grin. "I didn't mean to startle you."

"I get startled easy. My son used to laugh that I'd jump when he'd walk into the room. I tend to get into a zone or something. Not your fault."

Rick reached up and shoved his damp hair off of his forehead. "How's the ankle?"

"Um ... I ..." Maggie blinked at him for a minute. Her cheeks were flushed, he guessed from the chase, but then he remembered he was standing in front of her shirtless and in damp, clinging jogging shorts. "Fine. Th-thank you for the fl-flowers. I tried to contact you but the number I have wasn't yours."

"Oh, no problem. I'm just glad that you're okay." Rick shrugged.

Maggie nodded as if at a loss for words but then her eyes widened. "Oh, I came out here with papers for you to extend your lease"—she winced—"but, well, except for these two, they're gone with the wind. When would be a good time to come back?"

"For dinner," came out of his mouth without really thinking. "I was going to the grocery store later and I'd planned on grilling some steaks or chicken. Would you care to join me? I ask only that you help me with the side dishes. Grilling is about as far as my cooking skills go— well, unless you count breakfast," he added, but then realized that his comment sounded suggestive. "Not that I expect you to stay for breakfast," he added quickly, and for the first time that he could remember Rick Ruleman, rock star, blushed. "Sorry. I guess I'm ... so rusty that I creak."

"Then should I bring some oil?" Maggie asked, and then slapped a palm to her forehead. "That was a lame attempt at a joke. I didn't mean ..." She caught her bottom lip between her teeth and shook her head. When she burst out laughing Rick joined her.

"Okay, let me try this again. Maggie, would you like to join me for dinner tonight? I'll grill and you can help me in the kitchen."

"Yes, thank you very much. I would be delighted to join you," she replied. "May I bring something?"

"Dessert," Rick said, and then chuckled. "Let's just leave that one alone, shall we?"

Maggie tossed her head to the side and laughed. "What time would you like me?" she asked.

How about right now? went through Rick's head. Something in his thoughts must have been written on his face because her cheeks turned a pretty shade of pink.

"I mean to come . . . *arrive.*"

Rick laughed. He was so used to having a woman trying hard to be suggestive instead of the other way around and he found it so damn refreshing . . . and a really big turn-on. "How about around seven?"

Maggie nodded. "Perfect. I'll see you at seven."

Rick smiled. There was a moment of awkwardness when he didn't know what to do next. Shaking hands seemed silly and yet kissing her didn't fit either and so he simply nodded, but then on a whim leaned in and gave her a quick peck on the cheek. "See you tonight."

17
Man, I Feel Like a Woman

AFTER PULLING OUT ONTO THE MAIN ROAD, MAGGIE PUT her fingers to her cheek where Richard had kissed her. She tried to recall when she had last had a date with a man—a super-sexy man—and came up blank. "This isn't a date," she chided herself, "just dinner with a client." And what was up with every sentence that came out of her mouth sounding suggestive? Maybe it was because for the first time in such a long while she had sex on the brain. Not that she was going to act on it, but it felt pretty good to feel like a woman. She didn't think there was any juice left in those particular batteries but apparently all she had needed was a little recharging.

When she'd turned around and seen Richard standing there in nothing but skimpy running shorts she'd almost swallowed her tongue. He was just, well, to put it simply, *gorgeous*. Richard was fit without being bulky, handsome but with a little rough masculine edge that just made Maggie want to grab him and kiss him. She still didn't know what that tattoo said but she sure was curious. Maggie hadn't really been able to stop thinking about Richard ever since he'd carried her up the steps and tended to her twisted ankle. Luckily, when the beautiful bouquet of flowers arrived no one had been around to see that she'd been so moved that she'd cried.

And to think that she was having dinner with Richard at the beautiful cabin . . . Well, she just felt giddy with anticipation.

Wait. . . . What am I going to wear?

Maggie swallowed hard and looked at the digital clock on the dash. She had so much work to do at the office, but after doing a mental inventory of her neatly organized closet she realized with growing horror that she didn't have one single thing to wear. Maggie had business attire and casual clothes but nothing suitable for a date.

"It isn't a date!"

Still, she wanted something flirty but not too revealing. "Screw the paperwork. I'm going to check my e-mail and then go shopping."

When she pulled into the parking lot of Wedding Row, Maggie spotted Addison Monroe watering the pretty flowers in the clay pots perched in front of her shop. She decided to walk over and say hello.

"Hi, Maggie!" Addison looked over at her with a wide smile. "How's the ankle doing?"

Maggie lifted her foot and wiggled it in a circle. "Good as new."

"Glad to hear it," Addison said. "It sure is a pretty day."

"I know! I adore late spring, when everything is blooming. And your shop is really coming along. Do you mind if I take a peek inside?"

"Sure, I'll give you a tour. I can't believe that the grand opening is next weekend!" Addison put a hand to her chest and shook her head. "And your idea to have a Wedding Row open house at all of the shops was genius."

"I thought it would draw more customers if everyone banded together. It's going to be how it works, anyway."

"You're right. Flower Power is giving away free long-stemmed roses. Grammar's Bakery is having a wedding-cake tasting. Nicolina is holding a drawing for a beautiful necklace. We all went together and put an ad in the paper," Addison said as they entered the shop. "Any word on when we'll have a salon and photographer? Uncle Mitch said that there is a high-end salon based in Lexington that's interested."

"We're getting close to having a deal with the salon," Maggie answered. "Keep your fingers crossed!"

"I sure will." With a smile Addison held up crossed fingers. "So, what do you think?"

"Oh, Addison, this is simply lovely. You've done an amazing job. Elegant! I adore the chandelier. The antiques! Oh, the display of veils is just stunning." Maggie felt unexpected tears prick at the back of her eyes.

Addison put a gentle hand on her shoulder. "Are you okay, Maggie? Is something wrong?"

"I'm just overwhelmed at the beauty of it all. It's menopausal hormones too." She laughed as she brushed at a tear. Stepping closer to the wedding gowns, she touched a beaded satin skirt. "This is so pretty," she said, but felt embarrassed when her voice sounded wistful. "I always dreamed of having a fairy-tale wedding. I guess I'm just a hopeless romantic."

"There's nothing hopeless about being romantic. Maggie, you're a beautiful, vibrant woman. Your life is far from over. You might still get your wish."

Maggie waved her hand through the air and turned away from the display of gowns. "Oh, I do believe that ship has sailed. Life just doesn't go as planned, you know."

"Oh, I'm the poster child for that," Addison agreed with a chuckle. "I wouldn't have believed even a few weeks ago that I'd end up living in Cricket Creek, Kentucky, or owning a bridal shop. But here I am!"

"Well, I never thought I'd come back here to live and here I am too. At least my son, Tristan, and Savannah will be planning their wedding soon. I'll get to pick out a mother-of-the-groom dress."

"Oh, I already have a few in stock. I've ordered some traditional dresses but I'm leaning away from beaded, matronly styles and bringing in some fresh ideas. Would you like to take a look? I'd like to know what you think."

Maggie nodded. "What I really need is something to wear tonight."

"What's the occasion?"

"Oh, just dinner."

"A date, Maggie?"

"No . . . with a . . . client," she tried to say casually but felt the warmth of a blush creep into her cheeks.

Addison gave her a knowing smile. "Let me guess: a very handsome client. Someone you're interested in?"

"No . . ." Maggie scoffed. "I just, you know, want to look nice."

"Well, you're a beautiful woman, so no worries there. Oh hey. You know what? I might have something." Addison walked over to a rack of dresses and pulled out a peach-colored dress, belted at the waist. The scooped neckline would show a little bit of skin but not too much. "It's simple and feminine, and if you pair it with a denim jacket or maybe a white blazer it would be cute and not too dressy. It should hit just a little bit above the knee. Would you like to try it on? I think the color would look great on you, Maggie. I have it in several sizes, and you look to be about a size eight petite?"

"More like a ten, but, yes, these short legs need a petite size. I'm glad that you thought to carry petite. Selections at most stores are slim." Maggie nibbled on the inside of her cheek. Would a dress be too much like a date? What would Richard be wearing? "I do love the soft color and it's a flattering style. I'll try it on."

Addison smiled. "I'll look around to see if I have anything else that might work. The dressing rooms are behind the velvet curtains at the back of the shop. Let me see you when you try it on."

Maggie took the dress and nodded. "I will." She admired the rest of the shop as she headed for the dressing rooms. There was elegance everywhere but with an underlying warmth that would put jittery brides-to-be at ease. After taking off her clothes, Maggie looked at her reflection in the mirror and frowned. While she ate healthy for the most part and had an active lifestyle that kept her relatively fit, at her age her body was far from perfect. Still, she'd always worked hard to feel comfortable in her own skin. She slipped the silky material over her head and let it slide over her skin.

"Oh . . . very pretty," she said with a soft smile. Maggie was so used to suits during the day and sweatpants at night that she forgot how fun it was to wear something totally feminine. She pushed back the curtain and stepped out for Addison to see her. "What do you think?" She did a little spin.

"Oh, Maggie, you look so pretty. That peach color is perfect for you."

"I like your suggestion about pairing this with a denim jacket."

"Or a blazer if you want to wear this for work. A light sweater would work too. Maybe add a silk scarf."

"I'll take it! Wow, this was easy. I thought it would take me all afternoon!"

"Well, I talked it over with Mia and we decided that we would have a wide variety of dresses. I like when the bridesmaid dresses can be worn for other occasions too. I've even got some wedding gowns that turn into shorter dresses for the reception. How cool is that?"

"Oh, that sounds like something Savannah might like. I'm sure she and Tristan will come in for the open house. I'll be popping in all of the shops. If you need for me to do anything, feel free to tell me."

"Thanks, Maggie. Make sure you come over and tell me all about this dinner with your handsome client. Is he local?"

"Actually, Richard is renting Ty McKenna's cabin by

the river. He was only going to stay for a couple of weeks but he's going to spend the rest of the summer here. I'm thinking he might have an interest in buying, and I know Ty wants to sell."

Addison nodded. "Sounds like you're a busy lady, Maggie."

Maggie looked at her watch. "Yes, and speaking of, I'd better get going. Just let me change so you can ring this up for me."

With her purchase swinging from her arm Maggie hummed as she walked back to her office. She tried to get some work done but all she could think about was dinner with Richard, and after a couple of hours she hurried upstairs to get ready. She had a frozen apple pie that she'd bake while Richard grilled the steaks. After taking extra care with her hair and makeup, she slipped on the dress and added a denim jacket that she loved but didn't wear too often. She thought the look was flirty and fun and had to laugh at the sheer joy of having an evening out.

Feeling lighthearted and young Maggie played country music all the way to Richard's cabin! But when she arrived, a sudden fit of nerves took flight in her stomach. She might have told Addison this was a business dinner but Maggie secretly hoped it would turn into more than that . . . at least a kiss? She put her fingers to her lips. When was the last time a man kissed her . . . held her in his arms?

Shaking her head, Maggie picked up the pie and the paperwork. She knew she should be reminding herself that Richard was a client and would be leaving Cricket Creek at the end of the summer. She'd never allowed herself to become more than friends with a client, especially when there was a potential sale in the future. She'd lived by that rule for a long time and now wasn't the time to break it, she sternly told herself.

But when Richard answered the front door, looking incredibly handsome, all of her reasoning flew out the window. The light blue oxford shirt was tucked into jeans, giving him a sexy causal look that made Maggie swallow hard. The top two buttons were open, giving her a peek at the tanned skin. Her brain conjured up the previous image of him shirtless, with a sheen of sweat glistening over his chest, and she stood there even after he'd said something to her and stepped to the side. Maggie nodded even though she had no clue as to what he'd said, but she followed him into the gleaming, gorgeous kitchen that was a cook's dream.

Finally finding her voice she said, "I brought pie. Apple."

"Ah, one of my favorites and I don't indulge often. A slice of apple pie will be a real treat. Thanks."

"I would have baked it but I thought it would make the cabin smell wonderful."

"I've got the oven heated up for baking potatoes. We can pop the pie in after the potatoes are done. I thought they would be easy, along with a tossed salad and rib-eye steaks."

"Sounds delicious," Maggie answered, and tried to shake the sudden shyness. She put the paperwork on the granite countertop and wished she remembered how to flirt.

"You look amazing, Maggie," Rick said, even though he'd reminded himself over and over not to make advances. All he wanted was dinner and conversation. He was done with meaningless sex. He wanted something more substantial, beginning with friendship.

"Thank you." Her smile was soft, hesitant, like she wanted to say more. "And . . . and so do you," she finally said, but then averted her gaze.

Damned if he didn't long to sweep her into his arms and kiss her. She just looked so sweet but sexy at the same time. "Would you like a glass of wine?"

"Oh yes, please."

"Not knowing what you preferred, I bought a variety.

I have Chardonnay or Riesling chilling, or a merlot or a medium-bodied pinot noir if you prefer." He grinned. "And just about anything else in between."

"Oh, you didn't have go to all that trouble," Maggie protested, "but it was certainly nice of you to be so thoughtful."

"No problem at all." Rick could tell by her bright smile that it made her happy that he'd wanted to please her. He thought about the demanding, selfish women he was used to dealing with and pulled out the corkscrew. "Preference?"

"How about the Chardonnay while we cook, and the merlot with the steaks?"

"I like the way you think." Rick reached inside the Sub-Zero fridge and pulled out a bottle of chilled white.

"I just have to take it easy so I can drive home."

After searching for the corkscrew Rick said, "How about this: You kick back and enjoy yourself. There are three guest rooms upstairs. If you have too much wine to drive you are welcome to stay. And I promise to be a gentleman. No worries, okay?"

"Thank you, Richard. I have to admit that being a single mom made me pretty much a worrywart."

Rich handed her a glass of wine and then poured one for himself. "Here's to no worries." He raised his glass to hers.

"No worries," Maggie said, and clinked her glass to his before taking a sip. "Oh, this is good. Nice toasty finish," she said, and looked at the label. "Fat Bastard."

"I beg your pardon," Rick said, and then laughed with her. "I'll put on some music. We can enjoy our wine on the front porch while the potatoes bake and the steaks come to room temperature."

"Can I do anything?"

"Nope. I rubbed the potatoes with olive oil and sea salt. The salad is a spring mix from a bag and ready to go."

"You have everything under control. I came prepared to help out."

He grinned. "I wanted dinner to be simple so I could enjoy your company."

"Why, thank you." Maggie smiled and tried to hide her blush by taking a sip of her wine but Rick noticed and, God help him, but he was . . . What was the word? Smitten. He grinned at the rather old-fashioned word that popped into his head, but it fit. There was something about Maggie that made him smile just from being near her. Rick wanted to sit and chat with her, learn more about her.

When they sat down in the rockers on the front porch Rick silently but sadly acknowledged that keeping Maggie in the dark wasn't really right, but at this point he didn't see any way around it. Instinct told him that he could trust her but he also wondered how she would react if she knew that he was Rick Ruleman, and he guessed she would run for the hills. His carefully crafted bad-boy image was in many ways fabricated, but would she ever believe that? Probably not. Plus, this last rumor that he'd slept with his son's fiancée was a doozy that he wanted to die down. The last thing Rick wanted was to bring more heartache to Addison Monroe, so he reminded himself to keep the answers to any questions about himself vague. And as enchanted as he was with sweet Maggie, he should keep his distance. But when she turned and smiled, the keeping-his-distance vow vanished as quickly as the morning mist on the river.

"There's just something about a rocking chair on a front porch that makes life seem slow and easy."

"The view of the river off of the back deck is pretty amazing too." Rick nodded. "I have to admit that coffee out here in the morning and a glass of wine in the evening are pretty good ways to start and finish the day. It sure is peaceful here in the river valley."

"So, what will you do here all summer long, Richard?"

Rick took a sip of his wine and looked out over the front lawn for a moment before answering. "I'm going to work on getting my chaotic life back in order."

"So you needed a break from reality?"

"I sure did." He turned to her and smiled. "I like it so much I might never go back."

"To reality?" Maggie asked with a grin.

Rick chuckled. "Yeah. This is much better," he said, and decided to ask her a question before she pried a little bit too much. "I needed an extended vacation. So, how about you? Didn't you recently open your agency?"

Maggie nodded. "Having my own agency has been a dream of mine for a long time. I put it on hold while I raised my son up in the Cincinnati area. I knew the hours would be long and there would be a risk, so I waited until the time was right. Moving back here has been a good decision so far. And I'm working on expanding Whisper's Edge with my son."

"Whisper's Edge?"

"A retirement community that my father owned. Tristan bought it from him last year when he ran into some financial difficulty," she answered brightly, but something in her eyes told Rick that there was more to the story than a simple sale.

"So, you grew up here in Cricket Creek?"

Maggie gave him a rueful smile. "Yes, until I came home from college pregnant with Tristan. Let's just say that my father didn't react with . . . unconditional love. I moved out."

"I'm sorry, Maggie. That must have been tough. I'm guessing no help from Tristan's father."

She studied the contents of her glass for a moment. "I never knew who he was," she said softly. "I was at a college party and there was this punch that tasted like Kool-Aid, but I found out later that it was laced with Everclear. I don't remember anything about that night."

Rick felt rage bubble up in his throat at the thought of someone taking advantage of her. "My God . . . Maggie, this could have been date rape. Didn't anyone investigate?"

"Let's just say that my father didn't believe my version of the story. My mother left him when I was a baby and he'd become a bitter old man. It wasn't until I had a bout with breast cancer that he actually helped me one summer." She sighed. "I was hoping my illness would bring us closer and he'd bond with Tristan, but it didn't. Sad, but it's his loss."

"I'm so sorry."

"I was lucky. It was caught early." She shrugged and then smiled. "We all have our journeys, our crosses to bear. Tristan was a blessing and I love him dearly. I couldn't ask for a better son. And after surviving cancer—no relapses—I feel like I've learned to focus on the big picture and to try to be happy as best I can."

"You put your dreams on hold for him." He felt his heart lurch.

"Totally worth it." Her eyes welled up with tears. "Even if I could go back and rewrite history, I wouldn't change a thing. And now here I am in my fifties, getting to start a new adventure!"

"I admire your attitude, Maggie. I admire so much about you." He looked at her with a sense of wonder.

She chuckled. "My attitude was all that kept me going for a long time. But Tristan was such a joy and still is." He was sure that her radiant smile hid a lot of heartache. Rick was beyond impressed and even more drawn to her.

"Oh, don't look at me like I'm an angel. I had my days of despair and crankiness. I still do, for that matter. And I guess living through tough times makes me appreciate the good times even more."

"So, you've never been married?"

"No, I never really had the time for romance," she scoffed, but her smile faltered for the first time.

"And you were a little bit scared?"

She stopped rocking and stared down at her glass again. Finally, she lifted her gaze to meet his. "Yes," she admitted so softly that her admission blended with the evening breeze.

Not knowing what to say, Rick remained silent, wishing in some ways he'd never led her down this path.

"Of course, Tristan had questions, but as the years passed it became less important. The love we have for each other is really all that matters." She lifted one shoulder. "I just sometimes have a tough time with trust."

"Understandable."

Her gaze flicked away and she started rocking gently. Rick studied her profile in the waning light. She was such a pretty woman, so full of life. What a shame that she held back from experiencing romance . . . love. Judging by the way she loved her son, she would be an amazing wife. Caring, funny, sexy, smart. He couldn't ask, but he surmised that she hadn't slept with a man in quite some time. Rick thought about all of the meaningless sex he'd had and it turned his stomach.

"Oh, I'm sorry, Richard. I didn't mean to put a damper on the lovely evening."

"You haven't." Rick reached over and took her hand. "Not in the least."

Her eyes widened in a bit of surprise and then she smiled slowly, shyly. And while Rick knew he should withdraw his hand he simply couldn't.

Maggie McMillan was both fragile and incredibly strong. He was drawn to her in more ways than one. She had just revealed so much of herself to him, and he had secrets. Perhaps he should simply tell her. . . .

"Hey, don't look so serious," she said with a low chuckle. "Let's check on the potatoes and grab another glass of wine."

Rick squeezed her hand and nodded. "While you do that I'll get the grill heated up. Looks like we're in for a beautiful sunset."

"And you forgot to turn the music on. Put on something I can snap my fingers to," she requested with a laugh. "Music will get us back in a festive mood."

"So, you're a music lover? What kind?"

"Absolutely. A wide variety, depending on my mood. But I have it playing most of the day and sing along in the car. You? I noticed a guitar leaning against the wall. Are you good?" She raised her eyebrows and waited while he tried to decide how to answer. "Oh, don't be shy. I'll even sing along."

"I'm passable," Rick finally answered, and hoped she would forget about her request, even though playing some of the new songs he'd been writing appealed to him.

As the night wore on there wasn't anything about her that didn't appeal to him. From her easy laugh to her knowledge of baseball and her intelligence, Rick found himself wishing the night would go on forever. She didn't pick at her food and actually ate her steak with appreciation, unlike the women he was used to dining with, who for one reason or another eliminated just about every food group. Rick even enjoyed doing the dishes with her. When was the last time he'd done dishes?

"What are you grinning about?" Maggie asked with a tilt of her head.

"How you're making me enjoy simple things." He jabbed a thumb over his shoulder. "I have a whole stack of self-help books in the den and you've inspired me more than all of them put together."

"Really? Well, then, you need to tell me all about your life so I can be inspired over dessert and coffee."

"I'm not all that inspirational," he said and felt a flash of alarm. How would she react to his past?

Maggie suddenly put her hands to her cheeks. "Oh, I forgot to put the pie in the oven!" she exclaimed, and he was glad for the change of subject. *Saved by the pie . . .*

"That's okay. We can have it next time," Rick answered and just about held his breath while he waited for her response. "If, you know, you'd like to have dinner with me again," he added. Rick couldn't remember the last time he felt so unsure or so hopeful while waiting for an answer from a woman. The anticipation, the excitement, made him feel so alive! Going to a club or a four-star restaurant with some twentysomething never felt this good.

"I would be delighted," Maggie answered.

Rick let out the breath he'd been holding and smiled. He wanted to pull her into his arms but didn't want to go too fast. While he knew that sooner or later his secret would come out and that he would most likely move back to LA, for now he wanted to simply savor the time spent with her. "Would you like another glass of wine or an after-dinner drink? It's still relatively warm outside and there's a full moon, so we could head back outside."

"I would but then I wouldn't be able to drive."

She nibbled on her bottom lip, and he realized that some of what she'd told him about her past must be running through her head. He despised the fact that she could even think about something so terrible while with him.

"Hey, I promised to be a gentleman and I won't break that promise, Maggie."

She swallowed hard. "Those trust issues are rearing their ugly head."

"I understand."

"I'm sorry."

"There's nothing to be sorry for, Maggie." It killed him to hear her apologize for her feelings. Rick shook his head and then put his hands on her shoulders. "I had a great time with you tonight. Let me walk you to your car, even though I don't really like you driving these back roads by yourself."

"I'll be fine. I grew up on these country roads," she said. "But thank you for being concerned."

"I'm not just being polite, you know."

When she nodded ever so slightly Rick dropped his hands from her shoulders so he wouldn't give in to temptation and pull her in for the kiss he'd been longing to steal all night long. He helped her into her denim jacket and strolled toward the door. Out of the corner of his eye he spotted the unsigned paperwork and barely suppressed a grin. He'd just have to head up to her office right about lunchtime with the extended lease agreement.

Rick moved across the yard as slowly as he could without actually stopping, trying to milk every last minute with her. After the sunset the night had turned clear and cooler—perfect weather for snuggling beneath a blanket or building a fire.

Maggie gazed upward and sighed. "Wow, look at those stars and that amazing moon. The night sky is so pretty away from the city lights. Makes you feel small and insignificant."

"There's nothing insignificant about you, Maggie."

She looked at him with an element of surprise and smiled.

"Yeah, it sure is quiet and peaceful out here," he said when they stopped in front of her SUV. After hearing the beep of keyless entry, Rick reached over and opened the door for her. "I could get used to this."

"Living here?"

"Spending time with you," he said. "Tell me you'll do this again."

"I'll do this again." There was no hesitation in her voice this time.

"Ah . . . Maggie . . ." The need to touch her, to kiss her overcame his reasons for holding back. He dipped his head and captured her lips in a soft, sweet kiss, lingering just long enough to let her know that he wanted much more. He wanted her to feel beautiful and desired because she was both, but also that he was capable of holding back until she was ready. After she drove away, Rick poured the last of the wine into his glass and then came back out onto the porch with his guitar. He played by rote, humming softly while his mind wandered from the past to the present. Sitting on the front porch of a cabin in Cricket Creek, Kentucky was starting to feel a little bit less surreal and more like . . . home?

18

Ain't No Mountain High Enough

"SARA, COME ON ... SERIOUSLY? WHY IN THE WORLD would I want to spend my Saturday night at the grand opening of a bridal boutique?" Reid hefted the bag of chicken feed from the bed of the truck and then turned to face his sister.

"I don't know." She gave him an innocent look. "There will be free food. Cake! Who doesn't like cake? Plus, you can keep Cody company."

"Cody would rather be going over to Sully's to shoot some pool or throw darts. Now, if he wants to do that, I'm down with it. You can join us later."

"I want Cody to look at some of the bridal stuff with me and do some cake tasting."

Reid tilted his head to his shoulder to catch some sweat on his sleeve. "See, that's the difference. Cody is going to be a groom. I'm not, thank God."

"You know someday when you find the right person, you'll change your sad, sucky tune."

He reached for another bag. "Don't count on it."

"Seriously, Reid, you need an attitude adjustment.

You've been a grump all week. I was afraid for you to get anywhere near the kids."

He shrugged.

Sara paused long enough for Reid to brace himself. Her pauses meant she was gathering up ammunition. "I thought you might want to see Addison."

"You thought wrong," Reid answered tightly. Of course, that was a big-ass lie. But after their little agreement, Reid had steered clear of the cute wedding planner. As much as he wanted to be with her, he needed to give her time to think her proposition over before going through with it. He'd spotted her once when she'd come out to the farm to meet with Jason and Sara about the barn renovations, but he'd turned his tractor in the opposite direction. His keeping-his-distance plan had obviously worked. Addison hadn't contacted him. She'd probably thought better of the whole no-strings-attached scenario that was doomed for an epic fail, anyway.

There was only one problem: Reid couldn't stop thinking about her. And it was making him a little bit testy.

"Open house only lasts until seven, Reid. Just stop in for a little while, you know, to be polite, and then we can all go to Sully's afterward."

"No, thank you."

"Why are you being so stubborn?"

"Hanging out at Wedding Row isn't my kind of Saturday night."

"We're going into business with Addison Monroe, Reid. It's polite to show our support."

"You are going into business with her, Sara. And do I have to remind you that I'm still not convinced that this is a smart venture? Renovations like this are notorious for going way over budget. Instead of avoiding bankruptcy, you just might throw yourself into it." Reid tossed another bag of feed to the ground, making dust fly. His muscles no longer protested at the manual labor and, in truth, he'd felt healthier working outdoors instead of sitting behind a desk all day long.

"All right."

Reid looked at Sara's hands on her hips and jutting chin. He knew that stance all too well. "What do you mean, *all right*?"

"Nothing." She gave him a slight shrug but the chin stayed in place, meaning this was war. "I'll make other plans, then."

Reid propped his boot up against the tailgate of the truck and leaned his forearm on his knee. "What kind of plans?" he asked slowly.

"Cody's friend will agree to come out with us tonight. He has this . . . *thing* for Addison."

"Thing?"

"Yeah, Zack met Addison at Wine and Diner when she and I went out to dinner a couple of nights ago. Zack has been bugging Cody to get her number from me ever since. I'm sure he'll come out with us tonight. You remember Zack, right? A couple of years ahead of us in school."

"Yeah, I do. I remember he was an asshat."

"Why? Because you wanted his spot on the baseball team?"

"Yeah, well. I took it, remember?"

"After he broke his arm."

"A minor detail. Come on, really, Sara. Zack Martin?" She turned on her heel.

Dammit! Reid clenched his fists. "Sara!"

She slowly turned around. "Yes?" she asked sweetly.

"You told me that Zack has a different girl on his arm every week. He's a player. Why would you do that to Addison?"

"I already warned her and she was cool with it. She said that after this week of getting the shop ready she needs a night of fun. And since you aren't available . . ."

"You know that jackass is going to try to get in her pants." But wasn't he also a jackass who wanted to get in her pants?

"Addison is a big girl, Reid. She can handle Zack.

And, besides, Cody and I will be there." She paused for a second. "But if you're so worried about Addison, you can go out with us instead."

Reid knew he was being played by his twin sister. She knew him better than anyone, even after years apart. She shoved her hands in her jeans pockets and rocked back on her heels. To her credit, she didn't grin, even though she knew she'd won. "All right. But I'll drive separately and meet you at the boutique. I want to spend as little time in a damned bridal shop as possible," he grumbled.

"Okay." Except for a little twitch in her bottom lip she remained deadpan.

He had to grin. "And, by the way, well played."

"It was pretty easy." Sara grinned back but then tilted her head in question. "Look, it's obvious that you care about Addison. Why are you fighting it tooth and nail?"

"Addison is coming off a broken engagement and starting a new business. I'm trying to figure out whether I want to go back to investment finance or maybe move back to Cricket Creek. Not to mention that I'm a country boy and she's from Cali. We are worlds apart." He positioned his hands wide to demonstrate.

"So, you're considering moving back?" she asked hopefully.

"The operative word here is *considering*," he slowly pronounced every syllable. "Sara, I'm not sure what I'm going to do. How would that be fair to Addison?"

Sara walked over and hoisted herself up onto the open tailgate. "Keep going."

Reid leaned one hip against the edge. "That's not enough?"

"Nope."

Reid sighed. "That so-called ivory tower I was living in wasn't such a great place, Sara. Being in finance while the country was in a recession really sucked for me. I know I never came home all that much, but, Sara, I didn't do much of anything but try to find ways to keep clients from losing their hard-earned money. And I pretty much failed."

"None of that was your fault."

"It sure as hell felt like it."

"I'm sorry, Reid. I had no idea what you were going through."

Reid grimaced. "That was my fault too. I should have reached out, but instead I sort of retreated into a shell like a damned turtle."

"And here I thought you had turned your back on us when we needed you most."

"I'm sure that's how it appeared. But I worried every night about the fate of this farm. I worried about Jeff tossing everything away for a music career. I agreed with Mom that he should stay on the farm and help, and that Braden should stay in school. What I should have done was encouraged everyone to go after their dreams, but I didn't. I'm doing the same damn thing to you now." He swallowed hard and looked away.

Sara reached over and covered his hand with hers. "It's because you care."

Reid gave her a small smile. "After coming back here to the farm I'm not so sure that I want to go back to Lexington and work in an office. In other words, I don't know which end is up anymore. I shouldn't get involved with anyone until I get my own life straightened out." He raised his eyebrows. "Enough now?"

"Look, I know that you want everything to fit into timelines, graphs, and charts. But life isn't like that. Sometimes you have to reinvent yourself. I loved teaching and I love this farm. Now I get to combine those two things every day. Dad has a blast with the kids and it's helped his health. You know that Mom preaches that everything happens for a reason. I'm not so sure I buy into that . . . more like when life gives you lemons, make lemonade." She grinned. "And add some vodka for good measure. Sometimes you just have to make life your own personal cocktail."

Reid laughed. "Yeah, well, if you'd put my life on a timeline there are more valleys than peaks. My plan was to invest and make enough money to help Mom and Dad keep this place. For a while my plan was working really well. I invested my own money with more risk than I advise with clients, and the payoff was big . . . until the stock market crashed and I lost my ass. Then the loss was bigger."

Sara frowned. "Are you in financial trouble, Reid?"

He scrubbed a hand down his face. This part was hard to admit. "No, but I was for a while. Over the past couple of years I've recouped most of my *loss* but I'm nowhere near where I'd thought I'd be at this stage of the game."

Sara tilted her head and smiled. "Well, baby brother, the good news is that you have a lot of life left to live. It's time to get out of the valley and start climbing that big ole mountain again." Her smile faded a bit. "Hey, I reached rock bottom when Blake broke my heart by cheating on me. But Cody came along and he's such a good man. I'm so much better off and I love him to pieces. Your time will come but you have to be open to it and keep that big head of yours poked out of your shell, because it might come when you least want it to or expect it. So toss your timeline out the window and take a leap of faith."

He chuckled. "And what if I land on my ass with a big fat splat?"

"Are you referring to the time when I promised you the tree branch would hold you?"

"Yeah, to rescue that damned cat of yours. The branch broke."

"But you saved the cat."

"And your point, teacher?"

"You got a little bit bruised."

"And scratched by the cat."

Sara winced. "Maybe I shouldn't have used that example."

Reid gave her shoulder a brotherly shove. "I'm pulling your chain. I might have hated that cat, but you loved it and so a few scratches and bruises were worth it."

"See, now we're on the same page. Look, I don't know if Addison is the right one for you. But don't shut yourself off from the possibility. It's obvious that you're attracted to her and you care about her too. That's a pretty good start."

"Yeah . . ." He flicked his gaze away from her and fell silent.

"Okay, what aren't you telling me?"

"Addison proposed this . . . thing."

"What thing? Talk to me, Reid."

Reid wasn't sure he should tell Sara. After all, Addison seemed to have already reconsidered. Plus, it was kinda of weird talking about this with his sister. "Nothing. It was stupid, anyway."

"Hey, it's your twin you're talking to. I won't breathe a word to anyone. I promise. Not even Cody. I also won't let up until you tell me, so you might as well save us some time and spill."

Reid looked at Sara. "Addison wanted us to have this sort of no-strings-attached kind of deal. I told her I'd been off the market for a long time and was rusty at, well, the whole flirting or whatever bullshit. She wanted a sort-of pretend boyfriend, a rebound guy to keep her from making another big mistake. And she would be kind of my introduction back into dating."

"And you said yes?"

"Sort of. But I haven't heard a peep from her all week."

"Did you call her?"

"Hell, no. I wanted to give her time to reconsider her stupid plan."

"Wait. So you agreed but you think it's stupid?"

"Hell, I don't know, Sara. Yeah, sure it's stupid, but I don't know. It does have some merit, I guess."

"Well, she probably thought you had backed out."

"Oh crap. You think so?"

Sara nodded. "Um, yeah. Even in this day and age girls still wait for guys to call first."

"So, what do *you* think of the plan?"

"I think both of you just need to quit being so scared. You don't need any so-called plan. Just hang out. Get to know one another. It's pretty simple when you get right down to it."

Reid blew out a sigh. "What if she won't do that? Should I agree? I mean, I don't want to put my heart on the line for some game she wants to play so that no guys approach her."

"Do you want other guys to approach her? It sure didn't seem like you wanted her to hang out with Zack."

"Zack is an ass."

"You are avoiding the question even though I already know the answer." She swung her legs back and forth while staring him down.

"So, what the hell do I do?"

"Reid, you're going to put your heart on the line, no matter what the two of you call it. If you want to see where this is going with Addison, then agree to that nonsense. I think it's just a thinly veiled reason for her to give herself permission to hang out with you, anyway. I'm sure she made a no-guys-for-a-while vow after the breakup." Sara rolled her eyes. "Much better than my *every*-guy-for-a-while downward slide until I, thankfully and pretty quickly, came to my senses."

"It was called me carrying you out of Two Keys in Lexington."

"Whatever . . . We all have our ways to cope. Some ways are, you know, better than others. So . . . she's willing to see you if she pretends it's all for show, or whatever reason she's come up with, so she can feel some sort of safety."

"So, in other words, I should just do it and hope for the best?" Did he even want it to become something more?

Sara raised her hands in the air. "Geez, Reid, quit

overthinking. Just roll with it." She shooed her fingertips at him. "Now go get showered and all prettied up." She leaned over and gave him a quick kiss on the cheek. "I'll see you tonight."

Reid nodded but sat there for a minute while mulling over what Sara told him. Little John came bounding his way and defied gravity by leaping up into the truck bed. Booker trotted over and looked longingly up at them, knowing there was no way he could jump up that high. When Reid laughed and patted his thighs in encouragement Booker actually tried, coming an impressive foot off of the ground before landing sideways and rolling over. He got up and gave Reid an *I-totally-meant-to-do-that* look.

"You know what, Booker, you old crazy hound?"

"Woof!" Booker jumped again, a tiny bit higher, and somehow came back down on all fours.

"You just inspired me. Go against the odds and give it your best shot. Is that what you're sayin'?"

"Woof!"

Reid jumped down and scratched the old hound behind the ears. "Gotcha. Now I guess I'd better get cleaned up and try to make my amends. Beats me how I manage to get into hot water without even trying."

After a long, steaming shower Reid towel-dried his hair and then added a little bit of gel, something he hadn't bothered to do in a long time. He shaved his neck but decided to leave his five o'clock shadow, in hopes that Addison thought the stubble was sexy. He brushed, flossed, gargled, clipped his nails, and then splashed on some Acqua di Giò. With a sigh, he gave his reflection a critical once-over. Between his mother's cooking, Wine and Diner, and Grammar's Bakery, he'd put on some weight, but with farm work he'd bulked up rather than getting soft around the middle. He was tan from all of the time spent outdoors and his hair had lightened to a golden brown. The brackets of tension that had been present around his mouth had vanished. Reid had to admit that coming back to Cricket Creek and working on the farm agreed with him in more ways than one.

Usually a grab-it-and-go kind of guy, Reid put way more thought into what he was going to wear than he had in a very long time. He pulled out his favorite Lucky Brand jeans and tugged them on but then tried on four different shirts. "Quit being such a girl," he grumbled, but part of the problem was that he filled out the shirts to the point of them being almost too tight across his shoulders and biceps. He thought a golf shirt would be too casual for the grand opening, so he finally settled on a light blue Western-cut shirt with dark blue piping and mother-of-pearl-covered snaps. He knew one thing: He sure as hell didn't miss wearing a suit and tie.

Reid grimaced after looking at the digital clock on his nightstand. "How did it get to be past six thirty?" He would have to hustle to get to the shop before closing time. Sara was going to be pissed. After tugging on his best cowboy boots Reid hurried out of the cabin and jumped into his truck, wishing he'd drunk a beer while getting ready.

Sure enough, as Reid pulled into the parking lot everyone else appeared to be leaving. After he parked, Reid paused to reply to Sara's half dozen messages asking where in there world he was. Reid replied that he was running late and would meet her at Sully's after stopping in to say congratulations to Addison. He jogged over to the florist and quickly purchased a bouquet of spring flowers.

Reid entered From This Moment with three minutes to spare. A few people were milling around, making their way toward the entrance. With the bouquet in hand he looked around for Addison, and finally spotted her at the back of the shop, straightening up inventory. Her back was to him as she hung colorful dresses from a rack on wheels back to neat rows against the wall. Bridesmaid's, he guessed, since the entire middle of the shop displayed wedding gowns.

Addison wore a sleeveless dress in burgundy, simple but elegant, nipped at her waist and flowing to just above the knee. Usually straight, her shiny dark hair hung in soft, loose curls halfway down her back. She wore black open-toed, high-heeled sandals that looked difficult to walk in, and, judging by her sudden glance down and grimace, not too comfortable.

Soft music played through speakers and the shop smelled like coffee and cake. Everything looked so pretty and feminine, making Reid feel like a bull in a china shop. When Addison went on tiptoe to put a floppy lace hat up on a shelf he tilted his head, admiring how the silky material of her dress molded to her very nice butt. He decided he'd better make his presence known and walked closer to her. "Hello, Addison."

"Eek!" Clearly startled, she spun around, tossing the hat like a Frisbee right at Reid.

He caught it. "I want you on my Frisbee golf team."

"I didn't mean to do that." She put a hand to her chest. "You scared me," she admitted with a smile that quickly dissolved to a frown, as if she suddenly remembered to be pissed at him. "You really need to stop sneaking up on me."

"Sorry."

"At the risk of sounding rude, what are you doing here?"

"It's an open house."

"Was . . ." She pointed up to a really big round clock boasting large Roman numerals. "I'm closing."

He stepped forward. "Hey, um, are you mad at me?"

"No," she said, but her clipped tone indicated otherwise.

"Look, I'm sorry I didn't call. I—"

"Oh, just the phrase a girl wants to hear. Whatever . . . no big deal." Again, her tone said that it was a big deal. She reached out and snatched the hat. This wasn't going well.

"Okay, um, these are for you." When he thrust the flowers forward something flickered in her eyes.

"Thank you." *Ah* . . . at least her voice softened.

"The cake smells good," Reid said uncertainly, wishing he was better at this.

Addison waved the hand with the hat toward a table near the windows. "Help yourself. There's coffee or champagne if you prefer."

"Would you have a glass with me?"

"I'm busy."

Reid glanced around. "Everyone is gone, Addison."

"Except for you."

"Do you want me to leave?"

"Yes." She took a few steps away from him but then gave a little cry of pain and started to limp.

"Oh God. Are you okay?" Reid rushed forward and put a hand on her elbow.

"It's these shoes. They're killing my feet and I have a blister the size of Montana on my left heel."

"Montana?"

"Maybe Texas," she said weakly.

"Well, damn, Addison, sit down. I'll bring you some champagne." When she took a step and hissed, he said, "Hey, wait. Hold on to my shoulders."

"What?"

"I'm going to kneel down and take the stupid shoes off."

"They're not stupid; they're Jimmy Choo. I should have broken them in, but Mom sent them so I wanted to wear them."

"Let me guess—they cost the earth."

"Ha. Who are you to talk in your Tony Lama boots?"

"How did you know that?" Did she know they'd set him back nearly a grand? He'd bought them back in the heyday, before his life went to hell in a handbasket.

"I'm going to stock boots for brides who want a cowgirl theme. If I'm not mistaken those are ostrich."

Reid grinned. "You're not mistaken. I want to be buried in these suckers. You should be flattered. I bring them out only for very special occasions. But they don't hurt my feet."

When Reid eased one shoe from her foot she moaned. "Oh God, that feels so good."

"I get that a lot." Reid glanced up at her and she laughed. "You wanna go for two?" he asked. He looked at the heels. "That's gotta be at least five inches."

"Only four," she corrected, and laughed.

"I know what you're thinking. . . . Don't say it."

"Okay, I'll just think it."

Reid looked at the shoes. He had to admit they were damned sexy.

"But, yes, let's go for two." She gave him a low moan when he gently eased the shoe off of her other foot. "Oh, that's heaven."

"Addison, you do have a nasty blister. Why didn't you change out of these pieces of torture?" He stood up with the shoes dangling from his fingers.

"I didn't really notice the pain until people started leaving. And then my feet were suddenly on fire."

"This girl is on fire . . ." he sang, and she tossed her head back and laughed. Thank goodness the ice was broken. He usually wasn't exactly good at flirting, but there was something about Addison that somehow made him relax after being in her presence for only a few minutes. He didn't think he'd ever burst into song with a woman before but getting her to laugh was worth making a fool of himself. "Now go sit down in that huge chair over there. Hand me the flowers. I'll bring you some champagne."

"I won't argue," she said weakly and walked gingerly over to the big wingback black velvet chair trimmed in gold. After she sat down she eased her feet up onto a matching ottoman. A weary sigh escaped her while she leaned forward and massaged her feet, exposing a nice display of cleavage. Reid swallowed hard and almost dropped the flutes of champagne. He downed the cold bubbly liquid in three gulps.

"Here you go," Reid said.

"Thank you." She accepted the glass and took a sip. "Ah, nectar of the gods," she said with a tired grin.

Knowing he was taking a chance Reid lifted up her feet and scooted onto the big ottoman. Her eyes rounded slightly but she didn't kick or scream, so he went on to his next move . . . massaging her feet.

"If you're trying to get back in my good graces, that's totally working."

Reid chuckled softly. "I am."

"Then don't even think of stopping."

"I won't." He pressed the pad of his thumb to the ball of her foot, rolling it back and forth.

"Dear Lord . . . I think you missed your calling." She leaned against the back of the chair and sipped her drink, watching him through half-lidded eyes. She looked so tired that Reid longed to scoop her up in his arms and carry her upstairs to bed. The massage therapy wouldn't stop with her feet.

"Sara said you wanted to go over to Sully's and have a night out on the town. Are you game?"

"Not unless you want to carry me piggyback again."

"I would."

Her expression softened even more. He hoped it wasn't just from the champagne. "That would be funny." She giggled, and he knew she was a bit slaphappy but it was so damned cute on her.

Reid chuckled. "Have you eaten?"

Addison jammed her thumb over her head. "Cake."

"Is that champagne going straight to your head?"

"Yeah, it's awesome. May I have another?" She raised her glass.

"Absolutely." Reid refilled both glasses. "What are the raspberries for?" He pointed to the bowl.

"Oh, you drop one into the bottom of the flute. To look pretty and to go with the filling in the cake."

"Ahh . . . of course." Reid plunked one into her glass.

"No raspberry for you?"

"I don't fruit my drinks."

"Yeah, well, you do have to worry about that last swallow."

"Sounds like you know this from experience." Reid handed her the glass and then sat back down.

"I seem to learn everything the hard way." When she started to put her feet on the floor he shook his head.

"No you don't. Put those tired toes back where they belong."

"In your lap?"

"Absolutely."

"I'm too bone weary to argue. Pretty soon I'll be tipsy. Wait. I think I already am. Was that your grand plan?" She tipped the glass up to lips that were tinted with something pink and glossy.

"No, my plan was to take you to Sully's. But I'm flexible." He hesitated but then decided to take that leap of faith that Sara preached to him about. "In fact, Addison, I know exactly what you need."

19
Ya Gotta Have Faith

"AND WHAT MIGHT THAT BE?" THE RETURNING TOUCH OF his hands on her feet sent a warm, delicious tingle that started with her toes and spread throughout her body. She felt as if she were melting like butter on a pancake, the pain in her feet forgotten.

"A swimsuit."

"Thanks, but I don't think I'm up for swimming laps."

"You could use a long, hot soak in my hot tub. It saved my sore back when I first started working on the farm. I thought I was in pretty decent shape, but apparently I was wrong."

Addison watched the play of muscles beneath his shirt as he worked his magic on her feet. She remembered what he looked like bare chested and her fingers itched to lean forward and tug on the mother-of-pearl-covered snaps on his shirt, making them pop open one by one. And then she'd press her mouth to that tanned skin of his. . . .

"I promise you, it will make you feel like a new woman."

"Oh, I bet you could. I mean, it would. The tub . . . I

mean." *Dear Lord.* She tipped her flute back and drained the rest of the champagne.

To his credit he kept a straight face. "It works wonders."

"Oh, I admit that sounds so inviting. I haven't stopped all week and my weary body is starting to protest. I unloaded a million boxes."

"A million, huh?"

"Maybe two."

Reid chuckled. "You should have called me to come over and help."

Reid's offer caught Addison by surprise. "Would you have?" she asked softly.

"Yes," Reid replied, and then lowered his gaze to her feet. When he gently traced his fingertip over the blister Addison melted a little bit more. "You need some ointment on that one." He might be a little moody, but he was a good guy, caring about everything, unlike Garret who seemed to only care about himself.

"I can't do it."

Reid looked up at her. "Hey, I want you to know that I only thought the hot tub would make you feel better. I wasn't trying—"

"I mean that whole pretending-to-be-a-couple thing I came up with. I just can't do it."

"Oh, so you've had a change of heart?" He asked casually, but there was something in his eyes that made Addison's pulse pound.

"You could say that."

"I want you to know that I didn't call because I wanted you to rethink it, Addison." He stoked the arch of her foot, waiting for her answer, but she didn't know what to say. The foot massage was making her brain short-circuit. "Let me guess: You couldn't even begin to pretend to like me." His joking tone was at odds with the searching look he gave her.

"You guessed it. I'm a terrible liar."

Reid pressed his lips together and nodded.

"The truth is, I don't want you to be my rebound guy, Reid."

"I think you're making yourself pretty clear," Reid said with an edge of something . . . disappointment?

"No, I don't think I am. If I have a relationship with you I want it to be the real thing, not some silly sham. I suppose I made up that stupid scenario to try to come up with a way to spend time with you without feeling a sense of guilt for jumping into something so soon. But I already like you way too much, and that's dipping into dangerous territory."

"Wait. What did you just say?"

"It's too soon. I need to get my head screwed on straight." She tapped her temple.

"No . . . the other part. The part about liking me. Let me get this straight. You don't want to date because you like me too much? *That's* your reason?"

"It sounds silly spoken out loud, but yes."

"That's insane."

Addison scooted up in the chair. "Well, it's your fault! At first I was just physically attracted to you but I thought you were, well . . . kind of an ass. Then you had to become all likeable too and there's that dimple when you smile." Addison sighed. "And then . . ." She trailed off and shook her head.

"It was the piggyback ride, wasn't it?"

"Yep, that sealed it for me. And now this . . . just when I was pissed when you didn't call. Why couldn't you just stay a jerk and we could have had some really hot sex?"

Reid laughed.

"I'm serious."

"I know. That's why it's so funny."

"Not only that but I wanted to find out . . ."

Reid sat up straighter. "What?"

"Nothing. No more champagne for me."

"Tell me."

"No!" The word sliced through his gentle request. She

scooted forward but he held her feet captive. "Let go of my feet, please."

"I won't let go until you talk to me."

She crossed her arms over her chest. "Fine."

"Meaning you're going to tell me."

"No, I'm going to wait you out." Addison blinked at him for a few seconds. Along with all of that handsomeness he looked pretty stubborn and she kind of had to pee. Then again, she'd been mocked in the tabloids; what was one more little embarrassment? "Okay, well, I think that men get bored with me after a while, especially in bed," she said in a huge rush. She hoped he didn't understand because she wasn't going to repeat it.

"You're joking, right?"

She nibbled on the inside of her lip.

"Hold on. Wait. *That's* what you meant about the experiment you wouldn't tell me about? You wanted to see if . . ." Reid swallowed. "If you would give me a happy ending?"

She nodded slowly and then covered her face with her hands. "I think this is the single most embarrassing moment in my entire life. And, trust me, I've had a few big ones."

"You wouldn't disappoint me, Addison."

She peeked at him through her fingers. "Maybe not at first."

"I promise. Not in the short term or the long run."

"You can't know that."

"We're going to find out."

Addison dropped her hands and stared at him. "No, I can't let you do that."

"I'll take one for the team."

"We called the whole thing off!"

"That's right. We're not pretending anymore. Addison, look. I know that you're right. The timing is off for us. I get that you want to back off and get your life together. I have some decisions of my own to make. But Sara said something to me earlier and it stuck."

"What did she say?"

"When life gets shitty you have to take a leap of faith."

Addison frowned. "Sara said that?"

Reid gave her a crooked grin. "I'm paraphrasing, but yes. She said that my life is all about numbers and graphs, and sometimes life just doesn't always add up perfectly." He sighed. "I guess it's just that I watched my parents' financial struggle for so many years. I started to hate the farm, but damned if they didn't dig in their heels and hang on by the skin of their teeth."

"It's called a labor of love. My mother could retire if she wanted to, and my dad spends each day surrounded by music, art, and photography. It's not about the money. It's about loving what you do."

"Yeah, but I thought they were all going crazy! With Jeff heading to Nashville, Braden quitting school, and then Sara leaving her teaching career, I thought I was the lifeboat in a sea of insanity." He scrubbed a hand down his face. "I was wrong."

Addison put a hand on his arm. "It's never wrong to care, Reid."

"That's what Sara said, but, Addison, I was wrong to try to hold them back. Jeff recently played a gig at Tootsies in Nashville. Braden is happy being back here instead of taking business classes that he didn't care one lick about. I argued against the Old MacDonald education program and it makes money and, more importantly, has done wonders for my dad's health. I was wrong about everything, so that pretty much means that the barn wedding idea must be a good one, since I was against that as well."

"You're being way too hard on yourself."

"That's the way I roll."

"Well, give yourself a break at least for the rest of the evening."

He gave her a slow smile. "So, you think you're boring, huh?"

"Oh, stop." Addison rolled her eyes up to the ceiling. "I can't believe I told you that."

"Well, I'm going to really enjoy proving you wrong."

Addison's heart thudded. "So, where do we go from here?"

"My cabin."

Addison was referring to the future but then squashed it. Aiden and Garret had made her gun-shy and insecure. Reid was right! They didn't deserve the power to rule her life.

"Hey," Reid said at her sudden silence. "I was teasing, Addison. I want to take you to my cabin, but let's just see where the night takes us. No expectations, okay?"

"Okay." Addison nodded and gave him a smile. "What about food? Do we need to stop somewhere?"

"Are you kidding? My mother keeps my fridge stocked full of her home cooking. I have some fried chicken that will make you weep." He patted his stomach. "I'm busting out of my clothes."

"I think it looks good on you," Addison assured him, and then groaned. "I'm really having trouble keeping my thoughts from coming out of my mouth."

"No way. I want to know what's going on in that pretty head of yours. So, here's what I'm thinking. Let's get your swimsuit and head out of here."

"I need to wrap up the cake."

"I see the plastic wrap over there. I'll do it. I'll tidy up while you get what you need."

Addison smiled. "I'll get out of this dress and toss on some comfy jeans." She scooted to the edge of the chair and gingerly put her sore feet onto the cool floor. He helped her stand up. "I'll be back in a few minutes."

Reid nodded as he headed over to the table and started tossing paper plates into the green garbage bag Addison had started filling earlier. "I'll hold you to it."

"Bring the leftovers and the rest of the champagne." She hobbled over and picked up the flowers.

"Excellent idea. I'll even pack up the raspberries." He

swiped his finger in some frosting and licked it off. Addison watched as he sucked the top of his finger, and suddenly felt warm all over. "Mmm, really good. Now go get what you need."

"My bathing suit?" Addison asked over her shoulder.

"Totally optional."

"Ah, then I think I'll leave it behind."

Reid gave her a slow smile, showing off that sexy dimple. "Addison?"

"Yes?" Her heart pounded. There might be no expectations, but it was pretty obvious where the evening was headed.

"Hurry."

"No problem." Addison took the stairs as fast as her sore feet would carry her. But the fatigue she'd been feeling suddenly vanished. Her second wind had her slipping out of her dress, letting it pool in a pretty puddle at her feet. She smiled when she put the flowers in water. She wasn't even going to try to kid herself. Right or wrong, she was happy that Reid showed up.

After tugging on her favorite, worn boyfriend jeans she grabbed a T-shirt and gently slipped her feet into rubber-soled flip-flops. "Ahhh . . ." Not knowing if she would actually muster up the nerve to soak in the hot tub naked, Addison located a royal blue bikini, one of two that she had with her. The rest of her clothing and some other personal items were being shipped by her parents but hadn't arrived just yet.

After pulling her curls up into a ponytail she tossed some toiletries into a canvas bag, glad that her shop was closed on Sundays until business picked up a bit more, so she could have a day to rest up. Wait . . . *her* shop. Addison smiled. It was hard to believe that her life had taken this sudden and exciting turn.

Tonight, however, she wasn't going to think or worry about anything and just enjoy spending time with the handsome man waiting for her downstairs. *Sometimes no plan is the best plan of all.*

A soft knock at her door had her smiling. "Come in," she called, and when Reid entered she felt a little flutter in her stomach.

"All of the perishables are put away and I took the garbage out to the Dumpster. We do need a bag for the leftover cake and champagne."

"Thanks. Follow me into the kitchen."

He smiled and simply stood there and looked at her.

"What?"

"You looked incredible in that dress and sexy heels, but I like you even more in jeans, a T-shirt, and flip-flops."

Addison swallowed hard when he walked slowly toward her. He was going to kiss her. She'd seen it in his eyes, felt it in the rapid beat of her own heart. *Oh God . . .*

This is it.

This was what Mia had been talking about. Could Reid Greenfield be the real deal? Could she finally, truly be falling in love? Addison felt a little flash of fear when all kinds of what-ifs started buzzing around in her brain. But when Reid pulled her into his arms and kissed her all she could think about was how good it felt. She knew it was an old-fashioned notion, but being wrapped in his arms made her feel safe, secure, and happy to the point of being giddy.

"I've been thinking about seeing you, kissing you, all week long."

Addison put her hands on his broad shoulders and raised her eyebrows. "So, how was it?"

"Even better than I imagined." He leaned in and captured her lips in another sweet, lingering kiss. "Are you ready to go?"

She nodded.

"Good. We should get there in time to see the sunset over the river. By the way, I like what you've done with this loft."

"Thanks! It helps having a really nice antiques shop

right next door. I can't wait to have more time to shop at the thrift stores up on Main Street."

"Ever been to a flea market?"

"No, but it sounds like fun."

"There's a big one at the county fairgrounds every weekend. We'll go when you get the chance. I'm pretty good at refinishing furniture."

"I'd like that," Addison said, and took his offered hand.

"Good. It's a hobby I enjoy. And gives me a chance to impress you." He picked up the canvas bag for the cake and they headed downstairs.

The waning sunlight softened the brightness of the late-spring day, slicing through the tops of the trees along the riverbank. Lush and full from recent rain, the woods along the rolling hills blended into various shades of green. "I never knew that Kentucky was such a pretty state. My only visit was to the Kentucky Derby in Louisville."

"You'd enjoy driving through horse country in Lexington. The horse park is beautiful."

"Do you miss it?"

Reid glanced at her. "Sometimes. I really liked going to college there. I have my favorite restaurants." He grinned. "The Tolly-Ho is open twenty-four/seven and has some of the best burgers on the planet. And you haven't lived until you've had the cheesy tots with bacon and chili."

"That sounds like it could kill you."

Reid laughed. "No, it's what you do before you go to The Ho at four in the morning that could kill you. Of course, on the other side of the ledger is Malone's, consistently voted one of the best steakhouses in the country. And while the Derby in Louisville is sweet, my favorite is going to the races at Keeneland. Don't even get me started about Kentucky basketball."

"No, I think it's really cool to be proud of and love where you come from. I still think of Chicago as home. I know I sure miss deep-dish pizza from Giordano's and I'll forever be a Cubs fan. While I don't have anything against chains, I think it's more fun to eat at local haunts. I stopped at a lot of fun diners while I drove across the country. I know it's difficult for mom-and-pops to compete financially so I always support them."

"I agree one hundred percent." Reid nodded as he turned the truck off the main road onto little more than a dirt path. "Cricket Creek struggled for a long time. If it wasn't for the baseball stadium this town might have all but dried up."

"That's what Mia told me. So, your cabin is back here?"

"It's part of our property, but I'm taking you the back way. My dad used it as a fishing hideaway but I've been improving it little by little. Braden helped me add the lower back deck last summer."

"Oh look! There are three deer!" She pointed out the window. "Oh, and a baby."

"They're all over. Be careful that you don't hit one. They like to cross the road to get to the cornfields. You know that deer-in-the-headlights saying?"

"Yeah."

"That's what they do."

"Thanks—I'll remember that." Now that they were almost to his cabin Addison felt a flutter of nervous excitement. When the A-frame cabin came into view Addison turned to him. "You were being modest. It's gorgeous."

"Thanks." Reid shrugged. "I've got a ways to go but it's getting there." He came around and opened the door of the truck, offering his hand to help her down. "It's open. Just take your purse and I'll grab the rest."

Brick pavers led to matching steps and a wide wrap-around porch. "Oh, the outdoor furniture is really cool." She turned to Reid. "Is it from repurposed wood?"

Reid nodded. "Yeah, we were doing that before it became the in thing to do. Last spring Jeff, Braden, and I built the bench to match the chairs Dad built years ago. The wood came from an old shed we tore down."

"I love it." Addison ran her hand over the smooth surface of the wood. "Wow. You do nice work."

"After crunching numbers behind a desk, working with my hands is like therapy for me. Braden and I extended the upper back deck for Mom and Dad's anniversary a few years ago. I added the hot tub when Dad started having health issues. He needed to relax. I took a week's vacation, but Braden had to actually do the finish work."

"I think it's commendable that you took vacation time to do something nice for your parents." Actually, it was also kind of sexy.

"I should have come home more often but I buried myself in work."

"If you don't stop beating yourself up I'm seriously going to smack you."

Reid grinned and he passed through the door she was holding open for him. "After fixing the place up for my parents, I showed up and moved in." He flicked on a light. "Go figure."

"Reid, I'm sure they don't mind at all."

Reid chuckled. "My mom might. This is where Dad would come to escape, especially after Sara got engaged and all they talked about was the wedding."

"Ohmigosh, this is so pretty." She looked up to view the open, beamed ceiling. The walls were constructed of knotty pine paneling. Floor-to-ceiling windows flanked a fireplace. "Wow. Does the fireplace see through to the back deck?"

"Sure does. My dad built this cabin over thirty years ago. It's a basic A-frame design but he added some pretty cool details. We added another tier to the deck for grilling just last summer." He walked over to a galley kitchen to the left and put the canvas bag down on a breakfast bar. After putting two bottles of the champagne into the fridge he turned to her. "I'll put some chicken in the oven to warm up. I've got some of Mom's potato salad and some fresh-cut strawberries. Sound good?"

"Perfect. In fact, don't bother warming up the chicken. Cold is fine with me. I'm starving and anxious to get out there on the back deck and watch the sunset."

"Head on out there. I'll bring the food."

"No, let me help!" Addison insisted, and gave him a playful shove when he tried to block the entrance to the kitchen.

"If you insist." He grabbed her around the waist, lifted her up, and plunked her down onto the counter.

"Now, how is this helping?"

Reid handed her a bottle of wine and a corkscrew. "You can uncork this. The champagne needs to chill."

After doing her small task Reid poured the wine. She sipped the pinot grigio. "Oh, this is nice."

"Light melon and pear with a smoky finish."

She arched an eyebrow. "I'm impressed."

"Don't be. That's what it said on the back of the label. I'm mostly a beer or bourbon kind of guy but I'll enjoy an occasional glass of wine." He grinned. "Or champagne, if the occasion warrants."

Addison raised her glass. "So, you bought this just for me?"

"Yep, sure did," Reid said in a breezy tone, but the look he gave her was anything but casual. When it appeared as if he were going to elaborate he turned back to the fridge and opened the door. He pulled out a plate of chicken, followed by a plastic tub of potato salad. After opening the lid he dipped a fork in and offered her a bite. Addison leaned her face forward and accepted.

"Oh, mmm, good stuff." She pointed to the tub. "Another bite, please, and I want a piece of the hard-boiled egg."

Grinning, he fed her. "My favorite part too. I always have to fight Jeff for the eggs." He unwrapped the plastic wrap from the chicken. "Sure you don't want it heated up?"

"No, I can't wait."

"I know the feeling." He flicked Addison a glance that made her blush and then reached inside the cabinet for plates. The food might be cold, the conversation might be casual, but the air between them sizzled.

Addison picked up a plump strawberry and took a bite. "I love strawberries. And they're so good for you."

Reid turned and looked at her. "Oh, I forgot something," he said, and then pulled a little glass dish out of the fridge. He popped it into the microwave.

"What is it?" She sniffed the air. "Wait. Do I smell chocolate?"

"Dip for the strawberries." After the beep he pulled the dish from the microwave and dunked a berry.

"Hey, aren't you going to share?"

"Of course." Holding the strawberry, he closed the distance between them. "Open up," he requested in a husky voice.

Addison complied, moaning when the silky, warm chocolate rolled onto her tongue. She bit into the cold, sweet strawberry, giggling when Reid swiped a bit of dip onto her bottom lip.

"Let me get that for you." He leaned in and licked her bottom lip back and forth, nibbling, teasing, until Addison reached up and pushed his head closer. She kissed him back deeply, savoring the feel of him, the *taste* of him, loving his mouth even more than the decadent dip. She spread her thighs so he could get closer and then wrapped her legs around his waist. With a low moan, he cupped her ass, scooting her forward without breaking the kiss.

Pulling her head back, he found her neck with his mouth, kissing, nuzzling, sending a warm, delicious tingle of desire coursing through her veins. When he leaned back and tugged at her shirt Addison helped by pulling it over her head. She tossed it to the floor.

"Lean back and brace yourself with your hands."

Nodding, she did as he requested.

"God . . . Addison." Reid stood without touching her, looking at her as if drinking in the sight of her in her deep pink demi-bra.

While he looked at her with such longing and male admiration, emotion washed over her. Having lived in a society hell-bent on unattainable physical perfection, she'd felt below the LA standard. But Reid made her feel beautiful . . . sexy, desirable in a way she'd never experienced before. Here, in this town full of hardworking, wonderful people, she felt a sense of belonging.

And it felt amazing.

Shyness left the building, replaced by a feeling of feminine power. While Reid watched hungrily, Addison unhooked the front clasp of her bra, allowing her breasts to tumble free. She shrugged out of the straps and let him look his fill. She longed for his touch, his mouth, and as if reading her thoughts, he dipped his head and captured an eager nipple in his warm mouth. She gasped at the hot jolt of pleasure, leaning back farther, giving him full access.

And Reid took it.

Placing his hands on either side of her, he licked, sucked, and then added a light nibble for good measure. Addison closed her eyes, enjoying every little sensation, sighing at the soft brush of Reid's hair against her cheek and the light tickle of his stubble against her skin. The subtle, masculine scent of his cologne filled her head, teased her senses. Opening her eyes, she longed to see his body, to touch his skin . . . and to taste him everywhere.

But Reid had other ideas.

He deftly unbuttoned and unzipped her jeans and then tugged. Addison lifted her hips to help while he pulled the denim off and onto the floor, leaving her in nothing but a pink thong. "Wow . . ." he said.

"Somehow I think you're overdressed for the occasion." Addison reached up and pulled the snaps open on his shirt, revealing his chest.

"You're getting better at that."

"Practice . . . I need lots and lots of practice." *Oh my* . . . his tan was darker, his physique even more ripped. "And snaps instead of buttons. Snaps are awesome."

"I have tons of these shirts. I'll wear them all the time for you."

With a low chuckle she reached out and ran her hands over him, loving the feel of warm skin over firm muscle. He sucked in a breath and then dipped his head and kissed her with an eager hunger. When Reid slid his hands beneath her ass Addison wrapped her legs around him.

"I want you in my bed."

"Good. I'm ready for another wild ride."

He laughed as he picked her up, carrying her as if she weighed nothing, making her feel girly and sexy at the same time. "Then I'll give you one you won't soon forget."

Ever forget, she thought with a sigh. She buried her face in his neck. "You smell so good." She sucked his earlobe. "Taste even better."

"Why does this bedroom suddenly seem a million miles away?"

"A million?" she teased from his earlier comment to her.

"Maybe two," he grumbled, but a moment later they were in the master bedroom. A shaft of light sliced through the darkness, illuminating a rustic log-shaped frame and matching headboard. After lowering her gently to the bed Reid tugged a chain on a small lamp perched on a nightstand, casting a soft glow in the room. While he shrugged out of his shirt Addison reached for the snap on his jeans. Her heart thudded when her hand brushed over the hard bulge, letting her know how much he really did want to make love to her. She shoved the denim over his hips, taking the boxers with it. He sucked in a breath when she stroked him lightly, rubbing a fingertip over the head of his penis. When the pearly drop appeared he groaned. "Baby, slow down. You've got me too worked up and I want to last for you."

"I'll try." She withdrew her hand and watched as he removed his boots and kicked his jeans to the side.

"I need protection. I'll be right back."

Addison carefully pulled back a beautiful patchwork quilt and folded it at the end of the bed. She wondered who had made it, and, unable to turn off her business side, couldn't help thinking that wedding quilts would sell well in the shop. She made a mental note to ask Reid. Later.

She slid beneath the cool sheets, loving the sensual feeling of her skin against the smooth cotton. Her body ached with need. She'd never wanted a man more than she wanted Reid, and when he emerged from the bathroom she watched him walk across the hardwood floor with hungry eyes. When he pulled back the sheet and covered her body with his, she gasped with the sheer pleasure of having his nude body sliding against her flushed skin.

He kissed her deeply, thoroughly, with long strokes of his tongue and moved lower, kissing her breasts, her torso before spreading her thighs. He played with the thong, tracing the lace with his fingertips, driving her mad with desire. "Take it off," she pleaded, arching her hips to help, but he slipped his palms beneath her ass and lifted her, letting his tongue replace his fingertips.

"Reid!" Her throaty plea had him chuckling. He kissed her through the silk and she wiggled, somehow thinking with her sex-addled brain that her little shimmy would make the thong fall off. He finally slid it down her legs with one long swipe and tossed it over his head.

Reid came up to his knees, gazing down at her. "Let your hair down for me, baby. I want to bury my face in it."

She tugged the band from her ponytail and spread her dark curls over the white pillowcase. "You are so gorgeous." After looking at her for a long, heated moment

Reid lay down beside her. He trailed his hands lightly over her skin, making her desire grow hotter, brighter. When he grazed her mound with his palm she sucked in a breath. She could feel the steely hard length of his erection against her thigh, hot and ready. Just when she considered shoving him onto his back and riding him, he rolled over and covered her body with his.

And then he kissed her ... a long, hot, bone-melting, toe-curling, all-consuming kiss.

When she wrapped her legs around his waist he entered her, moving slowly but deeply. Addison wrapped herself around him breast to chest, skin to skin. The aching pleasure intensified with each stroke. He nuzzled her neck, murmured her name, and she arched her hips, wanting more of him ... all of him. He made love to her slow and easy, as if savoring every stroke, each caress bringing her closer and closer to climax. She ran her hands up his strong arms, down his back. Muscles bunched, rippled. Her nipples, sensitive, hard, slid against the silky hair on Reid's chest and drove her wild with desire. She arched her back and slid her hands to his ass, pressing, urging him to go faster, take her harder.

"Addison!" His throaty cry of release sent Addison over the edge. Wave after wave of pleasure washed over her and she clung to him, kissing him, never wanting to let him go.

20

I Want to Know What Love Is

THE INTENSITY OF HIS RELEASE SENT REID'S HEART RAC-
ing. Stunned, he stayed buried deep within her silky
heat. Dipping his head he took one sweet nipple into his
mouth, and when she cried out he kissed her, on and on
until his arms started to shake. Reid rolled to his side,
pulling Addison close, spooning. He held her against
him, trying to gather his scattered thoughts into one big
explanation of where they should go from here, but then
tossed it aside. Tonight he was not going to think but
instead give himself the luxury to simply *feel*.

Sliding Addison's hair to the side Reid kissed her
neck. "I'll be right back. Don't go anywhere."

"Like my legs could carry me," she said with a throaty
laugh.

After cleaning up in the bathroom he headed out the
other door to the kitchen, desperately needing a bottle
of water. He grabbed one for Addison and then grinned
at the uneaten dinner. After finding a tray he piled the
plates with food and headed back into the bedroom.

"Ah, my hero again," Addison said as he approached
with the feast. She came up to a sitting position. The

sheet covered her breasts but he could see the lush outline beneath the white cotton.

"At your service, madam."

"Oh ... so you're my slave?"

"Absolutely," Reid said. "Your wish is my command."

She scooted into a cross-legged sitting position. "Well,
now, I like that. I like it a lot." When she reached for a
chicken leg, the sheet slipped. With a little squeal she
tugged it upward.

"You've got to be kidding. I've seen every inch of that
super-sexy body of yours."

"I know, but ..." A pretty pink blush crept up her
neck and into her cheeks. She shrugged, making her
breasts brush against the sheet.

Reid felt a sexual stirring in his blood and was surprised how quickly his depleted body responded to the
sight of her naked in his bed. But he wanted her to enjoy
her dinner and so he reluctantly asked, "Would you like
me to get you a shirt?"

Ducking her head, she nodded. "Please."

Reid had no problem parading around naked. He
slipped from the bed and opened the chest of drawers,
locating a short-sleeved Western-cut plaid shirt instead
of a T-shirt, thinking he'd like to do that snap-popping
thing on her later.

"Thank you," she said, and shrugged into it.

"You sure look good in my shirt," he told her with a
grin.

"Are you quoting the Keith Urban song?"

"Yes. So you really do like country music?"

"Why do you seem so surprised?" she asked as she
dabbed at her mouth with the napkin.

Reid swallowed a bite of potato salad. "I don't know.
I guess it goes back to my preconceived opinion that you
were a Hollywood socialite with your nose in the air."

Addison shook her head. "You couldn't be farther
from the truth."

"I know that now. I'm sorry."

"Well, I had the image of big-bellied farmers in baggy overalls, spitting tobacco. So I was dead wrong too."

"I do own some overalls," he admitted. "But I also own a tux."

Her eyes widened.

"What—you can't picture this country boy in a tuxedo?"

"Wrong, I totally *can* and it's getting me all hot and bothered. Don't you know that you have the kind of look that could grace the cover of *GQ*?"

Reid waved a chicken leg at her. "Yeah, right. With a pitchfork in my hand?"

"Those blue eyes, that sexy stubble." She reached over and caressed his cheek. "Those dimples, and don't even get me started on that hot body of yours, Reid."

"Seems like you've given this some thought," he teased.

"In passing," she said, but laughed. "But, seriously, I have to tell you that it's refreshing that you don't obsess over your looks or body. It gets really old and exhausting. Luckily my parents believe in health and fitness but not some silly obsession with never aging or having an ounce of body fat."

He chewed on a bite of chicken. "Will your parents be visiting soon?"

"Right now they're in Hawaii on a second honeymoon," she said, but glanced away.

"What's wrong? Are you feeling homesick?"

"No, not really."

He put a hand on her arm and squeezed. "Oh, wait. . . . Don't tell me. Are they taking the honeymoon that you would have been going on?" He asked casually and out of concern, but the thought that she had almost married someone else bothered him.

"Yes."

"Do you miss him, Addison?" He didn't want to fall for someone who still loved someone else.

"I suppose I do in some ways." She lifted one shoulder. "It's weird to have someone in your life, care about them, and have it all go so wrong and then to no longer see them, speak to them, and have to figure out where to file the good memories."

"I understand. Life sure is unpredictable. Sometimes it's hard to know which fork in the road to take."

"I do think that I've learned from it, though."

"What did you learn?"

"What love . . . *isn't*."

Reid reached over and tucked a lock of her hair behind her ear, lingering on the petal-soft skin of her cheek.

"Love isn't simply having fun. And it isn't just friendship or even passion."

"So, then, what is love?"

"All of the above. It's caring so much about that person that you'd do anything to make them happy and support them in so many ways. You've seen your parents work together to keep this farm. My dad took a step back to allow my mother to shine. I see it with my cousin Mia and Cameron. She misses him so much, but baseball is his dream and she loves her job and so they somehow make it work even though it's got to be really hard. Uncle Mitch left Chicago and moved here to Cricket Creek to be with his wife. Nicolina is more important to him than power or money."

Reid nodded, thinking he'd been so wrong about her. "You didn't really answer my question. But you don't have to, Addison."

"Reid, I can tell you with absolutely certainty that I am not in love with Garret. In fact, I never was. I realize that now. He falls into the category of what love isn't." She gave him a level look but remained silent when he wanted to know more. She handed him a strawberry.

Instead of taking the strawberry from her he brought her hand to his mouth and took a bite. She finished the rest of the strawberry and then reached for another one.

"So . . . have you ever been in love, Reid?"

"There were a couple of girls in college that I dated for a while." He shrugged. "I guess I thought so at the time, but nothing became serious, much to my mother's sorrow." Reid shook his head. "Poor Mom. She is so anxious for a grandbaby. But twins run in her family. My grandmother is a twin. So she might get two for one after Sara gets married."

"Well, I'm an only child, so I'm the only hope."

It occurred to Reid that she'd make a good mother, patient and loving. He'd never talked to a woman about having kids before but, then again, he'd never really thought about marriage. He'd also never had a picnic in his bed with a woman either. Or had the urge to cuddle or massage tired feet. But he wanted all of those things with Addison.

Reid inhaled a deep breath. He wasn't thinking; he was finally feeling. Did he have it in him to take that scary-ass leap of faith?

Yes, he did. But should he tell Addison how he felt?

"Reid, hey, don't look so freaked-out. We can stop talking about children. I don't know how we got on the subject but it's clearly wigging you out," she said in a lighthearted voice, but there was a rather forlorn look in her eyes. She fell silent.

"You've got it all wrong."

"It's a pattern with me," she said with a small laugh. "So, are you going to enlighten me?"

Reid gave her pretty face a searching look. He decided that he'd wait to tell her what he wanted and how he felt. He wanted to give her time to forget about the past and build trust between them. Besides, showing her was much better than telling her, anyway. Reid wanted to treat her in the manner she should have been treated all along. Instead of being expendable or used, Addison deserved someone who would treasure her for all that she's worth.

"Reid?" She tilted her head to the side.

"No, but I am going to kiss you." He leaned in and

captured her mouth in a sweet, lingering kiss. "Addison?" he whispered in her ear.

"Mmm?"

"Last one in is a rotten egg."

She opened her eyes. "Last one . . . ? Oh, in the hot tub?"

"Yes, I've got it heating up." Reid scrambled from the bed and held out his hand.

"What about the food? We didn't eat it all. I don't want to waste any of it."

Reid nodded, liking that about her as well. "You're right." He tugged on his boxers and then started gathering up the leftovers.

Addison helped him put everything away, looking so damned cute walking around in his shirt that he wanted to scoop her up and make love to her again, but he knew she would benefit from the hot tub and so he refrained. Barely.

"Okay, now . . . last one in is a rotten egg," he said, and took off like a rocket.

"Hey, no fair. My feet hurt," she shouted after him.

Reid stopped in his tracks and turned around.

"I forgot." When he hurried back with the intention of scooping her up in his arms, she scurried past him, laughing over her shoulder.

"Oh no, you don't." Reid quickly caught up and snaked his arm around her waist. She squealed when he picked her up, but he silenced her with a kiss. "So, you don't play fair. I'll have to remember that."

"Yeah, well, I didn't want to be a rotten egg."

"Baby, there's nothing rotten about you," he said as he carried her out to the back deck. After setting her down he folded the cover back from the hot tub. Steam rose in the air, and when he turned the jets on she sighed.

"Oh, this is going to feel amazing," she said, but then looked at his boxers. "Oh, my swimsuit is in the cabin."

Reid arched an eyebrow and then took off his boxers. "Naked is the only way to go." He took a step closer to her and tugged at the shirt, exposing her body one snap at a time. He eased the shirt over her shoulders and let it slide to the deck and then pulled her in for a kiss.

"Oh my gosh. Can anybody see us?"

"Nobody but the bears."

"Bears?" she squeaked.

"Just kidding."

"Okay," she said, but looked right and left, making him chuckle.

Reid stepped into the tub and then held out his hand to assist her. "Careful, it can get slippery."

Addison took his hand. "Ahh, you were right—this feels heavenly," Addison said after she sat down in the bubbling water. She eased onto the bench seat and leaned back. "Oh yeah, this is the ticket. I feel as if my bones are turning to Jell-O."

"You can thank me later."

Addison laughed. "Oh, I plan on it," she said with a smile that held all sorts of promises. She closed her eyes and leaned her head back against the edge of the tub. Moonlight caressed her face and shoulders and the delicate column of her throat. The gurgling water played peekaboo with her breasts, giving him tantalizing glimpses. Her mouth looked pink and wet from the spray of the water and her cheeks were flushed from the heat. She'd piled her hair up in a sloppy bun but loose, dark tendrils clung to her neck. Reid watched her, drinking in the sight but allowing her to relax, when he wanted to scoot over there and slide his naked body against hers.

The feelings he tried so hard to suppress seemed to grow deeper by the minute, expanding and reaching into places he didn't know existed. He'd been semiserious a couple of times, like he told her, but what he left out was that no one brought out the feelings of protectiveness, possessiveness, and flat-out desire. He'd never had a woman occupy his thoughts the way Addison did or make his heart race just from looking at her.

Addison opened her eyes and their gazes held, locked.

His heart thudded when, without speaking, she closed
the gap between them and straddled his lap. Her skin felt
like wet silk sliding against him. She came up on her
knees and held on to his shoulders, offering her breasts.
Reid cupped them in his hands licking, sucking, rubbing
his thumbs over her nipples until her breath came in
short gasps. He felt her thighs tremble and she sank into
the water, wrapped her arms around his neck and fell
into a long, hot kiss.

Reid wanted to thrust upward and take her right
there, but he didn't have protection and so he held back.
She kissed his neck while moving erotically against him,
letting her breasts slide against his chest, and then slid
her fingers in his wet hair, kissing him once more. Reid
caressed her back, cupped her ass, letting his hands explore her wet, warm body.

The jets suddenly went silent, leaving only the light
sound of water lapping with their movements. Moonlight spilled over them and the music of the night lingered on the gentle breeze.

"Let's take this inside," Reid said in her ear.

"Yes . . . please."

"Ah, sexy and polite too. What more could I ask for?"
Reid teased, and she laughed. But, truly, *what more could
I ask for*? He felt his guard slipping away. Where she had
come from and who she had been engaged to no longer
seemed to matter. "Uh, unfortunately, I forgot towels.
Do you want me to run inside and get you one?

"No, I'll brave it," she said, "but we'll get the floor
wet."

"A small price to pay," Reid said and then scooped
her up.

"I can walk!"

"I like having your naked body in my arms."

"Just hold on tight, huh?"

"And never let go." He hadn't meant to say that part
out loud. Instead of giving her time to think about it he
hurried into the cabin, dripping wet and laughing all the

way. After grabbing two big, fluffy towels out of the linen cabinet he handed her one. "I brought your bag in here in case you needed anything," he said. "I'll give you some privacy." He cleared his throat and said, "You're welcome to spend the night."

"Do you want me to?"

"Absolutely."

She smiled.

"Good, I'm going to turn off the hot tub and lock up. Do you want anything?"

"You."

God . . . he thought but leaned over and gave her a kiss. "I'll be back in a couple of minutes."

Addison nodded, and he saw a flash of something in those big brown eyes that looked like hope. Over and above anything else he didn't want to be another man who disappointed or hurt her. The increasing intensity of his feelings for Addison caught him by surprise. He was a guy who liked to think things through, study, analyze, so it left him feeling a bit vulnerable and exposed. But with it came an odd sense of freedom. After so many years of holding back from taking even a little risk in both his professional and personal life he was really ready to listen to Sara's advice and take a leap of faith.

When Reid returned Addison was curled up beneath the covers, sound asleep. He gazed down at her and smiled. She looked angelic, lying there with one hand tucked under her chin. Her bare shoulders reminded him that she was naked and his blood stirred. But he wouldn't wake her. She needed the rest.

But tomorrow? Now, that would be a different story.

After brushing his teeth he slid beneath the sheet and pulled her close. She stirred, mumbled something, and then sighed. While making love to her again would have been awesome, Reid acknowledged that having her sleeping in his arms was a close second.

21

Flower Power

WHEN THE BELL OVER THE DOOR DINGED MAGGIE LOOKED up from the model home plan she'd been studying.

"Look what I've got for you!" said Gabby Goodwin, the cute little owner of Flower Power. She had to lean her head to the side to see beyond the big bouquet of colorful spring flowers.

Maggie took off her reading glasses and stood up. With a hand to her chest she asked, "For me?"

Gabby wiggled her eyebrows. "Yes, indeed. Someone sure does like you." She put the vase down on the desk and smiled. "Care to elaborate?" She tucked a golden curl behind her ear and waited.

Maggie took the small envelope from the tall plastic tong and then opened it. "Looking forward to dinner and dancing in the moonlight tonight. Richard," she read silently. "Oh, just a client," Maggie said, but felt a warm glow slide across her cheeks.

"Sure, he is," Gabby drew out the comment with a smile. "Dinner and dancing in the moonlight? That sounds incredibly romantic if you ask me."

"How did you . . . Oh right. You wrote this down for him when he called it in." Maggie tried to make light of it.

"Is he hot? "

Maggie felt her blush deepen. "Yes . . ." Her voice turned into a small squeak.

"Sweet! This is when I love delivering flowers. Men . . ." Gabby rolled her eyes. "They think the best time to send a lovely bouquet of flowers is when they've messed up. Wrong." Gabby wagged her fingers.

Maggie laughed.

"Yeah, I've had flowers handed back to me— No, make that thrust back at me. One woman walked over and tossed them out the back door! Right in front of me! I wanted to tell her to just give them to someone else . . . a neighbor or something, but you don't want to mess with that kind of crazy."

"So, you're saying that the time to send flowers is for no reason at all."

"Absolutely." Gabby nodded slowly. "I mean, it's great to do that too, you know, on Valentine's Day or your anniversary. Even then they should put some thought into it. Just a simple thing like a favorite color or a special note. Guys just don't get that women are pretty easy to please."

"Sounds like you're talking from experience."

Gabby scrunched up her cute little nose. "I'm the poster child for dating douche bags. Oh well . . ." She smiled and pointed to the arrangement. "But this guy sure has got it going on. Flowers for no reason? Dancing in the moonlight? Damn, girl . . ."

Maggie laughed again. "Oh, Gabby, someone's missing the boat by not snatching you up. Someday your prince will come."

Gabby raised her arms akimbo. "Tell me about it. I sure have kissed some frogs."

Maggie chuckled. "The arrangement is lovely but you didn't have to personally deliver it to me."

Her bright smile faltered. "Well, I'm the only one in

the shop today. Until business picks up with weddings, I'm a little bit slow. I do have prom coming up so that will help." She shrugged. "I put a be-back-in-ten-minutes sign on the door. And besides, I wanted to ask who the mystery man was. Actually, I think he had an assistant call in the order because the credit card name wasn't Richard but some company name."

Maggie laughed. "No mystery—just a client renting a cabin down by the river."

"Right, and he sent you a huge bouquet of flowers? Dancing in the moonlight? I sure wish I had clients like that. Well, I'd want something other than flowers," Gabby added with a tinkle of laughter. "I have enough of those. Give me chocolate!"

"Chocolate is the cure for anything!" Maggie smiled. She'd frequented Flower Power, loving the fresh scent and beauty of fresh flowers in her loft. Plus, she knew that until Wedding Row was up and running full steam ahead the shop was struggling a little bit. She'd gotten to know Gabby over the past few weeks. "You do wonderful work, Gabby."

"Thanks!"

"What made you go into the flower business? Other than you have quite the eye for color?"

Gabby's eyes misted over. "My mama. She was a single mom and worked so hard waiting tables at Sully's just to make ends meet. I would bring her wildflowers I'd pick because I knew they'd make her smile. I'd put them in a mason jar and set them on the kitchen table so she'd see them as soon as she walked in."

"That's such a lovely reason, Gabby." She smiled. "Tristan used to bring me dandelions. There's nothing sweeter than getting flowers from a child, even if they're weeds."

"True, but it's also pretty doggone nice to get flowers from an admirer," Gabby said with a grin. "I sure wish my Prince Charming would come along."

"Oh, he will. Most likely when you least expect it."

"Ah, so there's hope for me yet?"

Maggie nodded. "There's *always* hope. Now get on back before you miss a customer."

Gabby hugged Maggie and then stepped back. "I will. And make sure you come over for coffee and tell me all about Mr. Dancin' in the Moonlight soon. Okay?"

"I promise."

"Good," Gabby said with her usually bubbly smile back in place. "See y'all later."

After Gabby left Maggie tried to go back to the home plans but her eyes kept drifting back to the flowers. This time there wasn't a twisted ankle or any reason other than Richard was anxious to see her. The knowledge sent a flutter of excitement dancing around in her stomach. They had been taking things slow but the pull of attraction was undeniable, even when they talked for hours into the night. Richard listened and seemed to really care about her, but she realized that there was so much more that she wanted to learn about him. Once in a while she sensed an edge of sadness and she vowed that tonight she would draw him out and learn more about his past.

Over the years Maggie had felt a pull of attraction here and there. She'd been on a few dinner dates, but while Tristan was young she didn't want to upset the apple cart, since except for being studious and quiet he was well adjusted and excelled academically. Tristan's well-being and making enough money to live a modest lifestyle had been Maggie's main concerns. After Tristan had left for college Maggie could have made changes in her social life but the insecurity of not dating for so long made her incredibly gun-shy.

Maggie reached over and touched the soft petals of a purple iris. She supposed that her mother's desertion and her father's lack of love and affection had something to do with her reluctance to seek a relationship. When you felt unloved it was difficult to put your heart on the line to take a beating.

Maggie sat back in her chair, toying with a pen. Fear was such a powerful emotion and so tough to stifle. She inhaled a shaky breath. She needed to shake off the shackles of the past and conquer her fear of rejection. A trickle of fear slid down her spine, but then she sat up straight and tossed the pen down. She needed to stop being wishy-washy! She was attracted to Richard Rule and he obviously felt the same way. She needed to just go for it. Determination melted the cold ball of fear. After all, she and Richard were just two middle-aged people looking for companionship, and if it became more than that she needed to embrace it rather than run. This was her chance. She'd be crazy not to take it.

After all, thoughts of Richard had occupied Maggie's daydreams all week long. Lunch with him on Monday when he'd brought the paperwork to her only made her think of him more. Long conversations on the phone lasted into the night, creating an intense sensual longing that had her tossing and turning in her bed. The vision of him shirtless, however, plagued her the most.

And the kiss . . . *Oh, the kiss*.

Maggie heard a groan and then realized it had come from her own throat. She'd relived the sweet, sensual kiss over and over. That one kiss had the power to reach inside her heart and open something she'd kept locked tightly away for such a long time.

Desire.

"Oh, my . . . my." The need to fan her face wasn't from a hot flash.

Maggie finally gave up and shut down her computer. She locked the door and flipped the OPEN sign to CLOSED. Instead of trying to work she might as well head on upstairs and take a long, hot bubble bath. She planned on exfoliating, shaving, plucking, smoothing, and primping. In anticipation of seeing Richard again she'd purchased some sexy lingerie. A trip to the cosmetic counter at Macy's resulted in a sultry new fragrance and the knowledge of how to create a smoky eye. The eyeliner still proved tricky but she thought she'd finally gotten the method down. Blending, she had been instructed, was the key.

Maggie had always prided herself in presenting herself well as a mother and real estate agent, but this getting-sexy thing was fun! She only hoped she could pull it off. But Richard had a laid-back way about him that put her at ease. At lunch he'd had her laughing and feeling more carefree than she could remember. He'd requested that she bring jeans and tennis shoes along in the event they wanted to walk, and a bathing suit if she wanted to lounge in the hot tub. Of course, purchasing a new bathing suit had taken hours of trying on dozens of styles. She'd finally selected a modest one-piece halter-top style in a deep shade of emerald green.

The hot weather slipped into an evening warm enough for the baby-blue vintage scoop-neck sundress she'd bought at Violet's. The sleeveless dress dipped low in the back, showing just enough skin to make her purchase a white, loosely knit sweater to wear over top. She'd remove it only if she mustered up the nerve. White wedge sandals and a matching purse rounded out the outfit.

Maggie looked in the mirror and fluffed her hair. She added more lipstick and then a bit more blush with a fat brush. "Not too shabby," she said, trying really hard not to be nervous. In the back of her mind—and she kept it there—was the knowledge that this night could lead to more than a lingering kiss. They were adults, after all.

Maggie knew her body was far from perfect. Although she was no spring chicken, the sultry perfume, silky lingerie, and carefully applied makeup boosted her confidence. She gave herself one more once-over in the mirror and then looked at her watch. "Oh boy. Time to go . . ."

On the way to the cabin Maggie turned up the radio loud and sang along, partly because of her good mood but mostly to keep her mind off of getting incredibly, uncontrollably nervous. Because Maggie had made the decision that she wanted to make love to Richard Rule. Tonight.

But when she pulled into the lane leading to the cabin her heart started to pound. *Okay, maybe not tonight,* she thought, and then gripped the steering wheel harder. Maybe she should just shoot for another kiss in the moonlight?

"Just go with the flow," Maggie whispered to herself as she pulled up in front of the cabin. "Dinner, maybe a dance on the back deck. You don't need to be thinking about . . . *sex*," she grumbled.

With that in mind she killed the engine, hefted her purse and tote bag over her shoulder, and then proceeded to walk with slightly shaky knees up to the front door. After taking a deep breath, she squared her shoulders and knocked.

"Maggie!" Richard smiled as he held the door open for her. "Come in."

Apple and cinnamon wafted her way. "Oh, it smells heavenly in here."

"It's the apple pie from last time." He leaned close and kissed her on the cheek. "This day sure dragged while I waited impatiently for your arrival."

Maggie nodded since the touch of his warm lips against her skin interfered with her ability to articulate.

"You look lovely, Maggie." He took the canvas bag from her and of course their fingers had to brush, and she felt a tingle all the way to her toes. It didn't help that he looked so super-handsome in khaki shorts and a short-sleeved pale blue shirt that made his eyes appear even bluer. His short-cropped black hair was getting longer, giving him a boyish charm that softened the pure masculine line of his jaw.

"Thank you. And thank you for the flowers. They were beautiful and such a lovely surprise."

"I'm glad you liked them. Would you like a glass of wine out on the back deck?"

"Oh, I meant to bring a bottle."

"No worries. I have quite the selection, if you recall."

Maggie smiled and fell into step with him toward the kitchen. She sat down on a stool by the large island.

"I opened a Cabernet Sauvignon about an hour ago to breathe, but if you'd rather have white I have a Chardonnay in the fridge."

"Oh, the Cab sounds nice."

"I couldn't find a decanter so I poured some into the

wineglasses. I wanted the wine to soften." He grinned as he handed her a glass. "The two glasses sitting there were a constant reminder that you were coming but weren't here yet. It was like they were mocking me."

Maggie laughed. The fact that he was making no bones about how much he'd been looking forward to their dinner put her at ease.

Richard sat down next to her and lifted his glass. "To a wonderful evening ahead."

Maggie tapped her glass to his and took a sip of the full-bodied wine.

"Do you like it? Be honest, because I don't mind opening another bottle. I knew this vineyard produced a wine a bit more fruit forward, with less of the earthy finish. I hoped you would enjoy it."

"I'm hardly an expert but I appreciate bold flavors. This is nice."

When he seemed relieved Maggie reached over and put her hand over his. "Don't worry. I'm easily pleased but I won't waste calories on something I don't like."

"I know one thing. You're easy to be around. I really enjoy your company, Maggie."

"I feel the same way," she said.

"I thought we'd have grilled salmon, a tossed salad, and wild rice? But if you're not a salmon lover I have a couple of steaks in the fridge as well."

"Oh no, salmon is a favorite of mine. The menu sounds delicious. And you said you couldn't cook?" She pointed to the apple pie cooling on the counter. "Browned to perfection. I don't think you're giving yourself enough credit, or maybe you were holding out on me."

Richard lifted one shoulder. "I have to admit that I've been surprising myself lately."

When he reached for his wineglass his tattoo caught her eye once more. He seemed so refined, so educated, and the unexpected tattoo gave him that edge that she found compelling . . . and so damned sexy. "What does your tattoo say?"

Richard turned his forearm over so she could see. "Work hard, play harder," he said with a slight wince. "Not one of my best decisions."

"The tattoo?"

"Yeah, well, maybe but I was referring to the motto. It should be the other way around, I think."

Maggie traced the script with the tip of her finger. "I don't know. I spent most of my life working and not playing. Maybe you're not as wrong as you might think. Any other tattoos?"

Richard gave her a playful grin. "Want to find out?" he asked, and then put a hand over his face. "Pretend I didn't say that. I didn't mean to sound crass."

Maggie reached over and pulled his hand away. "It's okay. I asked, remember? Let's forget it and go outside with our wine."

"Okay." He appeared relieved and Maggie wasn't sure if it was because he regretted his playful remark or if he was embarrassed about other tattoos.

Either way, Maggie remained curious not only about the tattoo but the rest of his life. After they sat down in the padded lawn chairs on the back deck he remained quiet, making Maggie wonder what was on his mind. "If you're wondering, I find tattoos sexy."

He turned and gave her a slight grin. "I was wondering. Of course I've been wondering about a lot of things lately."

Again, Maggie sensed unease, as if something was troubling him. She wondered what he was hiding away from in the woods. "You don't have to walk on eggshells around me, Richard. If there's something on your mind, you can speak it. I'm a good listener. And I'm here if you need a friend. I want to know everything about you."

"Thank you. True friends are hard to find," he said, and then looked out over the river as if deep in thought. Maggie watched him take a sip of wine. He swallowed, licked his bottom lip, and turned to face her.

22

Dancing in the Moonlight

RICK WANTED TO TELL THIS LOVELY WOMAN EVERYTHING: who he was, why he was here, his past, his regrets, and the recent plans he'd been dreaming up lately. Most of all he wanted to pull her into his arms and kiss her.

But what would she do if she knew all of those things?

Right or wrong, and he admitted to himself that there was some wrong involved, he decided that Maggie needed to get to know the real man, not the image, the rumors, or who he'd been pretending to be for so many years. The past few weeks he'd felt as if he'd shed his skin and was ready to start fresh.

"So, if I may ask, why are you really here in Cricket Creek?" Maggie asked quietly.

Rick thought about how to answer. It was only fair that if she came out here and spent time with him she knew some of the truth, which, for now at least, was pretty much based on where he was going and not where he'd been. "I was at a dead end in my career and so I decided to come here and reflect on my life. Make some much-needed changes."

"Change can be difficult. Frightening. I hope you discover what you're looking for."

"It's a work in progress, but I'm getting there." He was actually pretty excited about the idea that had suddenly come to him in the middle of a sleepless night. He wanted to share it with her so badly but now wasn't the time.

"I can relate." She nodded but didn't pry, even though he could see in her eyes that she wanted to know more.

"But right now all I care about is spending the evening with a beautiful woman."

"Oh, are you expecting company?"

Rick laughed. There was something so real and wonderful about her. "No, she's already here." Rick expected her to dip her head and blush or look away but instead she held his gaze.

"Why, thank you." The breeze caught her hair, blowing it across her face. She brushed the strands away, laughing as if life was simply wonderful.

Something was different about her tonight, not just in the extra care she'd taken with her makeup, but a certain confidence that wasn't present before. And he liked it. "Let's get dinner started—what do you say?" When she nodded Rick stood up and offered his hand. She took it and it felt so good having her small hand in his firm grasp.

"Is there something I can help you with in the kitchen?"

"Nope, I want you to simply sit back and watch. I want to spoil you a little bit," he said, and realized it was true. She'd been a hardworking single mom and deserved to be pampered. And he was just the man to do it.

"Well, now." Maggie slid onto a stool and folded her hands. "I won't have any problem doing that."

"Sitting back?"

"No. Watching you."

Rick looked at her and she held his gaze once more. He felt a strong pull of desire, and when she smiled it was all he could do not to walk over there and draw her into his arms. He found her slightly suggestive flirting much more stimulating than bold sexual moves. Anticipation was highly underrated. As he gathered the items he needed Rick could feel her eyes watching him with appreciation, putting an underlying sensual vibe in the room that felt almost tangible.

"More?" Rick held up bottle of wine.

"Please." When she slid her glass across the smooth granite Rick reached for it but deliberately let his fingers linger on hers. After pouring he looked at her a beat longer than he needed to. When he saw the slight rise and fall of her chest he suspected she was feeling much of the same.

Rick unwrapped the white butcher's paper from the salmon. "Wild caught," he told her, and she nodded.

"Perfect. I detest when they add that artificial coloring to the farm-raised variety."

"I thought I'd make a dill sauce. Sound okay with you?"

"Absolutely." Maggie toyed with the stem of her glass. "Again, I'm impressed."

"It's just Dijon mustard, mayo, and fresh dill. Easy but full of flavor." Rick pointed to the box containing wild rice. "Easy as well, but I will say that I've discovered a love of cooking that I didn't know I possessed. The rice will simmer while I grill the fish." He grinned. "And the salad is from a bag again. Spring greens that I'll toss with mandarin orange slices and almonds." He turned away and located a wooden salad bowl. "I'll get the salad tossed, put the rice on, and then we can go outside on the deck while I grill the fish." He snapped his fingers. "Oh, and I bought a loaf of French bread from the bakery up on Main Street. Don't let me forget it."

"This is such a guilty pleasure watching you work."

"There's nothing to feel guilty about. I'm enjoying myself. Open up." Rick leaned across the island and offered her a mandarin orange slice. God, the touch of her warm tongue against his fingers sent a hungry jolt of desire straight to his groin.

"Mmmm . . . so good. May I have another?"

"You sure can." Rick slid a second slice into her mouth, nearly groaning when she sucked ever so slightly on his thumb.

"That's it." Maggie shook her head. "I can't stand it any longer."

Rick's heart thudded and he looked at her expectantly.

"I have to come over there and help."

Before he could find his voice to protest, Maggie stood beside him. "Tell me what you want me to do."

"That's a loaded question."

She laughed. "How about if I slice the bread?"

"I could think of other things, but okay."

"You're being awfully frisky, Mr. Rule."

"Do you like it?"

"I do . . ."

Rick's smiled but it felt a bit forced. He didn't like not being honest with her but told himself it was necessary for now. "The bread is on the counter behind me."

Maggie nodded and made herself at home, finding the knife, cutting board, and bread basket. While he tossed the salad she sliced the bread. They stood close, nearly but not quite touching. Rick decided he needed to remedy that whole situation and reached from behind her to pick up the small bag of almonds. His arm grazed against her arm that held the end of the loaf.

"Would you cut me a thin slice? I didn't realize how hungry I was until just now."

"Sure." When she turned and handed him the bread he stepped closer.

"Thanks. Oh, this tastes as good as it looks," Rick said. "I wanted to hold off but just couldn't stand it any longer."

"Sometimes you just have to try to find out," she said holding his gaze. "Richard?"

He swallowed the bread. "Yes?"

"I do believe that my body is about ready to catch fire with the need to kiss you. *Hot and bothered* doesn't even begin to describe how I'm feeling right about now. I'm ready for an appetizer and I don't mean cheese and crackers."

"You don't have to ask twice." The wild and wonderful kiss exploded in his brain. Rick could not get enough. They stumbled backward, sideways, drunk on desire until somehow, either by accident or grand design, they ended up in the great room on the sofa, in front of the gas fireplace that he'd turned on low earlier.

The waning light from the setting sun cast a soft glow through the windows.

"You're a beautiful woman, Maggie." He placed his hand over the wild beating of her heart. "From the inside out."

"A glass of wine and muted lighting helps," Maggie joked, making him laugh. God, how he loved being with this woman. It occurred to him how much he'd missed out on over the years by not being in a relationship with someone close to his age. He'd been such an arrogant dumb-ass.

And then he kissed her once more, a hot, sensual meeting of their mouths yet edged with tenderness. She threaded her fingers through his hair and then moved to his shoulders, his back, touching, massaging, exploring. "I do believe I could kiss you all night long."

"Mmmm, I like the sound of that." Rick held Maggie close and kissed her neck, loving the taste of her skin and the light floral scent of her hair. Although he longed to make love to Maggie he didn't want to rush them into anything. After so many years of fast living, he was finding that taking his time was even sweeter. It felt so good having her snuggled next to him, but he eventually summoned his willpower and asked, "Should we finish making dinner?"

"Just give me a few more minutes of being in your arms."

"No problem."

She rested her head on his shoulder and sighed. "This is so relaxing."

"Mmmm, I totally agree." Rick kissed the top of her head and smiled. The heat of the fireplace warmed their bodies, and a sense of peace like he'd not known in forever washed over him. In that moment he knew without a shadow of a doubt that he wanted Maggie McMillan in his future. Now all he had to do was find the right time to tell her about his past.

23

That's the Good Stuff

"**T**HIS UP-AT-THE-ASS-CRACK-OF-DAWN STUFF IS FOR THE birds," Reid grumbled as he slapped his baseball cap on his head. "And so is leaving you."

Addison turned from filling his coffee mug and wrapped her arms around him. "I totally agree with you."

"You've been doing a lot of that lately."

Addison tilted her head up. "Agreeing with you?"

"Yeah, it's pretty cool. Does that mean you kinda like me?"

Addison lifted one shoulder. "Eh, maybe a teeny little bit." She measured an inch with her thumb and index finger. "You might cross my mind like once or twice ... or maybe a hundred times a day."

Reid tucked a lock of her damp hair behind her ear. "Only a couple hundred? Well, then, I do believe I'll have to leave you with something to think about." He flipped his cap around, dipped his head, and gave her a deep, lingering kiss that held a promise of things to come. Pulling back, he pressed his forehead to hers and said, "God, I don't want to go ... This sucks so bad."

"Well, then, I think I have to give *you* something to

think about while you're riding around on that big green tractor." She took a step back and reached for the knot on her robe. With a slow smile, Addison parted the terry cloth, giving him an eyeful.

Reid groaned. "You're not making this any easier, you know."

"Just get your chores done and get your cute butt back here." She handed him the coffee.

"So, you think my butt is cute?" Reid turned around and pointed to it.

"Your butt is awesome, just like the rest of you," Addison assured him, and then gave him a quick, light kiss. "Call me when you take a break."

"I will," Reid promised, and then headed out the back door. Addison watched him walk to his truck, thinking he looked so sexy in his Wranglers and boots. He looked up and waved just before he opened his door. Addison raised her hand and smiled. Right timing or not, she was falling in love with Reid and she was powerless to stop her feelings from growing. It was hard for Addison to believe that just a couple of months ago her life had been pulled apart at the seams, but day by day, stitch by stitch, everything was coming together. Happiness surrounded her like a warm blanket and she hugged it close to her heart.

After pouring a cup of coffee she sat down at the breakfast bar and looked over some notes. Since the open house a few of weeks ago, business had been brisk, leaving her little time to head out to the Greenfield farm, but Sara kept her informed on the progress of the barn renovations. So far they were on schedule, with Sara having an autumn wedding. Mia and Cam had decided to get married at Wine and Diner but were going to wait until the barn was ready and baseball season over to have their reception there as well. Later that week Addison had a meeting with Tristan and Savannah, who were thinking about having a winter wedding with a holiday theme. Addison smiled at her notes by Savannah's wedding. Three of her bridesmaids were residents of Whisper's Edge, the retirement community where Savannah served as the social director, and Addison thought it was just the sweetest thing.

While Addison acknowledged that she dearly missed her parents, life in Cricket Creek was so much more to her liking than living in LA. She enjoyed the slower pace in the tight-knit community and simply loved running her own shop. Ideas never stopped coming. She planned to add prom dresses next year. Reid's mother ran a quilting bee and they were working hard to make wedding quilts for her to sell. Her only challenge was running out of shelf space!

She inhaled a deep breath, crossing her fingers that her ended engagement with Garret was now old news and remained that way. Addison didn't want anything to intrude on the peace she'd found in Cricket Creek. Apparently she was a small-town girl at heart but just never knew it. Thankfully, she hadn't heard any more about Garret's reality show, giving her hope that the idea never really got off the ground. Maybe Rick Ruleman had had the clout to squash the show, but, come to think of it, Addison hadn't seen him in the pop news lately either. She'd never know which one of the Ruleman men had started the rumor of her having an affair with Rick, but since it had seemed to die down, Addison wasn't about to stir that pot. She found it in really poor taste that neither of them had bothered to call her with an apology but, then again, she supposed she wasn't surprised. It was sad, though, because Addison really did believe that Garret was a much better person than he allowed himself to be, and she hoped someday he figured that out.

Since she'd already shared a steamy shower with Reid, all Addison had to do was put on makeup and get dressed before heading down to the bridal shop. Because she still had more inventory to unpack, Addison opted for leggings and a loose-fitting floral blouse belted at the waist and comfortable ballet flats.

"Gotta love this commute," she said as she bounded down the stairs. Her seamstress was on an as-needed basis and Cassie, the college student she'd hired as a sales clerk, worked limited hours. Most days it was still just her in the shop, but the press release she'd sent out had resulted in interviews for the local paper and in *Kentucky Monthly*, so she anticipated that business was going to pick up even more in the near future.

After unlocking the front door Addison turned on some soft music and then starting arranging some lovely headpieces she'd received yesterday. Mia had informed her that Southern ladies loved bling and she should stock a full line of tiaras. Addison had to admit that they were pretty cool.

A few minutes later Gabby from Flower Power walked into the shop, carrying a vase packed full of wildflowers. "Hey there, Addison. I've got a little somethin' for you," she said in her cute Southern singsong voice.

"They're lovely!" Addison said as she walked across the floor. "Oh, I just love the mason jar as the vase and the raffia bow! This would make a wonderful table arrangement for rustic barn weddings."

Gabby nodded. "Funny, but this was all I had to use as a vase when I picked flowers as a kid. Now it's super-popular." She shrugged. "I guess I was just ahead of my time," she added with a laugh.

Addison smiled when she silently read the note that said: *Thinking about you one hundred times already. Reid.* "Aw . . ." Addison smiled and didn't realize she had brought the note up to her chest.

"There must be somethin' special about you ladies here in Wedding Row. I just delivered flowers to Maggie, the real estate lady, the other day. What's up with you girls, anyway? And would you please send some of it my way?"

Addison grinned. "Oh yeah. I saw Maggie walking past my shop with some good-looking guy last week."

"Yep, I'm guessing it was the same guy. Apparently he's staying in a cabin down by the river."

"Oh, okay." There had been something oddly familiar about him that she couldn't put her finger on. "Not local, then?"

"No, I think he's from California. He had a secretary or someone call in the order for him."

"Oh, hmmm . . . May I ask his name?"

"Richard is all I know. Seems like a real nice guy, though. He sure is sweet on Maggie," Gabby replied.

"Good for her."

"Well, I can see why. She's one of those people who just lights up a room, you know?"

"Kinda like you, Gabby."

"Oh, go on . . ."

"I'm serious. I'm surprised that some local boy hasn't snatched you up."

Gabby dropped her gaze for a minute and then shrugged "Maggie says that my prince will come someday. But, hey, I sure do love having my own shop. Speaking of, I'd better get on back. I'm lookin' forward to doing weddings with you, Addison!"

"Me too, Gabby." Addison walked her to the door and gave her a quick hug. She was such a sweet girl with a bubbly personality. Gabby was going to be fun to work with. The warm sunshine on Addison's face prompted her to prop open the door and let in the fresh air. She waved to Nicolina, who was doing the same thing.

"Gorgeous day!" Nicolina called to her.

"Sure is!"

"Let's get the girls together for lunch or maybe cocktails soon."

"I'd like that," Addison called back. She made a mental note to ask Gabby if she'd like to join them.

Addison went back inside to her task. A shipment of bridesmaid's sample dresses was due in late that afternoon. Sometime during the week Mia and Savannah were both coming in to try on some wedding gowns. Humming along with the music, Addison bent over to get the last of the headpieces out of the box.

"Would you look at how beautiful this is!" said a female voice that sent excitement rushing through Addison. *Mom?*

"Did you have any doubt?" answered the unmistakable voice of her father.

"Mom? Dad?" Addison stood up so fast that her head hit the inside of the cardboard box and she fell backward, landing on her butt. The tiara that she was holding slid across the hardwood floor, stopping at her mother's feet.

"Check this out." With a laugh her father picked it up and placed it on her mother's head. "Suits you, my beautiful Indian princess."

She gave him a shove but looked into a nearby mirror. "Oh, I believe it does."

Addison watched them for a moment. There was something different in the way they were acting toward each other.

Her mother held out her arms. "Are you going to come over here and give us a hug? We've missed our baby girl so much!"

With a little squeal of delight Addison scrambled to her feet and ran over to her parents. "I didn't know you were coming!"

"We wanted it to be a surprise," her father explained, and gave her a huge hug, lifting her up and spinning her around like when she was a child.

"Mom!" Addison turned to her mother and hugged her in a dancing circle. "Look at you and Dad—so tan! Did you enjoy Hawaii?"

"Your dad had to drag me from work but I'm so glad he did. We had a wonderful, relaxing time." She leaned over and snaked her arm around his waist. "Just what we needed."

"This is awesome that you're here!" Addison nearly jumped up and down with excitement. "I can't believe it! What do you think? Do you like it?" Addison grabbed her mother's hand. "Do you?"

She tilted her head to the side and laughed. "No, I don't like it, Addison. I love it! Give us a grand tour!"

Her father pointed to his camera. "Do you mind if I take pictures?"

Addison shook her head, bubbling over with excitement. "No, of course not. Just make sure you send them to me." She led them through the shop, chattering on about every detail. Her parents gushed at everything, making her nearly burst with pride. She stopped at the display of jewelry. "These pieces were made by Nicolina, Uncle Mitch's wife."

"Oh, simply beautiful. I'm very impressed. You know how I adore unique jewelry."

"Her shop is in Wedding Row too. You should go see it. How long are you here for?"

Her mother pulled a face. "Oh, sweetie, just for tonight, I'm afraid. I have to speak at a conference tomorrow in Nashville, so we rented a car and we're planning on driving there in the morning."

Addison raised her eyebrows. "We?"

"Yes, I promised your dad that if he would travel with me more often I'd cut back and stay home more often." She looked up at him. "After Hawaii we decided that we liked traveling and spending time together."

He chuckled. "Well, now, Mel. Imagine that."

Her mother smiled up at him. "I do think absence has made my heart grow fonder."

His answer was to lean down and give her a quick kiss.

"You guys are so cute." Addison's heart swelled. Seeing the rekindled love in her parents' eyes gave her a surge of hope. She'd known that her mother's busy work schedule was taking a toll on their marriage. "So the Hawaii trip did the trick? At least *something* good came out of my engagement to Garret."

"Have you heard from the little twerp?" her mother wanted to know.

"Mel . . ."

"Sorry. I just . . . Oh, never mind."

"Not a peep," Addison answered. "I'm not even sure if his reality show is actually going to happen."

"I sure hope not," her father grumbled. "People should pick up a good book instead of watching that crap."

"Dad, I couldn't agree more. Not only that, but Garret is actually a talented musician. He could do so much more with his life. But that's no longer my worry," Addison said, and then changed the subject. "Why don't you go upstairs and check out my loft apartment? It has a river view."

"I'd rather see it with you," her mother answered. "Why don't we come back later and have appetizers? I'll bring them. We want to head over and see the stadium and track down Mitch for lunch. How late are you open, sweetie?"

"Only until five tonight. My hours will get longer when business picks up."

"Well, then, let's do appetizers and then go out to dinner," her mother suggested. "Don't you agree, Paul?"

He nodded. "I'll call Mitch and see if he and Nicolina can join us. I'm sure Mia will want to come too."

"Sounds good!" Addison said. "I'm beyond excited to see you both." She walked them to the door and did another happy dance, but then paused. Should she invite Reid? Would asking him to meet her parents be too forward? And what would her parents think about her already seeing someone new?

Addison walked over and sat down in the big chair where Reid had massaged her feet. She couldn't walk past it without thinking of him.

"Hey there, Addie. Why are you looking so glum?"

Addison looked up to see Mia walking toward her. "Do I look sad?"

Mia sat down on the ottoman. "Well, more like pensive. Dad just called and said that your parents are in town."

"You just missed them."

"Well, then, why the sad puppy-dog face? Aren't you glad to see them?"

"Yes, I'm super-pumped! Mom always did like surprises. What brings you here?"

"Oh, I have someone interested in a wedding. I could have called but I wanted to get out of the office for a little bit. After losing in extra innings last night both Noah and Ty were grumpy."

" I still haven't used the tickets that Reid and I won. I've been meaning to do that."

Mia reached inside her purse. "Here's a schedule."

"Hey, bring me a stack and I'll put them on the front counter."

"Super idea. I'll do that. Speaking of cutie-pie Reid, how are things going? Does your pensive mood have anything to do with him?"

Addison shifted in the seat and nodded slowly. "I can't make up my mind whether to invite him to appetizers and dinner tonight."

"Why? Because you think it will freak Reid out?"

Addison played with the fringe on a throw pillow. "Yes, maybe, and my mom and dad might think I've gone off my rocker, already seeing someone."

Mia reached over and gave Addison a shove. "Would you just listen to yourself?"

"What do you mean?"

"Let me ask you something. Do you want Reid there tonight?"

Addison nodded. "Yes," she answered softly.

"Then don't worry whether Reid will get freaked-out. If he does then you know where you stand with him right now. Knowing is so much better than wondering. And as for your parents? You need to remember to please yourself, not everyone else."

"I know . . . I *know*. Habits are hard to break, Mia." She put her fingertips to her temples. "This is why I should have taken a break from guys, like I told myself."

"Life just doesn't work that way. Look, and remember this: If your parents do voice concern or even disapproval, it's out of love so don't get mad at them. But ultimately, it's your choice."

"How'd you get so smart?"

Mia sighed through her grin. "Made lots of mistakes and cared about all the wrong stuff. Like having a closet full of shoes. Because my dad showed his love for me by buying me gifts I thought that things—possessions—made me happy. In the end, Addison, all we want is each other." She started fanning her face. "Oh boy, this is going to make me cry!" She swiped at a tear.

Addison leaned over to give her cousin a hug. "I've missed you so much. Thanks for being here for me."

"Hey, Reid might not give you the answer you want, and Uncle Paul and Aunt Mel might balk a little bit, but they are two of the most nonjudgmental people I know."

"Why is love so scary? It feels like I'm jumping off of a cliff."

"Because it means so much to us. But sometimes you just have to go for it. Like Cam says, you have to swing for the fences if you want to hit a homerun, but that also means you'll strike out."

"I'm sooo damn tired of striking out."

Mia stood up and acted as if she were holding a baseball bat. "You just have to keep swinging!" She swished her arms through the air and put a hand to her forehead and pretended like she were watching the flight of the ball. "Would you look at that? Homerun!"

Addison giggled. "You've been spending way too much time at the baseball park."

"I know. That's why I came over here." She clasped her hands together and grinned. "Oh, I almost forgot. Nancy Walker is the woman I wanted to tell you about. She just got engaged!"

"A friend of yours?"

Mia nodded. "She's the secretary over at the city building. I met her when I bailed Cam out of jail."

"That just sounds so wrong."

"Yeah, quite a story to tell our grandchildren, right? 'Grandpa and I met when he came to my rescue after tossing a Coke into a customer's face. Oh yeah, and then I jumped on the asshat's back and tried to pull his ears off. I bailed Grandpa out of jail, we got stuck in an elevator together, and the rest is history.'"

"Mia, you crack me up." Addison laughed. "So, Nancy the secretary is getting married?"

"Oh yes . . . I got a bit off track. I do that a lot. Drives Cam crazy. Nancy has been in love with Tucker, the maintenance man at the city building, for, like, forever. Nancy gave Tucker such puppy-dog eyes when I was waiting for Cam. I told her that she should, you know, flirt a little. She said some nonsense about that ship having sailed ages ago but I saw them out together not long afterward. Isn't that just the coolest thing? And now they're getting married! Nancy and Tucker are tying the knot." She raised her hands above her head. "I just love it. Anyway, Nancy proudly showed me her ring when I saw her at Wine and Diner, eating lunch the other day. I told her she'd better invite me! And then I gave her one of your cards."

"So, do you think they'll want something simple?"

"Oh no." Mia waved a hand through the air. "Nancy said that Tucker wants her to have her dream wedding. When I told her about the barn renovation she thought that setting would be perfect. They both grew up in Cricket Creek so it should be a fairly large reception. They're talking next spring."

"Their story is so romantic! I'll make a note of it and tell Sara. So, I guess I shouldn't give up, then, huh?"

"Exactly."

"Well, Reid is still skeptical, but at this rate and with some good publicity, I think that next spring we'll be pretty much booked up."

Mia nodded her agreement. "Dad is really trying hard to find a photographer. I wish Uncle Paul lived closer. Your dad does some wonderful work."

"Maybe he knows someone. We should bring it up tonight."

"Speaking of, I need to get back to the stadium or I'll end up staying late, and I don't want to miss a minute visiting tonight."

Addison stood up. "I need to get back to work too."

"Hey, Addie, I didn't mean to get into your business. I just want to see you happy. Your deserve it."

"No, I'm so glad you stopped in. I needed someone to talk to. I'm going to invite Reid. And you were right, you know."

"About what?"

"It's all about the kiss."

Mia's smile turned soft and dreamy. "Yeah, it sure is."

24

Head over Heels

SARA SAT DOWN ON THE FRONT PORCH SWING NEXT TO
Reid and handed him a glass of sweet tea. "Why are
you staring at the cell phone like it's a snake about to
strike?"

"I just listened to a voice mail from Addison." He
looked up from the phone and took a swallow of the
cold tea, letting it cool his parched throat. The weather
had turned considerably hotter, leaning more toward
summer than spring. "Damn, that's good. Mom still
makes the best tea, strong but not bitter and not too
sweet. How does she do that?"

Sara gave him a deadpan look. "Forget about the tea.
What did Addison say?"

Reid inhaled a deep breath and blew it out. "Her parents are in town for the night. She wants me to have
appetizers at her place and then go out to dinner with
them."

Sara raised her arms in the air. "So?"

"What do you mean . . . so? Dinner with her parents?
Oh, and Mitch Monroe, his wife, Nicolina, and Mia are
going to be there."

"Again ... so? You're not intimidated by them, are you?"

Reid gave her a scowl. "No, of course not. I mean, it did cross my mind that Addison would never be interested in a country boy like me, but I've gotten over that."

"Good, because that's nonsense. Not only that, but did you forget that you graduated from the University of Kentucky with honors?"

"I mean, I'd really like to meet Melinda Monroe, but ..." He took another drink of his tea and sighed once more.

"But what?" Sara rocked the swing back and forth, waiting.

"Stop swinging."

"It a swing, Reid. It's what you're supposed to do."

"No, I'm serious. I don't feel like swinging."

Sara planted her feet on the ground, making the swing come to an abrupt halt. "You wouldn't be so testy if you'd just stop fighting this tooth and nail."

"I know." Reid nodded. "Don't get me wrong. I'm starting to have some hard-core feelings for her."

"You're in love with her."

Reid glanced at Sara. She knew him inside out so there wasn't any reason to deny it. "Yeah, I am."

"Let me guess: Meeting the parents puts a serious spin on your relationship with Addison and it scares the pants off of you."

Reid looked at his tea, wishing it were something stronger. "I'm not scared, exactly. I'm worried."

"About what?"

"Addison's been through so much. I don't want to cause her any more heartache. Maybe I need to slow this thing down."

"I think I know what's going on here and I feel like it's partly my fault. I called you out on not being here for the family, thinking all the while that you were living a cushy life when you were struggling to save your clients from financial ruin. You've had the weight of the world

on your shoulders way too long. Just live your life, Reid.
Addison wouldn't have invited you if she didn't want you
there." She patted his leg. "I might be a teeny bit preju-
diced but I think Addison is one lucky girl to have you in
her life."

He shrugged and took another swig of tea. "I'm being
an idiot, aren't I?"

"Funny how you can read my mind. I guess it's part of
being a twin," Sara said with a small smile. "Now go take
a shower. You're a little gamey."

Reid got up but then gave the swing a shove, making
it swing wildly back and forth.

"Hey, I almost spilled my tea!" Sara shouted, just
when Braden walked out the door.

Braden looked in their direction and shook his head.
"You two will never change."

"Where are you going, smelling all good and with gel
in your hair?" Sara asked.

"I don't have gel in my hair."

Sara rolled her eyes. "You're going to be spittin' some
game at the ladies. Oh wait. Are you seeing Ronnie?"

"Not tonight. I'm just up to Sully's to shoot some
pool," Braden replied. "Wanna come, Reid?"

"Thanks, but I'm heading over to Addison's," Reid
replied, giving Sara a silent *don't-say-anymore* look.

"Don't forget, you're playing Farmer Braden tomorrow.
Dad has a doctor's appointment. So don't be out too late."

Braden shook his head. "You're not my mom."

"Thank God," she muttered, as she walked down the
steps. "Hey, did you just flip me off?"

"I merely waved good-bye," Braden called back to
her.

Reid had to laugh. He'd missed the banter between
his siblings.

"Don't encourage him," Sara grumbled, but she had a
smile on her face. "Why do I love you guys so much?"
She stood up and gave Reid a hug. "We need to get Jeff
home sometime soon."

"I think Braden said Jeff might have a gig at Sully's coming up. That would be cool for us all to be together."

Reid nodded. "Yeah, it would."

Sara watched Braden drive off in a cloud of dust. She shook her head. "I wish he'd settle down a little. Find a girlfriend."

"I asked and Braden told me he dates, even though he said it's called *hanging out* or *talking*. Who knew that dating was an old-school term?"

"Well, I wish he'd *hang out* with something other than eye candy and find someone with substance."

"I'm sure he will. Well, I'm going to head on over and shower."

"Let me know how it goes. Just have fun, okay?"

Reid nodded. "I've been trying to take that leap of faith you keep talking about. It's not easy."

"We're all a work in progress, Reid. But I know one thing: It sure is good to see you smile again."

"Feels good too." He gave Sara a quick hug and then headed over to his truck.

Later while Reid showered, he thought about how he'd been living his life over the past few years. Looking back, the collapse of the economy had been boldly written on the wall. Melinda Monroe had tried to forewarn the public but in the midst of a boom no one wanted to believe a naysayer. During the worst of the recession Reid had lain awake at night, wondering how to salvage the savings of those who had entrusted him with their hard-earned money. Anxiety became his constant companion, sucking the life right out of him. "That and your stubborn pride," Reid grumbled at his reflection as he shaved his chin.

But Sara was right. Coming home had pumped joy back into his life, making him realize that his family should have been his lifeline all along. He would never make that mistake again. At this point he couldn't imagine moving away again but he couldn't just help Braden out on the farm forever. He would have to find a way to make money. While Reid wiped off the traces of shaving cream with a warm washcloth, he thought about all of the time he wasted being lonely and miserable. "No more wasting time." Blinking at his reflection, Reid held on to the edge of the sink and decided that he needed to tell Addison about his growing feelings for her. Surely she knew from his actions but he suddenly felt the need to tell her. They'd never had a conversation about their future, but it was time.

After putting on his best pair of khaki pants and a dark blue oxford shirt, Reid realized he was early and decided to stop at Flower Power and pick up a bouquet of flowers. He whistled all the way to his truck, feeling lighthearted and happy. He had just pulled into the parking lot of Wedding Row when his cell phone rang. After pulling it out of his pocket he smiled. "Hi, Addison. What's up?"

"I need your help."

Reid sat up straighter at her urgent tone.

"Everything okay?"

"Well, I think I've bitten off more than I can chew. Oh no! Wait!"

Reid pressed the phone closer to his ear, trying to hear what was going on in the background. He heard some clattering noises, a *clank*, and a muffled curse. With his heart pounding Reid got out of the truck and decided to pass on the flowers. "Addison?" he shouted into the phone, but when he reached From This Moment, the doors were already locked. "Addison? Are you okay?" he asked when he heard another clatter. He jogged around to the back entrance to her apartment and took the stairs two at a time. Luckily, the door was unlocked. He swung it open and sprinted into the apartment. "Addison?" He spotted her in the kitchen.

"Yes. Oh sorry," she said into the phone. "I had an emergency."

Reid hurried over, startling her when she turned

around and spotted him standing there. He had to grin. She had a streak of flour on her cheek and a dusting in her hair and her kitchen was a huge mess.

"Just when the cupcakes were done, the stew started boiling over. I was trying to get everything under control but then I tripped over the cord to the mixer and, well . . ." She raised her palms upward and shook her head. "I am one hot mess."

Reid would have laughed but her bottom lip trembled. "Ah, baby. What can I do?"

She sniffed and leaned her head against his chest. "I hurried up and finished early in the shop and decided I'd surprise everyone with a home-cooked meal. I went to the grocery store and picked up the items I needed and I was so pumped, but I guess it has been a while since I've cooked for this many people."

"How long is a while?"

"Well, like, in . . . never. I mean, you wouldn't know it by the state of the kitchen but I'm a decent cook, but usually just for my parents and me. Stew seemed like an easy thing to do but then I got ambitious and decided to bake cupcakes for dessert. Chocolate cupcakes are my dad's favorite. Then I thought I'd throw together some biscuits." She angled her head over to the mixing bowl. "And I wanted icing . . . and suddenly I was in way over my head," she said, drawing out the word *head* in a sorrowful tone.

"Oh, baby . . . don't worry, I'll help. Just tell me what needs to be done and I'm on it." He tilted her chin up and gave her a tender kiss. "Let's turn on some music, open a bottle of wine, and have some fun with this."

She smiled. "You're a lifesaver."

Reid pushed a tear away with his thumb and then kissed her again. "You taste like chocolate."

"I swiped some of the cake batter from the bowl," she said in such a guilty tone that Reid couldn't hold back his laughter.

"Do you have any idea how cute and lovable you are?"

Addison inhaled a deep breath. "Well, I have a confession to make."

Reid kissed the tip of her floured nose. "What's that?"

"I wanted to impress you with my mad skills."

"Trust me, you already have."

When she smiled, Reid almost told her that he loved her, but he held back.

"So, you'll help?"

"There's nothing I wouldn't do for you," he admitted, coming as close to a profession of love as he dared.

"Where have you been all my life?" Her tone was teasing but there was something in her eyes that made Reid's heart pound. She felt the same way! But then she quickly turned around, as if not wanting him to see the truth in her eyes. Reid understood. She was gun-shy. He needed to be patient.

"Waiting for you," he answered in an equally light, teasing tone. When she turned back around and looked at him neither of them said another word, but love was hanging in the air between them. "Put me to work, Addison. With our big family, Mom puts us to work in the kitchen. I know my way around. Speaking of, your family knows I'll be here, right?"

Addison nodded. "They know that you're Sara's brother and that we've been seeing each other."

"Does that concern them?" He tried not to feel any anxiety about her response.

Addison put her palms on his chest. "My parents love me and want me to be happy. That's all they care about. Just be yourself."

"That's all I know how to be," Reid said. No matter what happened in his life he'd never go back to withdrawing into a shell, hiding out from life.

"Perfect."

Less than an hour later the cupcakes were frosted, the stew simmered, and the biscuits were on the cookie sheet, ready to pop in the oven when the time arrived. "You need to let me clean up while you shower."

Addison wrapped her arms around his waist and looked up at him. "There is nothing sexier than a man doing dishes."

"I think you just talked me into doing the dishes every night," he said. "Well played."

She giggled.

Reid shooed her toward her bedroom. "Now go. I've got it under control." As he watched her walk toward her bedroom Reid realized that he liked this domestic spin that cooking for company put on their relationship. He'd never even considered what it would feel like to be married.

Until now.

He waited for a shot of fear or apprehension but it failed to come. He smiled as he dried a bowl and put it in a cabinet. Nice . . .

About thirty minutes later Addison walked back into the kitchen, wearing white jeans and a billowy teal blouse belted at the waist. She wore her hair up in a loose bun. The only thing flashy was the diamond tennis bracelet that she'd told him was a gift from her parents for her twenty-first birthday.

"What?" Addison asked, making Reid realize he'd been staring.

"You're gorgeous, Addison. I can't take my eyes off of you."

She came over and smoothed her hands up his chest. "I know the feeling. I can't keep my eyes or my hands off of you. It's going to be tough not being all over you when the company arrives."

Reid groaned and was about to dip his head for a kiss when the doorbell chimed. He felt a slight twinge of nerves, but when the Monroe clan came into the room, full of hugs and laughter and introductions, he felt at ease. Addison took a tray of appetizers from her father.

"I brought artichoke dip and pita chips," Mia said. "It's still warm."

"My favorite," Addison said.

Mitch handed Reid a bottle of bourbon. He looked at the label. "Pappy Van Winkle's twenty-three-year-old? Are you kidding me? That's as smooth as it gets."

"Oh, he's been on the bourbon trail twice," Nicolina said with a shake of her head.

"I love the history behind the distilleries," Mitch declared, drawing a laugh from Paul.

"Yeah, right. You love the bourbon."

"What's not to love?" Mitch asked, but then looked at Reid. "You're a Kentuckian. You know what I'm talking about."

Reid nodded. "I sure do. There's nothing better than a fine bourbon." He held up the bottle. "This one is one of the finest. Wheat is used rather than rye, giving it a sweeter taste. This twenty-three is really hard to come by."

Nicolina laughed again. "He loves telling people he's a Kentuckian now."

"Makes me feel badass, like on *Justified*," Mitch said, making them all laugh.

"Something smells amazing," Melinda said. "Sweetie, did you cook dinner?"

"A big pot of beef stew. Reid came to my rescue and helped." Addison nodded. "I thought we could talk easier here than in a noisy restaurant. Is that okay?"

"Perfect," Melinda answered, making Reid notice the similarities between mother and daughter.

"I hoped Bella might be able to come," Addison said to Nicolina.

"Mitch couldn't take another day of seeing her sad face and insisted that she fly out to Iowa to see Logan play. He's with the Iowa Cubs now, hoping to move up from the farm team to Chicago."

"Impressive." Addison peeled back the foil from a veggie tray and put out cocktail plates. "I will forever be a Cubs fan. So, Uncle Mitch, the Cricket Creek Cougars aren't affiliated with Major League Baseball?"

"No, it's an independent professional league," he answered. "Noah Falcon wanted to give players a second shot at making the minor leagues. Logan, for example, was drafted into the minors but came back too soon from an injury, almost ruining his career. Noah and Ty gave him a second chance and it paid off."

"Cam came with a bad attitude and a chip on his shoulder," Mia said. "He just needed someone to believe in him."

"The Cougars scout smaller schools, hoping to find talent that gets passed over," Mitch continued. "Of course, only a small percentage of them will make it, but the rest get to enjoy playing competitive baseball for a few more years."

After breaking out the bourbon the men chatted about baseball and the women toured the apartment. Reid knew that Addison's parents were being polite and casual but he could tell that they were checking him out. He didn't blame them because he would do the same thing.

After dinner they lingered over cupcakes and coffee. Reid enjoyed talking about finance with Melinda. He found the entire family entertaining, friendly, and fascinating. Other than getting Addison alone, he was actually sorry to see the evening end.

"I wish you were in town longer," Addison said as the company headed for the door.

"Me too," Melinda admitted. "We'll be back as soon as we can. I'm really impressed with your shop, Addison. With the popularity of lavish weddings From This Moment should do quite well. Uncle Mitch and I were chatting earlier and I'm thinking this is just the beginning . . . but we'll talk about that later."

Reid frowned, wondering what Melinda was referring to, but the exit turned to tearful hugs and he put his worry aside. As soon as the door closed Reid pulled Addison into his arms. "Don't get me wrong. I think your parents are amazing people and I enjoyed your family, but I've wanted you all evening long."

Addison wrapped her arms around his neck. "Well, now you get me all night long. Are you up for it?"

Reid pulled her close. "All it will take is one kiss."

"Are you going to kiss me?"

"Remember, all you ever have to do is ask." He grinned. "But that ripping-off-my-shirt thing works for me too."

Addison laughed but then she fell silent and looked up at him with those brown eyes. "Kiss me, Reid."

Reid dipped his head and met her mouth in a sweet kiss that quickly heated up into something hot and hungry. Groaning, laughing, they pulled, tugged, and shed clothing, leaving a trail all the way to the bedroom. They fell onto the bed in a heap of tangled arms and legs, kissing with a wild, all-consuming passion. Reid had never kissed this way, felt this way, and when he entered the welcoming heat of her body he knew that he never wanted to be with another woman. Nothing could compare to . . . this.

Reid made love to Addison deeply, intensely. He watched the play of emotion on her beautiful face through half-lidded eyes drinking in every detail. And when she slid her arms to the side and fisted her hands in the covers the sight would remain in his memory forever.

25

Against the Wind

"ANGIE, YOU PROBABLY DON'T REMEMBER WHEN THIS WAS done by pulling hair through a rubber cap," Maggie said, while the cute hairstylist slid a foil beneath a few strands of Maggie's hair.

Angie dipped a fat brush into a bowl, painting and weaving with quick efficiency. "No, but I've actually had clients that ask for it and call it having their hair frosted."

Maggie chuckled. "Well, I guess I'm dating myself. But, then again, when I was a teenager I used to spray Sun-In onto my hair. Oh, how times have changed. I wonder if they still make that stuff."

"Products are so much better now. A lot less harsh on your hair, for sure." Angie gazed at Maggie in the mirror. "Well, I think you're ready to process, my soon-to-be blond bombshell. Would you like a magazine to read?"

"Please." Maggie nodded and the foils clinked together, sounding like a whispering wind chime.

Angie handed her a *People* magazine. "Sorry. It's a few weeks old. I'll see if I can find another one."

"Don't worry. This is fine." With a dismissive wave Maggie smiled, then started flipping through the pages, looking at the pictures and shaking her head at Lindsay Lohan's latest blunder and wondering why the public found the Kardashians so fascinating. The photo of shirtless Huge Jackman had her pausing to appreciate his amazing chest.

"Oh, very nice." Angie looked over Maggie's shoulder as she unfolded a foil and checked the progress. "I'm kinda into older dudes. Don't know why."

"Older dudes are sexy too," Maggie said. *Very sexy,* she thought with an inner sigh. When her mind drifted to the passionate night of lovemaking with Richard she almost had to fan her face with the magazine. Having lived through some tough times in her life—her mother's desertion, her father's wrath, single parenting, and fighting breast cancer—Maggie always drew inward for strength and forged on with a brave smile, even when she was shaking on the inside. She'd always longed for but never really thought that love would find her. Having Richard come into her life at this stage of the game felt like a miracle to Maggie and she treasured every single minute with him.

Love, it seemed, hadn't passed her by after all.

Maggie closed her eyes and swallowed hard. Richard had said he had something special planned for tonight. She simply could not wait to find out what he had in mind, but Maggie had the feeling it was going to be amazing. And if he told her that he loved her she was going to say it back because she was head over heels in love with Richard Rule.

Giddy with happiness, Maggie flipped the pages of *People*, not really seeing what she was looking at, but something gave her pause. Wait.... She turned back a few pages, thinking she'd spotted Addison Monroe. "Yes," she murmured, and took a sip of her water. Sure enough, there was the pretty little bridal shop owner. Addison was on tiptoe, kissing a leather-clad, long-haired, bearded man. Because Addison was so down-to-earth Maggie had forgotten that she was the daughter of famous finance guru Melinda Monroe, but who was the guy? He looked old enough to be her father. Maggie read the caption beneath the photo: *After recently breaking off her engagement to Garret Ruleman, rumors are flying that Addison Monroe is having an affair with none other than Rick Ruleman, Garret's rock-legend father. Both Addison Monroe and Rick Ruleman have been suspiciously absent from the LA area, while Garret has been dropping hints that the rumors are indeed true.*

Maggie shook her head. Addison sure didn't seem like the kind of girl who would do such a sordid thing. She was about to turn the page but there was something about the picture of Rick Ruleman that made her heart start to race. The hair might be long, he might have a beard, but she would know that smile, those eyes anywhere. Rick Ruleman.

Richard Rule.

"Oh my God," she whispered. The picture suddenly swam before her eyes and she felt as if her heart was going to jump right out of her chest. Her breath came in shallow gasps.

She had to get out of the salon before she fell to pieces.

Rick Ruleman had been hiding out in Cricket Creek . . . in plain sight. Of course, minus the hair, beard, and leather he looked like a totally different man. Did Addison Monroe know? Was Addison still seeing him on the sly and dating Reid Greenfield just for show? Was Reid being played for a fool as well? Questions buzzed around in her head like angry hornets stinging her brain with each horrible speculation.

"How we doing here?" Angie's cheerful voice barely registered. She opened one of the foils. "Oh yeah, looking good!"

Maggie nodded, unable to speak. She took a long breath and dug deep, thinking she'd spent most of her life hiding her anguish, her sorrow. She could do it again.

"Let's get you to the sink for a rinse and then I'm

going to make you love your hair. Hope you're doing something special tonight, because you're going to be one hot chick." She smiled. "Not that you're not already gorgeous."

Maggie managed to smile and go through the motions, answering questions and listening to Angie chatter away, but on the inside her heart thudded so hard that her chest ached. When she laughed at one of Angie's jokes Maggie's voice sounded as brittle as she felt. She wouldn't have been surprised if when she stood up from the chair her body would shatter into a million pieces.

"You're being awfully quiet, Maggie. Don't you like your hair?"

"Oh . . . oh no! I love it, Angie. My mind is just wandering off. I truly love it."

Angie gave her a smile edged with relief. "You had me worried for a hot minute."

Maggie paid and gave Angie a nice tip, sorry that she made the sweet girl fret. She blinked in the bright sunshine thinking that just a couple of hours ago she'd been so excited about her evening with Richard. Her hand actually shook as she opened the door of her SUV and for a couple of minutes she simply sat behind the wheel, trying to maintain her composure.

When Maggie pulled into Wedding Row she didn't even know how she arrived there. After getting out of her SUV she absently locked the doors and then glanced at From This Moment, wondering if she should go in and confront Addison. She inhaled deeply, trying to find the gumption, but came up empty. Instead, she walked on wooden legs up to her apartment, dropped her purse to the floor with a solid *thud*, kicked off her shoes, and then sank onto the sofa with a cry of utter despair.

Maggie rarely allowed herself the luxury of tears, or maybe the well had dried up long ago. After her mother left, Maggie would sit by the window, waiting, hoping for her to return, and then cry herself to sleep at night, holding the red teddy bear, the last gift her mother had given her. Looking back Maggie wondered if her mother had been bipolar. There were no words of comfort from her father but he was so consumed by anger that she supposed there wasn't room for any other emotion. Back then no one spoke about mental illness and perhaps if they had known, understood, her mother could have been helped. Instead she simply disappeared.

Maggie masked her pain with bright smiles and a sunny disposition, hoping to win her father over. In truth, getting pregnant with Tristan had been her escape, a blessing in disguise. She showered her sweet little boy with love and he gave it back freely.

The need to talk to Tristan now was so keen that Maggie shuffled over to her purse and dug out her cell phone. She returned to the sofa and stared at the phone. She refrained. Tristan was so happy, so content, that Maggie didn't want to do anything to bring him down. Still, she considered calling her son simply to hear the reassuring sound of his voice and to remind herself of the blessings in her life.

And then the phone rang, buzzing in her hand, nearly scaring her out of her skin. Maggie looked down. *It's Richard.* Her heart thudded. It wasn't Richard but Rick Ruleman. "No way," Maggie grumbled, and tossed the phone onto the cushion, but then glanced at it when it beeped, indicating a new voice mail. She thought about listening but didn't want to subject herself to hearing his voice or his lies.

With sheer determination, Maggie refused to shed a tear. She should be on her way to his cabin soon and she wondered what he would think when she failed to show up. Would he end up on her doorstep? Did he really have an affair with his son's fiancée? The fact that he'd moved to Cricket Creek pointed to a big, fat yes. Maggie laughed without humor. Wow ... what must Richard think of Maggie's middle-aged body compared to someone young and lovely like Addison?

Covering her face with her hands, Maggie shook her

head. She thought about getting her laptop out and Googling Rick Ruleman in an effort to learn more about his past but then squashed the urge. Maggie knew from experience that curiosity could eat you alive. For a long time mysteries had plagued her. She wondered what had happened to her mother. She'd wanted to know who Tristan's father was. It wasn't until the breast-cancer scare that she pushed those negative thoughts from her mind and chased them from her life.

"Just forget about him and go on with your life," Maggie said, so she could hear the words out loud. The pain, however, felt jagged and raw and she knew why. She'd let down her guard and for a few achingly sweet weeks she had believed that she had finally found love. For the first time in her life instead of running against the wind she'd been walking on air! All along she'd thought Richard was the real deal when in truth everything about him was a complete lie.

Maggie vowed to forget about him and throw herself into her work. She'd refuse his calls and pray that he didn't have the nerve to show up on her doorstep.

26
Long Time Coming

RICK BANGED ON MAGGIE'S DOOR, NEARLY CRAZY WITH fear. When she didn't show up for dinner and failed to answer his calls, worry got the best of him and he headed over here. He saw her SUV parked out back, so she must be home, and yet she wouldn't answer the door. What if she'd fallen or hurt herself? He banged again. "Maggie? Are you in there? Baby, I'm worried. If you don't open up I'm going to call the police or something." He shoved his fingers through his hair and waited. He called her cell but it went to voice mail. He was about to call 911 when his phone indicated a text message from Maggie. He opened it.

Please leave.

Why? What did I do? Whatever it is I'm sorry, he typed back.

I know who you are. You lied to me. Please leave.

Rick sank down onto the top step of the deck and stared at the phone.

I'm sorry, he typed again. Please open the door. Let me explain.

I never want to see you again.

Rick read her reply with growing despair. I will sit here until you open the door. Do you think I'd be here if I didn't care?

Rick stared at the screen, waiting for what seemed like an eternity for her to reply. When he heard the creak of the back door opening, his heart started pounding. He stood up so fast that he nearly lost his balance and had to grab the railing for support. "May I come in?"

Maggie gave him a curt nod. "Against my better judgment."

Rick followed Maggie into the apartment. She sat down in a chair and waved her hand toward the sofa. It hurt that she made the effort to stay as far away from him as she could. He wanted to drag her into his arms so badly that he had to clench his fists in order not to do so. He sat down, wondering where to begin. She looked so beautiful and so forlorn that it tore at his heart.

"Are you having an affair with Addison Monroe?" Maggie asked bluntly.

"No! God . . . no." He thought that damned rumor had died down. "How . . . Why would you think that?"

She shifted in her seat. "I was getting my hair done and saw a picture of Rick Ruleman, you, kissing her," she said with a flicker of embarrassment. "The caption read that you were the reason for the breakup of Addison and your son." Maggie shrugged. "I'm not one to read or believe that stuff, but, Richard"—she shook her head—"I mean, Rick, the fact that you moved to Cricket Creek soon after Addison arrived, well, made me wonder if the rumor was true."

Rick scooted to the edge of the sofa, wanting to reach over and grab her hands. "It's not," he said firmly. "It was some stupid idea my publicist came up with to keep my badass image intact. I fired him."

"Why didn't you come out and refute the rumor?"

Rick closed his eyes and swallowed. "I tried, Maggie." He sighed. "But then Garret made matters worse when he led the public to believe the worst."

"Your son would do that to you?" She appeared appalled.

"I'm sure it was in an effort to fuel ratings for his reality show."

"That's horrible."

Rick felt compelled to defend Garret. "I haven't been the best of dads," he admitted quietly. "I'm hoping to change that."

"So, I'm confused. Why are you in Cricket Creek if it has nothing to do with Addison?"

"It did. See, it was my intention to personally apologize to her and lie low at the same time. But she was faring so well that I didn't want to do anything to upset her." He shoved his fingers through his hair. "And maybe I was too ashamed to show my face. Maggie, after this all went down I took a hard look at my sorry-ass life and knew it was time to make some serious changes."

"Altering your appearance doesn't change you on the inside."

"I know." Unable to witness the hurt, the disappointment, in her eyes Rick looked down at the floor for an agonizing moment. Finding the courage, he raised his gaze to meet hers. "I admit that I haven't been a good father . . . good person for a long time. But, Maggie, I want to live differently. I want to reach out to Garret. I have plans that I've been working on for a while. I was going to tell you about all of it tonight." He waited for a heartbeat and then said, "Will you come back to the cabin with me?"

"No, Richard." She shook her head slowly.

"Why not?"

"Because you've been lying to me the entire time." She raised her hands upward. "I don't even know who you are. I'm sorry, but we're through," she said quietly but firmly. "You should . . . you should go."

"I'm so sorry." Rick nodded. "I understand how you must feel." He stood up. He wanted so badly to tell her how much he loved her and about the plans he had for the future. Big plans that he'd been so excited to reveal. "I'll leave, Maggie, but I want to thank you for at least letting me in so that I could attempt to explain things and to make sure that you were okay." He angled his head. "But I will tell you one thing that you're wrong about."

"What?" she asked softly.

"You know me better than anyone." With that, he walked to the door and let himself out. He stood on the back deck for a moment, holding on to the railing until his legs were steady. He hoped that she'd rush to the door and tell him that none of that mattered, only that they'd found each other. But she didn't.

And so he left.

But as Rick drove back toward the cabin his despair turned into determination. He loved Maggie McMillan and he was going to show her just how much he cared for her. But first he needed to put into action the plans he'd been working on for the last couple of weeks. His plans included his son, Garret.

"And it's about damned time," Rick said as he pulled up to the cabin, and felt a little bit better about himself. But after walking inside he felt a pang of sadness. The table was set for the dinner that never happened. Sighing, Rick looked away from the table and headed into the office and sat down at his desk. After gathering his notes he put in a call to Pete Sully. It was time to get the ball rolling.

27

Coming Home

"JEFF!" REID HURRIED ACROSS THE YARD WHEN HE SAW his brother's Ford F-150 come to a stop in front of the house. As soon as Jeff's long legs emerged from the truck, Booker and Little John pounced on him with so much canine love that Jeff started laughing.

"At least somebody missed me," Jeff said with a grin. He pushed past the dogs and gave Reid a bear hug. "How've you been, bro?"

"Good," Reid replied. "What brings you home from Nashville?" Reid asked, and then shook his head. "Wait. Are you the special concert that Sully's been talking about all week? The whole town is buzzing with anticipation. There was speculation it could be either you or Cat Carson."

Jeff hesitated and then tipped his cowboy hat back. "I've been sworn to secrecy but I'll tell you this much: Don't miss it." He hesitated again. "And make sure the whole family is there."

"Are you kidding? I think all of Cricket Creek is going to be there. There's a stage set up with a sound system that looks incredible. They're roasting a pig. Come on, I promise not to tell." Reid gave Jeff's shoulder a shove. "What the hell's going on?"

"If I told you, I'd have to kill you."

Reid sighed. "Okay, damn, you're a tough nut to crack."

"Just get there early. You bringing that girl you've been seeing?"

"I'll bring Addison. She's been talking about it all week too."

"Wow, would you just look at you?"

"What?"

"The mighty Reid Greenfield has fallen in love." Jeff shook his head. "Well . . . well, first Sara and now you. Mom must be happy."

"Hey, hold on, now. I didn't say I was getting married."

Jeff chuckled. "Speaking of that, how is the barn renovation coming along?"

"Ahead of schedule. They've got so many requests that Sara is talking about moving her wedding date up."

Jeff reached down and scratched Booker's ears. "Are you finally on board with the whole thing?"

Reid shrugged and then gave Jeff a wry grin. "Everything I've shot my mouth off about has become a success and this is no exception."

"You were just looking out for Sara."

"My heart has always been in the right place. But listen, Jeff. I'm sorry I didn't encourage you to pursue your singing career years ago. I regret that I took Mom and Dad's side and became part of Team Guilt that tried to keep you here on the farm. You're super-talented. I hope I didn't hold you back."

Jeff shrugged. "It means a lot to me to hear you say that but, in truth, you know how hardheaded I am. The more you preached against it the more I wanted to prove you and everybody else wrong."

Reid nodded but he knew his brother was being generous. "Ahhh, so then you owe your success to me?" He jabbed his thumb at his chest. "Do I get a cut?"

Jeff gave him a shove. "Yeah right. But seriously, make sure you're all at Sully's tonight." Although Jeff sounded causal there was a nervous energy about him that told Reid that whatever was going down was going to be something big.

"Damn, you have me curious. The whole doggone town is buzzing with excitement, no matter where you go. Can you give me a little hint?" He looked at Jeff expectantly. "You know I could probably wrestle it out of you."

"Not anymore, big bro. I work out. And I think I'm taller."

"Well, then, I guess I'll just have to wait. Everybody else is in the house getting ready. There's leftover meatloaf and mashed potatoes in there."

Jeff started hauling some of his stuff out of his truck. "Awesome. I could use some of Mom's cooking."

"I've got to go and shower up before I pick up Addison. I'll see you there. Oh and, Jeff?"

"Yeah?"

"I've still got you by a good inch."

"In your dreams! And I bet I can beat you and Braden arm wrestling."

"You're on!" Reid laughed. It would be good to have all of his siblings together. It sure had been a while.

After a quick shower Reid tugged on some cargo shorts and a blue golf shirt. Since the tail end of spring had started yielding some summerlike weather he dug out his flip-flops, glad to be out of his boots. After tossing a blanket and some lawn chairs in the bed of his truck he headed over to pick up his girl.

"Hey, baby. Aren't you ready?" Reid asked when Addison answered the door in her bathrobe. "Jeff told me it's going to be packed so we'd better get a move on." He leaned in and kissed her.

"Your brother is in town?"

Reid nodded. "Yeah, and he knows what this whole mysterious thing is all about. He wouldn't tell but said that the family should be there. It's definitely more than just a concert. I have a feeling there's going to be some sort of announcement."

"Wow, okay. I'll hurry. I was talking on the phone with my mom and the time got away from me."

"Everything okay?" Reid asked, since Addison seemed a little bit distracted, but she gave him a bright smile.

"Yes, we'll talk about it after the concert," she said. "I'll be ready in just a few minutes. It's still hot out, right?" she called over her shoulder.

"Yeah, perfect night for an outdoor concert."

True to her word Addison emerged from her bedroom less than fifteen minutes later. She wore a deep yellow sundress dotted with white butterflies and carried a white sweater. "I didn't have time to curl my hair."

"Are you kidding? I love it like that." Reid reached over and tucked a silky lock behind her ear. "You look amazing, Addison." He leaned down and kissed her bare shoulder. "Mmmm and you smell so good. I wanna gobble you up," he added with a playful nip. He spanned his hands around her waist and pulled her against his body. "God, I want to kiss you, but if I do I won't be able to stop."

She giggled and then reached up and rubbed her hand against his cheek. "Oh . . . sexy stubble."

"You said you liked it even though my mom will give me crap for not shaving."

"Mmmm, yeah, I like it when you rub—"

"Stop." He put a fingertip to her lips and groaned. "Don't say it. You've already got me half aroused."

"Only half?" She reached over and checked.

Reid laughed and then grabbed her hand. He loved that she had become open and playful with him. Being with her was coming naturally, easily, and he loved it.

He loved *her*.

And tonight he was finally going to tell her.

"You're right. The weather has been calling me outside," Addison commented as they headed for his truck. "I've been looking forward to the concert all day long, and after you told me what Jeff said I'm over-the-top excited."

"You've got me super-excited too." He shot her a wicked grin.

"Oh stop," she said, but the pretty pink color in her cheeks spoke otherwise.

Reid reached over and took her hand and brought it to his lips. After so many years of worry it felt so good to feel happy and as close to carefree as his personality would allow. So much of his mood had to do with the pretty woman sitting in the passenger's seat. "Wow," Reid said when they pulled into the parking lot of Sully's Tavern. "It's already getting packed." The main lot was nearly full but Pete had set up a grass field with additional parking.

Addison looked at him with raised eyebrows. "Seems like this is going to be quite the event."

"Let's hurry so we can get a spot near the stage," he said, and came over to open Addison's door. He handed the blanket to Addison and picked up the chairs. "Pete sure did do this up right," Reid commented. The field that butted up against the parking lot sat on a ridge overlooking the river. Chairs were to the side and colorful blankets were spread across the grass, giving the appearance of a giant patchwork quilt. Children ran around, laughing and chasing one another, while adults stood in groups, chatting and drinking longneck beers. The aroma of barbecue wafted through the air, making Reid's stomach rumble.

"Wow, look at that." Reid pointed to a stage that had been erected at the far end of the field. "I could see it from the road but up close it's even more impressive." Huge speakers flanked each side, telling Reid that this really was going to be something else. Beneath the conversation and laughter was a buzz of anticipation. "This is probably the biggest event in Cricket Creek since the opening day of the stadium."

"Sure looks that way," Addison agreed. "Oh hey, there's your family." She waved to Sara, who spotted them at the same time.

"Follow me," Reid urged, and weaved his way through the crowd, heading for a spot near the stage. They waved to several people, including Maggie, who sat with Tristan and Savannah. Noah Falcon sat with the Cougars baseball team, who were signing autographs for eager children. Mia Monroe tossed T-shirts and baseball caps to the crowd. It seemed to Reid that most of Cricket Creek really was in attendance. He placed the chairs in the row that his mother had saved for them and grinned. "This is something, isn't it?" They were greeted with hugs.

"I got y'all some food," Sara said, and handed them two plates with foil-wrapped sandwiches and bags of potato chips.

"The roast pig is amazing," Braden told them. "I'll go get you guys a couple of beers." He shook off Reid's offer of money. "This one's on me."

"I guess no one got Jeff to tell what in the world is going on?" Reid asked.

"I did my best," his mother admitted. "I even tried to bribe him with his favorite red velvet cake but it was a no-go."

"I told y'all just to be patient," Reid's father said. "We'll know soon enough."

"Not soon enough for Sara," Cody said with a laugh. "Poor little thing had been practically jumping up and down with excitement all day long."

"Can you blame me?" Sara slipped her arm around Cody's waist and looked up at him.

"I sure can't," Addison said as she accepted the ice-cold beer from Braden. "Thanks."

Reid tapped his bottle to hers. "To a memorable night."

A few minutes later a hush fell over the crowd when Pete Sully sauntered onto the stage and grabbed the microphone. "Welcome, everybody, and thanks so much for coming!" He had to put his hands up, waiting for the applause and whistles to die down. "Save your applause, 'cuz you're gonna need it. First, I need to give a huge thanks to Jason Craig and his crew for getting the stage built on such short notice. They worked their tails off. And thanks to my son, Clint, for working nearly around the clock getting this event put together." Pete grinned as he held up his hands once again, waiting for the crowd to quiet down. "Before we get started I want to tell you that I'm gonna have not one but several exciting announcements, so don't even think of going anywhere."

Reid looked at Addison with raised eyebrows. Everybody, even the children, fell silent while Pete paused for dramatic effect.

"This stage," Pete began, "is temporary. Very soon Jason and his crew are going to start on a permanent outdoor arena that will host some amazing talent, drawing from nearby Nashville and beyond. We have to clear some more land but we hope to be up and running by next spring!" He eased his hands in a downward motion for silence. "And I thought it would only be fitting to have one of our own do the honors of singing on this here spot for the very first time. Ladies and gentleman, fresh from Nashville, give it up for Cricket Creek's very own . . . Jeff Greenfield, along with his band, South Street Riot!"

The crowd erupted into wild applause when Jeff and his band walked onto the stage. Jeff grabbed the microphone from Pete and shouted, "How's it goin', Cricket Creek? Y'all ready to party?"

Reid put his pinkie and thumb to his lips and whistled before looking down at Addison. "Jeff sure knows how to work a crowd!"

Addison nodded her agreement. "You got that right!"

"I want to thank Pete and Clint Sully for hosting the first of many concerts to come right here in my hometown of Cricket Creek, Kentucky! We're gonna start off with a cover of Jason Aldean's 'My Kinda Party' to get ya'll up on your feet and then play a few of our own songs. But like Pete said, don't go anywhere because this is just the beginning of what's going to be an amazing night!" Jeff shouted and then signaled for the band to begin.

As predicted the crowd was up on their feet, dancing and singing to the popular song. Nobody even thought about sitting on the lawn chairs or lying on blankets. Reid listened to his brother's voice and smiled. Not too long ago he was just a kid sitting on the front porch, strumming his guitar for friends and family—most of whom were now in the crowd, singing and cheering him on. Jeff had one of those deep, rich, versatile voices that could rock it out or sing a slow, soulful ballad. Reid felt a sense of pride, but a twinge of guilt hit him when he remembered how he had preached against Jeff going off to Nashville. Never again would he ever discourage anyone from pursuing their dreams. *Failing is better than never trying,* Reid thought while tapping his foot to the music. Reid mused that it was funny because Jeff was actually more reserved and quiet than outgoing Braden, but he simply came to life up on the stage, like he owned it.

"How many of y'all ever been so much in love that you couldn't see straight?" Jeff shouted, and was met with cheers, and whistles. Reid grinned when Cody looked at Sara and raised his hand. "The next song is one of our own called 'Outta My Mind with Lovin' You,'" Jeff said, and launched into a heartfelt ballad that had the crowd swaying to the beat while listening to the story the lyrics told. And then, showing their diversity, they slid right into a banjo-filled bluegrass song that had people linking arms and dancing to the fast-paced tune.

Addison came up on tiptoe and said in Reid's ear, "Jeff is amazing. My dad would love to have their music in his store. I'm blown away by how good they are."

Reid smiled and then looked over at his mom and dad, who were beaming with parental pride.

"And the women sure are swooning," Addison added. "Jeff has star quality, for sure."

"Thanks," Reid said, and gave her a quick kiss. His mom caught his eye and gave him a subtle thumbs-up. Instead of shaking his head, Reid nodded his agreement, making her smile.

At the end of the energetic song Jeff tipped his cowboy hat and then raised his hand for silence. "This brings me to the second big announcement of the night. I'm proud and thrilled to announce that my band and I just signed with a record label." He waited for the cheers to die down and then said, "That's only the beginning. Let me introduce rock legend Rick Ruleman to tell you all about it."

There was a heartbeat of stunned silence followed by more wild applause. Reid stood still while his heart raced. He looked down at Addison, but she stared wide-eyed at the stage and seemed as surprised as everyone else at the unexpected news. But the guy that walked onto the stage didn't even begin to resemble the long-haired rocker that Reid remembered. *Wait. . . .* Reid tilted his head to the side. Hadn't he seen this guy a couple of times having lunch at Wine and Diner with . . . Maggie McMillan?

Reid leaned in close to Addison's ear. "Do you know anything about this?"

"I'm clueless, Reid. Truly," she added, and seemed a little bit shaken up.

"Hello there, Cricket Creek, Kentucky! Give it up for the amazing Jeff Greenfield and his band, South Street Riot!" After the cheering died down, he said, "I know I don't look like the Rick Ruleman you're used to seeing so I thought I'd better convince you." He took the electric guitar from a stagehand. He quickly went into one of his complicated guitar riffs that made the audience go wild. "That's from my first hit single, 'Jagged Edge.' But what you don't know is that 'Jagged Edge' was supposed to sound like this," Rick announced, and then signaled for Jeff and his band to join him.

The bluesy, soulful rendition of the famous song was

nothing like the huge hit that made Rick Ruleman a household name. Jeff harmonized, and Reid had to admit that the result was pretty damned awesome, and the crowd sure agreed.

"When my record label wanted hard rock I gave it to them," Rick explained after the song ended, "but my heart has always been in a different place. But when 'Jagged Edge' went gold, then platinum, the stage was set, if you'll pardon the pun," he said, and the audience tittered with laughter. "But now that I'm um ... of a certain age, I finally decided it was time to shed the long hair and leather—and, damn, that leather was hot and I don't mean in a good way," Rick continued, and the crowd laughed again. "I've decided to start my own record label, called My Way Records, and when Pete Sully sent me Jeff's demos I knew I'd found some amazing talent. We've been jamming all week long down at the cabin I've been staying in. With the help of my son, Garret, we'll be scouring the area for more talent and looking for studio musicians. Tonight is just the beginning of great things to come!"

Reid glanced at Addison, who was watching with avid interest. A few people who obviously knew about the rumors looked her way, and he drew her close, putting a protective arm around her in spite of the bit of discomfort he felt at seeing the famous father of her ex-fiancé standing up onstage. And apparently going into business with Reid's brother, not to mention bringing Garret into the fold.

"You might wonder how I ended up in Cricket Creek," Rick continued. "Well, I actually came here to apologize to Addison Monroe, my son, Garret's, ex-fiancée. There were some untrue and ugly rumors that I broke up my son's engagement by having an affair with Addison. The rumor was started by my publicist to create some publicity. I fired him. But when I saw Addison's lovely shop and knew she was flying under the paparazzi radar I decided to do her a favor and keep my distance.

But now I want to give a public apology to Addison Monroe for being pulled into the ugliness of something she had no part of and didn't deserve to be drawn into. Addison and Garret parted friends, and I'm so very pleased that she's doing well in this amazing town of yours!"

Reid tightened his grip on Addison, letting his fingers caress her arm supportively. She had a faint smile on her face but appeared slightly stunned. He could tell that she didn't like the attention, but she nodded and raised one hand in recognition of the apology.

Rick paused for the applause and then said, "And there is one more person that I need to apologize to. Maggie McMillan." He looked in the direction where Maggie stood with Tristan and Savannah. "Maggie, I'm so sorry that I didn't tell you my true identity . . . but, in reality, since I've been living here in Cricket Creek, I've stopped pretending to be someone else and I feel like I've come home." Rick looked at Jeff, who nodded to the band. "Since you won't listen to me, I'm going to cover a song by one of my favorite artists, the late, great Jim Croce." Rick then started singing "I'll Have to Say I Love You in a Song."

When they got to the last stanza Rick said, "Come on, Cricket Creek. Lend your voices and sing along. I need all the help I can get . . ." he said, and smiled down at Maggie, who was clinging to her son's arm while wiping tears with her other hand. When the song ended she blew him a kiss and the audience applauded wildly. "And now I'm going to give the stage back to Jeff Greenfield. There's a woman I need to hug."

28

The Real Deal

AFTER THE CONCERT ADDISON AND REID WERE INVITED to the private celebration being held in Sully's Tavern. While they waited for the party to begin, at Addison's request they sat in Reid's truck so that they could talk. Addison could feel Reid's apprehension and she couldn't really blame him. Rick Ruleman's sudden and altered appearance, along with his plans to build a recording studio, was quite a shocker. But before they could even get to the subject Addison's cell phone rang. "Oh, it's my mother." She looked at Reid.

"You should take it, Addison."

"Hey, Mom, what's up?" Addison answered, and was prepared to tell her mother she would call back later, but her mother's voice sounded even more excited than the conversation they'd had earlier when her mother said she'd wanted Addison to come out and be a guest on her show promoting small business.

"I have some more exciting news, sweetie. You know those pictures your father took of your shop?"

"Yes."

"Well, we were out eating lunch with the Grangers

earlier today and Julia is interested in opening another From This Moment here in LA and perhaps one in her hometown in Houston, Texas. She simply adored the lay-out and the mix of old and new."

"You mean like a franchise?" Addison asked.

"Yes! You could oversee the stores. Wouldn't that be fun?"

Addison frowned. "But I just opened the shop here in Cricket Creek. We don't even know if it will be success-ful. Maybe this is premature," she protested with a glance at Reid.

"Normally I would agree with you, Addison. But with the low interest rates and lots of strip malls begging for business this is the opportune time to go full speed ahead. And with the backing of the Grangers, well, you can't go wrong. Why don't you fly out here next weekend and chat with Julia about the prospect?"

"I . . . um, I don't know. This is so fast and sudden."

"That's how opportunities like these often happen. And they can be gone just as fast. Listen, I'm not trying to push, but you needed to know right away so you could think about it. You need to strike while the iron is hot, though. Call me later and we'll talk, okay?"

"Sure, Mom. I love you. Give Dad a hug for me."

"Love you too, Addison, and I miss you terribly. Bye, now."

Addison ended the call and then turned to Reid. She explained briefly.

"Your mother's right. The timing is perfect," Reid said.

"Not for us, though, Reid. It would mean extensive travel. I'd have to spend most of my time getting the other locations up and running."

He shrugged. "I know that. But this is a huge oppor-tunity and your mother was also right in that these things only come around so often. If you miss out you might never get another chance. This could be huge for you, Addison."

"But . . . but I'm in the middle of so much right here.

I have weddings to plan . . ." Her throat constricted at the thought of leaving him when their relationship was going so well.

"Sara won't have any classes at the farm during the summer break. I'm sure she could fill in at your shop while you're away."

"But she's busy planning her wedding and overseeing the barn renovation."

"The renovations are going smoothly. Believe me, Sara of all people knows how to juggle her time. She is an expert in multitasking."

"But I would miss you too much," Addison said softly, and gave him a trembling smile. She looked at him, thinking of how much time her mother and father lost over the years and it came close to ruining their marriage. She put her hand over his but he withdrew it, making her heart pound. *Please don't do this,* she thought. *Please care about me more than that.*

"Addison, you should go to LA and listen to your mother. She knows her stuff. She won't steer you wrong."

"But what about . . . *us*?" Addison asked in a strained voice.

Reid shifted in the leather seat. He was silent for a long moment and then said, "I've been meaning to talk to you about that."

Addison felt her heart rate speed up. "And?" she asked when he hesitated. She had felt that he'd wanted to tell her that he loved her for a while now. "You can be honest with me, Reid. We've grown so close. Don't hesitate to tell me how you feel," she urged.

"I . . . I'm moving back to Lexington. My firm called and wanted a final answer about whether I'm returning."

Addison swallowed hard and felt the impact of his words like a punch to her gut. "I thought you loved the farm." *I thought you loved me,* she wanted to shout.

"I do, but I came back to help get things under control. They are and then some. I'm not needed any longer. I can return to my job, knowing things are fine here."

"So, when were you going to tell me?" she asked in a shaky voice.

His gaze flicked away. "I was trying to find the right time, I guess."

"And so you thought after this amazing night with your family would be the best time to break it to me?"

"Addison, I had no idea what was going on here tonight."

She nodded, on the verge of tears. "Is this about Rick Ruleman being in town? I really didn't know, Reid."

"I believe you."

"Then—"

"We should get inside."

"Um, I'm not sure I want to go to the party. I have a lot to think about and I would really appreciate it if you would just take me home. Please tell Jeff congratulations for me, okay?" She forced a smile.

Reid nodded. "Sure. I understand."

He drove her back in silence. Absorbed in her thoughts and aching sorrow, Addison didn't speak a word. She hoped the entire way home that Reid would suddenly tell her how much he loved her and couldn't bear it if she weren't in his life. But he didn't.

When he pulled up to her apartment he came around and opened her door. "You don't have to walk me up. I know you want to get back to the celebration."

Something flickered in his eyes and Addison held her breath. "You're right." He leaned in and kissed her on the cheek—*the cheek!*—and her heart shattered.

Once again she'd believed in and let a man into her life, only to have her heart trampled on.

Later, while she sat cross-legged on her bed, reliving the evening, Addison wondered if this really did have anything to do with Rick Ruleman or the announcement that Garret would be working with him. Did Reid think that she'd go running back into Garret's arms? How could he think that?

Addison leaned back against the fluffy pillows and she suddenly had a moment of clarity. This apartment felt like home. She loved running From This Moment and wasn't remotely interested in starting a franchise. She wanted her shop to be personal and one-of-a-kind, not duplicated all over the country. Whether she made piles of money or just enough to get by, she loved her life and she wasn't going to make the mistake of doing something because she didn't want to disappoint her mother, even when it wasn't what she truly wanted. Those days were over. And if Reid cared so little about her that he could just walk away, then she'd overestimated how much he cared for her. How could she have gotten it so wrong yet again?

Unlike the dull ache of disappointment she'd felt with her broken engagements to Aiden and Garret, this felt like a searing pain jabbing at her heart.

Her throat hurt with the thickness of unshed tears and her eyes burned, but she refused to dissolve into a puddle of despair. Instead, she turned off the light, determined to get some sleep and to get on with her life. Her body, however, had different ideas. Addison tossed and turned, looking at the digital alarm clock with increasing anger. She wanted to fall asleep so badly but, in truth, there was something tapping at her brain. She punched the pillow, kicked off the covers, and then got cold and yanked them back up to her chin. She closed her eyes and then realized she was squeezing them shut, and groaned.

"Okay, relax," she whispered, but she knew that part of the problem was that she missed having Reid in her bed. His big, warm body lying next to Addison made her feel safe and loved. Without him she felt a bit lost and lonely. "It just doesn't make sense," Addison murmured with a tired yawn.

And then she sat up so quickly that she knocked pillows to the floor. The missing piece fell into place with a mental *clink*. "Well . . . duh . . ." She smiled slowly as she sank back onto the pillows. Her eyelids suddenly felt heavy and the soft pillow cushioned her head. She would head over to his cabin first thing in the morning and put an end to this stupidity.

Addison opened her eyes and blinked in confusion. Something didn't feel right. Rolling to the side she looked at her alarm clock. "Noon? I slept until noon?" Since it was Sunday the shop was closed, but still . . . she couldn't remember the last time she'd slept in this late. Of course, tossing and turning for hours had had a lot to do with it. But she had a mission and needed to get over to confront Reid with the truth. Tossing back the covers, she hurried to the bathroom and jumped into the shower, rehearsing in her head exactly what she was going to say to him.

Less than two hours later she pulled onto the Greenfield property and was going to head down the lane to Reid's cabin when she spotted Sara, who flagged her down. Addison rolled down her window.

"Reid's not here," Sara said glumly. "He left shortly after breakfast."

"Where did he go?" Addison asked, even though she already knew the answer.

"Lexington." Sara stood back for Addison to get out of the Mustang. As soon as she did Sara gave her a big hug. "I'm sorry he's being such a dipshit. Come on over to the porch. Nobody else is home except for me and the dogs," she said.

Addison gave Booker an absent pat on the head and managed a weak chuckle when Little John came bounding their way.

"Can I get you some sweet tea?"

"Maybe in a minute. Look, Sara, I have to admit that I was floored when Reid told me he was leaving."

Sara nodded. "He told me about the franchise possibility your mother told you about. Are you considering it?"

Addison shook her head hard. "No way. I like the laid-back small-town lifestyle. I love my loft apartment, and I'm looking forward to planning weddings. I don't want to travel all over creation, opening up new shops. I know my mother meant well, but for me there's only one From This Moment. Turning it into a cookie-cutter franchise just feels . . . wrong.

"How'd you come up with that name?"

Addison told her the Shania Twain song story and the dance with Reid. She smiled at the memory. "You know, I asked my cousin Mia how you know when it's the real deal, how you know you're really in love."

"It's in the kiss."

Addison raised her hands skyward. "How come everybody knew but me?"

"Because it's something you have to experience. And you've got that special something with Reid, don't you?"

Addison nodded slowly. "I love him, Sara. With all my heart."

Sara reached up and brushed at a tear and then raised a fist. "I knew it!"

"I need to go after him. Sara, in the wee hours of the morning I figured it all out. Reid pushed me away because he didn't want to hold me back." She put her hand up to her mouth and felt hot tears course down her cheeks. "I know he loves me." She patted her chest. "I just know it. And he let me go because he put me first over his own feelings."

"Which is why you aren't going after him."

"What?" Addison tilted her head to the side. "Why? He needs to know."

"Nope." Sara shook her head. "Let him go back to his desk job. Let him miss you like crazy. In the meantime we have lots of work to do."

"Like what?"

"Planning a wedding, silly girl."

"Yours?"

Sara waved a dismissive hand. "Are you kidding? Between me and Mom we have it all planned down to the very last detail." She tapped Addison on the chest.

"We're planning *your* wedding. The first wedding in the renovated barn needs to be yours."

"Um, but I'm missing something important called a groom."

"A minor detail." Sara grinned. "You haven't lived in Cricket Creek long enough to know that when we want to get something done the whole town bands together."

"But—"

"Do you want to marry my brother?"

"Yes."

Sara put her hands on her hips. "Problem solved."

"But shouldn't Reid be asking me that all important question?"

"I'm his twin. I'm asking for him. And I already know he loves you because he told me. Addison, he was even looking at my engagement ring one night, asking questions. I told him that Nicolina needed to design a ring for you and he agreed."

"He . . . he was talking about buying an engagement ring for me?"

"Yes. So will you marry Reid?"

Addison blinked at Sara and decided to take the bull by the horns. With a laugh, she remembered when she grabbed Reid's shirt and kissed him. "Yes!" Taking charge felt amazing. "Yes, I will marry your brother."

"Jason said that the barn will be ready in one month." She held up her index finger. "Let's get crackin'."

"What about things like a marriage license and all of those pesky little details?"

Sara grinned. "Another perk of living in a small town. I know people. I'll get the paperwork done."

"This is crazy, Sara."

"I know. Isn't it awesome?"

Addison laughed but then grew serious. "I don't want to railroad your brother into something he doesn't want. If he wants to marry me I want him to propose."

"I understand. Let's just set the stage. You saw how Pete had the entire town at Jeff's concert. We'll send out invitations and just call it an open house, a mock wedding to showcase the renovated barn. Invite your parents, giving them the same impression. If everything works out the way I think it will, shit will suddenly get real. . . ."

29

From This Moment

One month later

REID WAS IN A PISS-POOR MOOD. HE DIDN'T WANT TO AT-
tend this so-called mock wedding in the barn but
Sara insisted. His mother jumped on the Team Guilt
bandwagon and so here he was on the road to Cricket
Creek. To make matters even worse, the mock bride was
going to be Addison. Great . . . he could witness the love
of his life wearing a wedding dress while standing at the
altar. He thought about the ring he'd spoken to Nicolina
about and his stomach lurched.

Not cool.

Reid didn't even dare ask who was going to be playing the groom. Seeing Addison say her vows to another
man, even if it was fake, was something he didn't want
in his memory vault. It was pretty simple. He wasn't going to go.

Feeling just slightly better, he took the back way to
his cabin, not wanting to come into contact with Sara or
his mom. He got out of his truck and headed inside, glad
that someone had turned on the air-conditioning. "Yes!"

he said when he opened the refrigerator and found a cold beer. After he finished it, he was going to call Sara and give his regrets. Maybe he'd find a baseball game to watch, spend the weekend at the cabin, and then head back to Lexington.

The thought of returning to the city, however, held little appeal. He knew that he wouldn't be able to stay with the desk job forever, but for now he didn't know what else to do. Being home reminded him of Addison, but it was where he wanted to live. Reid knew one thing: He couldn't bear to lay eyes on Addison. He saw her in his dreams every night but seeing her in person . . . in a wedding gown? No, thank you.

She must be well on her way to planning the franchise, and even though it hurt to lose her he couldn't stand having her give up such an amazing opportunity. It didn't matter that he knew she loved him. Making her businesses take off would take one hundred percent of her dedication. Taking a dream away from somebody was a recipe for disaster in a marriage—or a family—and he wasn't about to do that to her. She spoke of how hard her mother's career had been on her father so she already knew the hardships of separation. He loved her way too much to put her through that, even though it was killing him.

Feeling pretty damned gloomy, he tilted the bottle up to his lips and took a long pull. After the drive the cold beer tasted good, even though it did little to improve his mood. He found the Cincinnati Reds playing Pittsburgh on television and rounded up another beer. "Damn, I've got to call Sara," he said with a wince. She was going to be pissed.

Taking a deep breath, he picked up his cell phone and called her.

"Hey!" Sara said, but instead of being on the phone she came walking through the door.

"Hey, yourself." Reid stood up and gave her a hug.

Sara licked her lips in that way that said she was about to ask him a favor. "Um, I have a tiny favor to ask."

"Sara, your favors are never tiny."

"Okay, I have a big favor to ask of you."

"Shoot."

"Well, you know this mock wedding?"

"About that—"

"The mock groom is . . . um, unable to come, so I thought maybe you could fill in."

"No way. No possible way."

"Please? It would mean a lot to me." She paused and said, "And it would mean a lot to Addison. We've been planning this beautiful wedding for the past month and we don't have a groom."

"Absolutely not."

Sara sighed and then said slowly. "We don't want to leave Addison standing at the altar all alone, *now, do we*?"

Reid set his beer bottle down. There was something in Sara's tone, something in her eyes that had his heart skipping a beat. No way . . . "Sara . . ." he said softly. "Are you kidding me?"

She shook her head slowly back and forth. "Do you love her?"

"Yes, you know I do," he answered gruffly. He closed his eyes and swallowed. "She consumes my thoughts. But—"

"She's not doing the franchise. She never even considered it. Addison loves it here in Cricket Creek. She loves *you*." Sara swiped at a tear. "You big idiot."

He froze. Well, then, why had he spent the last month being miserable? "But surely she's pissed at me for leaving."

"She figured out why and loves you even more for it. Reid, you gave Addison a choice instead of an ultimatum and she chose you. So, what are you waiting for?"

Reid shoved his fingers through his hair while his thoughts scattered everywhere. "But other than doing the books and helping out on the farm, I don't have a job."

Sara shook her head. "Well, baby brother, while you've been missing in action a lot more has gone on than just planning your wedding. The barn-wedding receptions have taken off like wildfire, and Dad is filling in dates with pig roasts for family reunions. Addison's shop is out of space for inventory so she's leasing the smaller space next door for handmade wedding gifts, including quilts made by Mom's quilting bee."

Reid tilted his head. "Wow. But what would I do?"

"Crunch your doggone numbers. Run the business side of things so we creative types can do our thing. And I'm sure your soon-to-be mother-in-law will have some ideas too."

Reid nodded slowly. Everything was falling into place. And the most important part was Addison. "You've got it all figured out."

"Well, somebody had to. Come on, Reid. You've got a wedding to go to."

His eyes widened. "But what about the ring?"

Sara reached in her purse and pulled out a box. "Handcrafted by Nicolina with Addison's personality in mind. It's gorgeous."

Reid opened the box and smiled. "It's the ring I had picked out."

"I know," Sara said gruffly, but then gave him a shove. "Before you got all stupid and left." She grinned. "You do, however, have to pay for it."

"But . . . the preacher? The paperwork?"

"Taken care of. Jeff and his band are playing at the reception. Wine and Diner is catering the food. Grammar's did the cake. The flowers, the tux are all furnished. Addison's dad is taking pictures. All we need is the groom."

"But they all think it's a mock wedding?"

"Until you get down on one knee and propose."

"This is nuts."

"Not really. Cody would have been thrilled if all he had to do was show up. Reid, simply ask yourself whether you love Addison and want to spend the rest of your life with her."

"Are you kidding me? This past month has been a nightmare. I miss Addison more than I thought was humanly possible."

"Then get your ass over to the barn." She looked at her watch. "I have to go get into my bridesmaid dress."

"You're in the wedding?"

Sara fisted her hands on her hips. "Of course! I've got your tux in my truck. I'll go get it."

After Sara hurried out the door Reid stood there in the middle of the cabin, in shock. But then a grin spread across his face from ear to ear. He was getting married to Addison Monroe. Today.

Joy filled his heart. He couldn't be happier.

Addison arrived at the beautiful barn wearing the simple but elegant dress of her dreams. Her bouquet of wildflowers shook slightly because she was so nervous. After all, a bride didn't ever arrive for her wedding wondering if there was going to be a groom. To her surprise, when she stood at the entrance to the barn, her father showed up.

"Dad, I thought you were taking pictures?"

"Your mother will be taking the shots of you coming down the aisle with me. Sara asked me to walk you down the aisle. Addison, tell me: Am I crazy or is this actually the real deal?"

"If Reid shows up."

"He did."

Addison put trembling fingers to her lips. "How did you know?"

"I got a sneaking suspicion when Sara asked me to walk you down the aisle. There were tears in her eyes and I pretty much had it figured out. So, you love him?"

"With all my heart." She smiled through happy tears.

"I am so happy for you, Addie," he said gruffly. He kissed her on the cheek and then offered his arm. "Well, then, let's do this." He opened the door to the beautiful barn. A narrow aisle was flanked by neat rows of white chairs. In front of them was a raised altar decorated with satin ribbons. Thousands of lights wrapped around the wooden beams twinkled overhead, and colorful Chinese lanterns of pink and white hung suspended from the ceiling. After the nuptials the chairs would go back around the white linen-covered tables for dinner and the reception to follow. Rustic met elegant, but Addison had eyes only for the man standing at the altar, smiling at her as if he were the happiest man alive.

As Addison walked down the aisle, Cat Carson, the friend of Mia's who had recently signed with My Way Records, started singing "From This Moment." Almost losing her composure at the beauty of it all, Addison clung to her father's arm. She caught sight of her mother, who was trying to take pictures but was dabbing at her eyes and had to hand the camera over to someone else. Mia, her maid of honor, and Sara both smiled, looking lovely in the dusky pink bridesmaid gowns. Jeff, the best man, and Braden were handsome in charcoal gray tuxedoes.

When Addison reached the altar, the preacher spoke to the audience. "We'll commence with the wedding vows in just a minute. But first we have a little detail to take care of," he said, and then stepped away.

Addison stood before Reid, who took her breath away in his tuxedo. In that moment Addison knew she had kept her promise to Garret. She hadn't settled for anything less than undying, all-consuming, everlasting, crazy love. Reid knelt down on one knee, causing a buzz of excitement to ripple through the audience.

"Being away from you the past month was the hardest thing I've ever endured. I love you with all my heart. Addison, will you marry me?"

With her heart pounding she nodded. "Yes, Reid."

"Give me your hand, please." Smiling, Reid reached in his pocket and pulled out a ring. He slipped an elegant champagne sapphire surrounded by tiny glittering diamonds in a rose gold setting onto her finger.

"Oh, it's stunning," she said, beaming at him while the crowd applauded.

Reid stood up and took both of her hands in his. "I should have been more specific. Will you marry me ... *right now*?" Laughter filled the room, along with the sound of sniffles.

Addison felt happiness fill her from head to toe. "Reid Greenfield, I will marry you right here, right now ..." She paused to brush at a tear and then gave him a trembling smile. "From this moment my heart will forever and always belong to you."

"You've made me a happy man." Reid leaned forward for a kiss, but the preacher stepped in.

"Not so fast. I know we moved quickly from a proposal to a wedding but we have a few details left before you claim your bride," he announced with a grin. "In just a few more minutes Addison will be yours for the rest of your life."

Reid stepped back and smiled warmly at her. "I can't wait."

"Then let's begin...."

Epilogue

One year later

"MOM, THAT POT ROAST WAS AMAZING," REID SAID, AND his mother beamed. "I'm stuffed."

"Thank you, Reid. Your father and I look forward to Sunday dinners, but having the entire family sitting around the table is a special treat. Isn't it, Barry?"

"Absolutely."

"Are we ready for dessert?" his mother asked and stood up. "I baked a couple of apple pies."

"In a minute." Reid put his napkin beside his plate and looked at Addison. "We have something to announce."

"Okay," his mother said with wide eyes.

Reid felt emotion well up in his throat when his mother reached over and took his father's hand and sank back onto her chair. "Tell them, Addison."

"We're having a baby!" Addison said with a bright smile.

"Oh! Oh! A grandchild!" Susan shouted with joy. "Oh, Barry, we're having a grandbaby!"

"Grandchildren," Sara added, and grinned across the table at Reid. "Twins like to do things at the same time."

"Oh my ... oh my goodness!" Susan jumped up, shouted, and raised her hands heavenward. She looked like she might either faint or explode from joy. "Barry, can you believe it? I am simply overwhelmed with happiness!" She did a little dance but then stopped and pointed at Jeff and Braden. "You boys are next. We want to fill this farmhouse with the pitter-patter of little feet, don't we, Barry?"

"We sure do," he answered gruffly.

A moment later everyone stood up and the room became a Greenfield hug fest. Reid looked over the top of his mother's head from where she hugged him tightly around the waist and met Addison's eyes. *I love you,* he mouthed, and felt a rush of emotion when she mouthed it back.

It didn't get any better than this. . . .

"*W*ILLIE! NO! DON'T JUMP!" THE LOUD, DESPERATE PLEA frightened social director Savannah Perry into sprinting toward the pool at Whisper's Edge. Willie's dangerous plunge attempts had been happening all too often. "Oh, baby, please don't! It isn't worth it!" Although the tearful wail had Savannah picking up her already swift pace, she did manage to notice a sleek sports car parked in front of the main office. The sun glinting off the silver hood piqued Savannah's curious nature but a splash followed by another wail of distress kept her placing one flowered flip-flop in front of the other. The thongs adorned with daisies were the result of last Wednesday's craft workshop but were not very good for running shoes. "Doggone it!" Savannah nearly tripped as she hopped over the curb but she refused to slow down. Willie was not a strong swimmer.

Breathing hard, Savannah pushed open the gate that should have been latched and looked past umbrella tables and lounge chairs. "On no!" She spotted eighty-year-old Patty Parsons teetering precariously close to the edge of the water at the deep end of the pool. "Please back up," Savannah warned, but hard-of-hearing Miss Patty was further hampered by the pink bathing cap covering her ears.

"I'll rescue Willie!" Savannah tried again, but Miss Patty's attention remained focused on her sinking dog.

"Oh, Willie, swim harder!" Miss Patty wrung her hands together as she watched her beloved basset hound trying to capture a yellow tennis ball that bobbed just past his nose. Willie's ears fanned out over the surface of the water and, although he doggy-paddled at a furious pace, his short legs and rotund body were no match for gravity. He sunk a little lower.

"Baby, forget about the danged ball! I'll buy you a dozen!" Miss Patty wailed but Willie was on a mission and paid his master no heed. Then, to Savannah's horror, the spry little lady pointed her hands over her capped head and bent her body toward the glistening water. "I'm coming for ya!" she promised, but although Miss Patty was in great shape for her advanced age, Savannah knew from experience that without her flotation noodle, she'd sink like a stone.

Savannah was about to have quite a situation on her hands. She cupped her fingers at the corners of her mouth and shouted at the top of her lungs, "For the love of God, don't dive in, Miss Patty! I'll save Willie!"

God must have been listening because Miss Patty suddenly straightened up and looked at Savannah across the width of the pool. With wide eyes she put a hand to her chest. "Oh, praise the Lord! Child, pul-ease save my Willie!"

Savannah kicked off her flip-flops, losing a hot-glued daisy in the process. "I will," she promised and, while holding her nose, she jumped fully dressed into the pool. Although she'd cranked up the heat for afternoon water aerobics, the sudden plunge still felt shockingly cold. Ignoring the discomfort, Savannah bobbed to the surface. She lunged for Willie and managed to wrap her arm around his midsection.

"You got him," Miss Patty shouted, but her glee was short-lived. Although Savannah kicked with all her might, she and her canine buddy sank beneath the water. Willie, apparently sensing doggy death by drowning, wiggled away. With a gurgled protest, Savannah followed in swift pursuit but Willie swam like a manatee while underwater. He didn't, however, manage to paddle his way back up to the surface and started sinking closer to the bottom.

Although her lungs protested, Savannah knew her only hope was to get beneath Willie and push him upward. She lunged forward and gave his furry rump a huge heave-ho, repeating the action while using her legs as a springboard off the bottom. The old Olympic-sized pool was deep and Savannah was short, so by the time she and Willie reached the side of the pool, Savannah was struggling. Her lungs burned but she somehow managed to give Willie one last hard shove closer to where Miss Patty was bent over paddling the water as if that would somehow help.

The effort sent Savannah sinking backward but she pushed off the bottom and stroked as quickly as her tired arms would allow. Savannah broke the surface and took a huge gasp of much-needed air. Wet hair obscuring her vision, she dipped under the water to slick the long dark red tresses back from her forehead. Just as she raised her head above water, another splash had her cringing. Not again! Savannah was flailing around in a circle, trying to get a bead on where Willie landed when, to her surprise, a strong arm snaked around her waist and pulled her against a hard body.

"Don't worry. I've got you," the owner of the hard body said next to her ear. Savannah tried to twist to see his face but his firm grip prevented her from budging. "Stay calm and put your arms around my neck. I'll get you over to the edge."

Savannah obeyed but then felt silly. The words *I'm not drowning* formed in her head but the exertion, coupled with the lack of oxygen, scrambled Savannah's brain. She attempted to talk once more but unfortunately only a breathy *drowning* got past her lips.

"Don't worry. I won't let you," her knight in soggy clothing promised in a whiskey-smooth voice laced with a touch of the South. Savannah loved accents because they represented a sense of home, and roots, something she'd never had until landing the job at Whisper's Edge. "Hang on and you'll be just fine."

"Okay," Savannah managed. She tightened her hold, forgetting that she didn't really need assistance.

"We're almost there." His warm breath near her ear sent a delicious tingle down her spine, and when he tilted his head back, Savannah was able to see his tanned face. "Don't worry." He gave Savannah a reassuring smile that was utterly gorgeous. In that brief moment when their eyes met, Savannah felt an unexpected flash of longing she couldn't quite explain. He must have felt something similar because his gaze dropped to her mouth and lingered. Time felt suspended and unfolded like one of those slow-motion movie moments that needed Maroon 5 music in the background. Savannah tilted her face slightly closer but before she could do something incredibly insane like lean in and kiss a perfect stranger, he turned his head and started swimming toward the ladder. "Thank God . . ." *Damn . . . didn't mean to utter that out loud.*

"Almost there," he assured her in a soothing tone of voice.

Savannah could see the hot pink silk zinnias adorning the top of Miss Patty's flip-flops. Several of the ladies had squabbled over favorite flowers during craft time, and Savannah had had to make them draw straws.

"Here you go." With firm hands circling her waist he gently guided Savannah to the rungs of the ladder. She could feel the heat of his body pressing against her back and the urge to lean against him was almost too strong to resist. Luckily, Willie's deep bark startled some sense

back into Savannah's befuddled brain. With a quick in-
take of breath she gripped the metal handrails and
hoisted herself up while hoping that her wet sweatpants
clinging to her body didn't make her butt look big. Be-
latedly, Savannah realized she wore a swimsuit beneath
her clothing and wished she had taken the time to shed
it before rescuing Willie. Too late now . . .

Trying not to think about her butt, Savannah sloshed
her way up the ladder, but when she tried to stand, her
shaky legs gave her trouble. To her acute embarrassment, she stumbled sideways like a drunken sailor.

"Whoa there." Her handsome hero placed a steadying
arm about her waist. "Are you okay?"

"Yes." Her voice, which had a low timbre to begin
with, came out sounding like a croak. Could this possibly
get any worse? It wasn't until she pushed her wet hair
from her eyes that Savannah realized that they had
quickly drawn a small crowd of elderly lady onlookers,
most of whom were dressed in swimsuits and clutching
colorful foam noodles for water aerobics.

Apparently, her day could indeed get worse.

Also available from

LuAnn McLane

CATCH OF A LIFETIME
The Cricket Creek Series

Top Chicago chef Jessica Robinson is back in Cricket Creek—and making her aunt's diner the go-to place for comfy gourmet fare. Former major leaguer Ty McKenna is no stranger to Jessica's cooking. At the Chicago hotspot where she worked, he was a regular—with a different girl on his arm every night. Now he's the manager for the Cricket Creek Cougars. And convincing the mouthwatering chef that he's a one-woman man may be harder than getting his team ready for opening day.

Available wherever books are sold or at
penguin.com

facebook.com/LoveAlwaysBooks

Also available from

LuAnn McLane

PITCH PERFECT
The Cricket Creek Series

Mia Monroe is done being Daddy's little rich girl. Buying an old car with the last of her money, she sets out for who knows where—until her clunker clunks out in Cricket Creek. With no plan and no credit cards, Mia has to find more resilience than she's ever needed before. And a little help from an attractive new acquaintance wouldn't hurt…

As first baseman for the Cricket Creek Cougars, Cameron Patrick has two jobs: win games and stay out of trouble. If he can do both, he might just make it back to the minor leagues. He knows Mia is trouble from the moment she catches his eye—but he can't stop looking. And maybe her kind of trouble is exactly what he needs.

"No one does Southern love like LuAnn McLane."
—Romance Dish

Available wherever books are sold or at
penguin.com

facebook.com/LoveAlwaysBooks

Also available from

LuAnn McLane

WHISPER'S EDGE
The Cricket Creek Series

Savannah Perry loves her job as manager of Whisper's Edge, a
retirement community in Cricket Creek, Kentucky. She has
become the adopted granddaughter of the retired residents—
they rotate having her for dinner and fight over who gets to
have her company on holidays. But the community is
struggling to stay afloat, even with all the changes in the
economy of Cricket Creek.

Tristan McMillan is tired of the grind as a trial lawyer. So he
decides to change the direction of his life and buys Whisper's
Edge from his grandfather. The property is suddenly prime real
estate, and Tristan has big plans for it. But his plans don't
include falling for sweet Savannah or her beloved community.
Can he get his priorities straight in time to save both?

"A romantic, light-hearted, feel good story."
—Romance Reviews Today

Available wherever books are sold or at
penguin.com

facebook.com/LoveAlwaysBooks